SEAN M. TIRMAN

Dreamweavers, LLC

"Where Your Dreams Are Our Reality"

Book Cover Design by ebooklaunch.com

No AI was used in the creation of this book.

First edition

ISBN: 979-8-9894899-4-7

Editing by Anne-Marie Rutella

This book was professionally typeset on Reedsy. Find out more at reedsy.com

For my mom, who was never afraid of being a big dreamer and taught me to dream the same.

For my dad, who taught me the value of hard work and how to make really, really corny jokes.

"A strong spirit transcends rules."

–PRINCE

Acknowledgments

As always, my first (and biggest) thanks are owed to my wife, Tristen. You're my best friend, biggest supporter, most crucial work-shopping gut-checker, and first reader. None of these words would have made it onto these pages without you.

I also owe thanks to my niece, Sabrina Higbee, for inspiring me to write something a little less gruesome and a little more hopeful. You don't know it yet, but I probably wouldn't have written this book if not for you.

As for my earliest readers—Ryan Tirman (my brother), Mom (my mom), Dad (my dad), and Sereli Rodriguez—thank you for all your time, effort, and honest feedback. Teamwork does, indeed, make the dream work.

Thanks again to Anne-Marie Rutella, my editor, for cleaning up after me and for your crucial input.

Thank you to Dublin, my shadow. You were the weirdest, floppiest, fastest, spookiest, most perfect cat. I miss you every single day.

And thank you, dear reader, for taking a chance on my book. It means the world to me. I hope you enjoy your time in the

Dreamscape.

Dream Log #1

Earth Date: Holocene Period, Age of Humankind, First Century, 17 CE (Earth calendar)

Corporeal Location of Subject: Tomis, Dobruja (Earth)

Subject: Human, male-identifying poet, aged approximately sixty (Earth years)

Start log.

A man stands atop the crest of a great valley, surrounded by towering, snowcapped mountain peaks. The sun, high above in the center of the sky, illuminates the whole landscape, its beams shimmering and glinting with a warm, welcoming, otherworldly glow. He gazes down into the verdant basin far below, admiring a lush forest replete with wildlife. He notices birds chirping, winds whistling through the trees, and the faint plucking of a lyre somewhere in the distance.

Raising his hands to his face, the man turns them over and scrutinizes their wrinkles, spots, bony joints, blue veins, and brittle nails. With his right hand, he pinches and tugs at the thin skin of his left hand. When he releases, the skin does not snap back. He frowns with disappointment and rubs the rimpled lump, massaging it back into place.

When he lowers his hand, he realizes he no longer stands atop the great valley's crest. Instead, he sails high above the valley, the wind gently caressing his face. He feels weightless, soaring around and through the clouds, diving toward the ground before launching back up into the deep blue sky. Now, he can barely hear the lyre. He looks down at the valley below and blinks.

When he reopens his eyes, he stands at the valley's center, surrounded by the lush forest. Various animals dart around and over him, staying just far enough to avoid his reach. The man senses their fear and their curiosity. He opens his mouth to speak—to comfort the animals and to let them know he is not a threat—but no words come out. The lyre he heard playing in the distance sounds much closer and more cacophonous.

The animals gather around the man, still staying just out of reach. There are squirrels, rabbits, birds, badgers, mice, deer, and even a small bear. The man, still unable to speak, waves at the growing crowd, and the animals wave back. The man smiles, and the animals smile in return.

A tiny mouse finally scurries forward, hopping around at the man's feet. The man reaches down and picks up the minuscule, friendly creature. He pets it and pats it on the head. But it is no longer a mouse. Now, it is a morsel of food—the man's favorite, a fig.

Thinking nothing of it, he pops the fig into his mouth and bites down, realizing too late that it has transfigured back into a mouse. The man feels the pop and crack of the mouse's body and bones. Around him, the animals scream. A dozen lyres strike a dozen dissonant chords.

The man tries to spit out the mouse, but his mouth is empty. And he is no longer in the forest. Now, he stands in a crowded agora—a marketplace lined with dozens of stalls, their vendors selling all manner of goods.

Although relieved at first, the man quickly realizes something that unsettles him: he is small, too small, and no longer human. He has become a mouse, standing inside a basket of figs.

A woman reaches into the basket and picks up the man-mouse alongside a handful of figs. She opens her hand to count the figs, looking down at the man with an eerie smile stretching from cheek to cheek. Satisfied with the count, she opens her mouth too wide, far wider than any human should be able to, and tosses the figs—and the man—inside.

The man-mouse braces himself, trying to stop the woman's surprisingly sharp teeth from crushing and tearing him to bits, but the pressure is too great. He pushes as hard as he can, squeezing his eyes shut, but he cannot free himself from the woman's jaws. He can feel his bones cracking and flesh tearing, just like the mouse he mistakenly ate. And just as he's sure that he's about to die, the pressure releases.

He can hear somebody playing the lyre again, a familiar song that brings him comfort and relief. Slowly, he opens his eyes. He is standing in a large, stately, well-appointed home—his home, he thinks. But it seems both familiar and unfamiliar simultaneously, almost like someone had rearranged his furniture without his knowledge.

Then, he remembers: this is a place he hadn't seen in decades. It was his childhood home and the last place he saw his brother alive.

With the jubilation of a child, he runs through the manor

and out into the courtyard toward the sound of the lyre. He passes his mother, lounging in the sun's glow coming through one of the home's windows. And he runs right past his father, pacing the halls and talking to himself as he was wont to do. He runs through the home's towering doorway, as big as it had been when he was so little all those years ago, and out into the courtyard toward the music he knows so well.

And there, sitting beneath an olive tree, he sees his older brother, somehow alive and healthy, plucking at the strings of the modest instrument.

The man, now a boy again, does not wait for his brother to set the lyre down. He tackles him, squeezing his torso as tightly as he can muster and sending them both rolling through the grass beneath the olive tree. Tears roll down his cheeks as he looks up at his brother, who smiles in return.

"Welcome home," his brother says.

End log.

Act One

Chapter One

Dreamscape Orientation and Dreamcraft 101

T he scene ends as the screen fades to black before flickering to a grainy off-white. In the room's center aisle, atop a wheeled metal stand, a dusty old film projector—its reels spinning—*clickity-clacks* to a slow stop. A great, shadowy figure toward the front of the room flips a tiny switch on the wall, and an array of fluorescent bulbs flutter to life overhead, eliciting a sickly hum.

Disoriented as if waking up after a long nap, Alora squints, raising a hand to shield her eyes against the harsh glow of the tube lights above her. As her vision finally adjusts, she takes note of her surroundings.

She sits toward the center of a drab, run-of-the-mill community college-style classroom, with four light gray walls—marred only by a smattering of informational posters, their print ever-so-slightly too small to read—and a coarse, practically burlap, taupe carpet.

An arrangement of student desks—uncomfortable with their cold, rigid plastic chairs and laminated pressboard writing surfaces—crowd the middle of the room. All of them, surrounding the projector stand, face the same direction:

toward a yellowed pull-down screen at the room's front.

Alora notices that most of the desks are empty. But all the people sitting in the occupied seats are strangely dressed, with what look like bedsheets of varying styles and patterns tossed over their heads. She looks down at herself to see that she, too, is draped in a bedsheet—an oddly familiar white one with pink polka dots. She chuckles to herself, finding the whole scene curious and almost comical—as if she sits in the middle of a roomful of cartoon ghosts.

But something else demands her attention, draining her amusement and sending a shiver down her spine. With the lights on, she can now see the figure standing in the front corner of the room next to the light switch. With a gasp— echoed by several of the bedsheet ghosts around her—Alora recognizes the creature immediately. She had seen versions of it fictionalized throughout her life, in books, on television shows, in movies, and even at church. But, she realizes, she never really believed in it. She never had any reason to, until now.

Standing at the front of the room—its great wings outstretched, horns protruding from its forehead, and skin the deepest shade of blue Alora had ever seen—is a demon.

Seeing the reactions its appearance elicits from the classroom full of ghosts before it, the demon lets out a disappointed sigh.

"Alright," the demon grumbles, "let's get this over with."

☠

"For the last time," the demon urges, "no, I am not a demon, and this is not Hell. You are not here to suffer for all eternity, nor is the earthly notion of Hell itself—with the fire and brimstone and trident-brandishing ghouls—even accurate in the least. My name is Morpheus, and I am a nonhuman entity who dwells in the Afterworld. More specifically, I am a department head—*your* department head—here in the Dreamscape, a subsidiary within the Afterworld."

One of the bedsheet ghosts toward the back of the room raises its hand. The demon—*no, wait,* Alora thinks, *not a demon*—tucks back its wings and walks before the projector screen.

"Yes," Morpheus answers. "You have a question?"

The ghost clears its throat. "Morpheus, like Laurence Fishburne from *The Matrix*?"

Morpheus lowers his head, rubbing his temples and closing his eyes tightly. "No," he finally groans. "I don't know who that is or what a...matrix is."

"Oh man," the ghost replies. "So, there's this guy, and he's like a computer hacker. But then one day—"

Morpheus cuts him off. "Maybe we should hold all questions until the end. What do you say?"

All the bedsheet ghosts nod in agreement, including Alora and the Larry Fishburne fan in the back.

"Okay, great," Morpheus continues, taking a deep breath before resuming with gusto. "What you just witnessed was a dream. In fact, it's the most important dream for everyone here in the Dreamscape, perhaps even the whole of the Afterworld. This is because it's the first one we show newcomers to help prepare them for what is to come. Congratulations, you are all official employees of Dreamweavers, LLC!"

Morpheus pauses dramatically, his arms and wings outstretched and fingers splayed wide, waiting for applause that never comes. The bedsheet ghosts stare back at the dark blue creature, all dumbfounded and speechless.

"And I'm your new boss. You know what, forget it. Roll the tape."

Morpheus snaps his fingers, and the film projector whirs back to life, a new spool somehow spinning on its reels. The horned being—who Alora still thinks looks suspiciously like a demon, although not quite the right color—steps back into the corner of the room, his wings once again tucked back. With a *crackle-pop*, a new video projects on the pull-down screen.

Cheery baby-blue-and-gold lettering, the kind you might see on a postcard or tourism billboard, wipes across the screen. *Welcome to the Afterworld*, it reads. And then, another phrase fades in toward the bottom, this one in quotes and a slightly smaller font: *On Earth as it is in Heaven*.

The lettering fades out, and another image fades back in. This time, it depicts a striking four-armed woman with golden skin and a warm, welcoming smile. She's dressed in a sharp-looking, tailored silk suit with a lotus flower pinned to her lapel. The ornate office chair she sits in also looks like a lotus flower. Behind her, there's a sprawling, verdant swamp full of gorgeous flowers, trees, swans, and elephants.

"Hello and welcome to the Afterworld," the woman says, parroting the graphic at the beginning of the video. "My name is Maya. I am the chief operations officer here at Dreamweavers, LLC, and it is my distinct pleasure to welcome each and every one of you into the fold of our little organization."

Maya rises from her lotus chair and walks across the screen.

The camera follows her as she passes a wall with the words *Dreamweavers, LLC* scrawled on it in big, bold lettering. She continues speaking.

"As you may have guessed by now," Maya's smile fades as she puts two of her four hands together in a prayer pose, "You are dead."

Alora hears the gasps—and a few nervous chuckles—come out of the bedsheet ghosts around her. The golden woman on the screen pauses as though she's aware of the reaction from those in the classroom.

"But not to worry," she finally continues, "Your life—or rather, your *afterlife*—is only beginning. You see, we here at Dreamweavers, LLC have an essential job to do, one that keeps us deeply connected to the corporeal world of the living. Here, in this realm, we conceptualize, develop, design, construct, implement, and analyze the somnambulatory experiences of those still hewed to the mortal coil. In short, we make dreams."

Maya extends all four of her arms, and the screen bursts into a shower of sparkles. The flourish reminds Alora of fireworks or pixie dust.

"While the complexities of this endeavor are legion," Maya continues, "our purpose is quite simple: we guide the living through their subconscious ordeals to help them better navigate the waking world."

The screen fades to black, and another image fades back in. This time, it's a cartoon—a hastily drawn and poorly animated one, at that. It depicts a mostly featureless person, little more than a smiley face on a stick-figure body, standing in an equally featureless bedroom. In one corner, the room has a small rectangle that Alora surmises is a bed, and there's a crude four-square window—*that's gotta be a window*, Alora thinks—

10

in the middle of the back wall. As the animation plays, Maya continues her monologue.

"When a living person on Earth goes to sleep," Maya says, as the little cartoon figure comes to life, magically changing into a nightgown and cap and hopping into bed, "their mind opens up to possibilities beyond the physical realm."

The little cartoon closes its eyes and starts to snore, little cartoon Zs floating around its head. Then, a series of tiny bubbles pop up, leading to a larger dream cloud thought bubble. The image zooms in, and the cartoon person appears inside, flying like a superhero above a city skyline.

"This is where we come in." Maya pauses as the image of the little cartoon person zooms back out, showing a smattering of beings—some winged like Morpheus; some that look like half-humans, half-animals; and others that look like bedsheet ghosts—working behind the scenes on some kind of movie set. Some of the beings tilt spotlights, others hold the rope keeping the flying cartoon person suspended, and others still stand around machines resembling television monitors, watching the whole scene play out on the tiny screens.

"So, how does all this work, you're probably wondering?"

The image cuts back to Maya, walking between two long rows of warehouse-sized sound stages beneath an impossible sky—somehow both day and night at the same time and dotted with comets, planets, and even great winged creatures, which remind Alora of flying mutant elephants or airborne whales with trunks and tusks.

Maya continues, "The short answer: astral projection paired with a unique and proprietary combination of modern After-world technology and ancient magics. The long answer: you'll soon find out."

The golden woman smiles slyly, snapping her fingers on all four of her hands, instantly transporting her back to her lotus chair from the beginning of the presentation.

"But before I go," Maya continues, "you've probably got one more burning question: What's in it for you?"

Maya's office dissolves, this time into a series of still images. The first shows an Egyptian painting of an enormous dog-headed man crouching next to a normal-sized human and a set of huge scales—a feather on one side and a human heart on the other. The next, a long line of people wait outside an enormous pair of golden gates guarded by a man with great white wings and a halo, checking a long list of names inside a massive book. A third features a woman riding on the back of a strange serpentlike dog across a gigantic, raging river.

Maya's voice continues as the images shift. "The Afterworld has many realms, and while the Dreamscape is one that exists to assist the living, it also serves as a realm of judgment—a place where the dead, those poor souls found still wanting before crossing over, are given a second chance. Do good work here at Dreamweavers, and you may escape eternal punishment. Rise to the top of your subsequent department, and rewards shall follow. A select few, the best of the best, may even earn Ascension."

A choir of voices rings out, and harps chime as Maya annunciates the word *Ascension*.

The screen dissolves back to Maya sitting in her office. She stares into the camera as she delivers her sign-off, "Will you be among the Ascendant?"

Once again, the pull-down screen cuts to black and then to white as the rickety, dusty old film projector *clickity-clacks* to a stop. Morpheus steps back in front of the classroom, his fingers interlaced and thumbs tapping together.

"Alrighty," he says. "Hopefully, that cleared some things up for y'all. Now, do we have any questions?"

All at once, the bedsheet ghosts raise their hands. Morpheus smirks and claps his hands together. A puff of smoke erupts before each of the bedsheet ghosts. When the smoke clears, Alora finds a ratty, water-damaged, hand-stitched, leather-bound book on her desk. She looks around to see that all the other ghosts have similar books sitting before them. Emblazoned on the cover is an assortment of indecipherable runes and words in a language Alora doesn't recognize.

"I'd bet my left wing that all the answers you seek are in your Dreamweavers, LLC employee manual. Have fun thumbing through the pages, and take your time. We do have an eternity, after all."

With a final puff of smoke, Morpheus disappears, leaving the bedsheet ghosts alone in the drab classroom.

Alora looks back at the book again to find that the esoteric symbols and lettering on the cover have shifted into more familiar arrangements and patterns.

Dreamweavers, LLC Employee Manual, it reads. And below that: *Your helpful, handy guide to navigating the Dreamscape, the art of Dreamcraft, our organization's bureaucratic structure, and much more!*

"This can't be real, right? It's gotta be some kind of joke," says Rasui, the ghost formerly known—at least to Alora—as the Larry Fishburne fan. Science-fiction imagery—rockets, astronauts, and shooting stars—dots his light gray bedsheet.

At Rasui's suggestion, all the bedsheet ghosts had gathered toward the center of the room, arranging a bunch of desks in roughly a circular shape so they could all see one another and work together—both at deciphering the situation they were in and their newly acquired, deeply mystifying tomes.

With the desks all facing one another, Alora noticed small nametags taped to their fronts. She tried to memorize them, even leaning over to look at her own. Seeing her name written down, it seemed correct but felt slightly odd. Like an oversized shirt, it fit, but not quite. She pushed the thought from her mind and tuned into the ghosts' conversation.

"Just look at the mission statement page," Rasui continues, flipping his book open and thumbing through the opening pages. *"To inspire humanity in dreams to better navigate the waking world.* That's it. That's the whole thing. And did you see the *Bureaucratic Organizational Chart* at the back?"

Rasui flips to the back of the book, landing on a page that looks more like an impossible labyrinthian maze than a flowchart. He picks up the book to show the rest of the ghosts.

"No way anyone can make sense of this," Rasui exasperates.

"Maybe this really is Hell." This time, it was Kanasu. Draped in an off-white bedsheet with an intricate multicolored geometric design, Kanasu had seemed gruff and standoffish since everyone had scooted their desks together.

"The blue guy—Morpheus—already said it wasn't and that he wasn't a demon," Alora disagrees.

"That's precisely what a demon would say," Kanasu retorts. "Plus, dude has wings and horns, and I think I saw one of those forked tails sticking out his backside."

"Do you think you belong in Hell?" Endri asks through his

black-and-white plaid bedsheet. So far, Endri seemed mostly unbothered by what was transpiring, treating it with an almost clinical approach. "Have any of us murdered anyone or caused any undue suffering that might earn such a punishment?"

"I can't even remember how I got here," Alora answers. "Do any of you?"

The ghosts around her all shake their heads.

"I can't remember much of anything at all," Endri comments.

"It's like there's this haze," Rasui interjects. "I have a vague, kind of fog of memories, but nothing specific…"

"So, none of us know how we got here or where we came from," says Alora, tugging at her polka-dotted bedsheet. "And we're all wearing these stupid sheets. They're stuck to our heads or something. What are they, glued on?"

"There aren't any doors in here." Alora and the rest of the bunch turn their heads toward the voice. It was the fifth and final ghost, Yume, who hadn't said much of anything until now. Instead, draped in a light pink sheet dotted with little drawings of fruit, she had risen from her desk and floated around the room, reading the strange posters on the classroom's walls.

"No windows and no doors," Yume continues quietly. "And no mirrors or reflective surfaces, either."

"The Hell theory is becoming more convincing by the minute—" Kanasu scoffs.

Still flipping through the pages of his book, Rasui interrupts. "Hold on, I think there's an index. Yes! Check this out."

"Did anyone see that black cat just now?" Yume asks, pointing toward another corner of the room, but nobody seems to hear her.

The ghosts gather around Rasui as he flips to the back of his book, finds a reference to "mirrors," and then flips back

15

through the book to find the page in question. Rasui reads the passage out loud.

"...unlike locales on Earth where the veil between the mortal realm and the Afterworld are thin enough for some powerful spirits to pass through, such as graveyards and hospitals, mirrors are impenetrable. However, as they can still serve as windows between the realms, they are strictly forbidden in the Dreamscape. If vanity demands it, Dreamweavers, LLC recommends that employees cast a Lookingglass spell or take a trip to Narcissus's Pond to inspect their appearance."

Rasui slams the book shut and throws his arms in an exaggerated shrug. "The whole thing is written like this."

"If this is Hell," Alora says, "why would they give us a handbook?"

"Torture," Kanasu interjects with a laugh. "Eternal, infernal torture. It's already working."

"Does anyone else feel invisible under these sheets?" Yume squeaks, twirling around like a dancer.

"What Hell are we even talking about?" Endri asks. "There are over four thousand different human religions. Even those with a concept of Hell don't agree on what it's like, right? So, which one is this?"

"My own personal Hell, it would seem," a booming voice rings out. The ghost group turns toward the voice at the front of the classroom as a puff of smoke erupts and dissipates. Standing in its place is a well-dressed older man with a close-cropped haircut, a curly white beard, and impossibly dark blue eyes. The man rubs his forehead as if in pain.

"Who the heck is this guy?" Rasui jerks his thumb at the newcomer.

"I already told you," the man answers, "my name is Morpheus.

Or did you miss that bit?"

"What happened to the, you know," Kanasu whistles, gesturing an approximation of horns and wings, "your whole getup?"

"I thought maybe y'all would be my first crew I didn't have to metamorphose for. Clearly, I was wrong." Morpheus groaned, gesturing to his new look. "This...form has traditionally been less distracting, so here we are."

"Are you going to tell us what's happening here now?" Endri asks.

"Well, I wasn't. I figured I'd let you all work things out for yourselves. But I've been ousted for shirking my duties. Again. Chernobog's blasted spies are everywhere, it seems. Plus, you're all just taking so damn long. I can give you the gist, but I'm afraid the explanation still won't answer all your questions. You humans always have so many damn questions—never can just let things be."

With a flick of Morpheus's wrist, the desks—even the ones still occupied by the ghosts—shifted back into place. The rest of the ghosts drift back to their seats, except for Yume, who seems content to stand off to the side.

"Don't all get comfortable, now," Morpheus says, stroking his beard. "We're not staying here. I just wanted to get the place in order before— Well, you'll see."

Morpheus claps his hands, and the classroom falls out from under everyone.

☠

"This is the Dreamscape," Morpheus announces as the class floats high above the landscape. Below lies a magnificent

17

expanse of vast jungles too thick and verdant to peer into, gravity-defying mountain ranges, extensive river systems that seem to crisscross up and over themselves like tangled yarn, shimmering crystal canyons that appear bottomless, and Technicolor deserts.

At the center of it all sits a majestic city whose architecture makes it look like a fairy-tale castle—and its surrounding city—stitched together with incredible magic. An ethereal, infinite expanse surrounds the metropolis. Simultaneously merging day and night, stars, nebulae, entire galaxies, and solitary planets drift within it. Alora can also see those strange flying elephant creatures soaring up and over the landscape, crowding the air space—*if there's even air out here at all*, she muses.

"Or rather, this is the Dreamscape as it appears at this particular moment," Morpheus continues. "Now, watch."

As if on cue, the landscape below begins to shift, some of its elements phasing through one another, others becoming impossibly intertwined, others still disappearing entirely, and new pieces seemingly coalescing from thin air. The mountains and rivers collide to become a vast ocean dotted with archipelagic islands; the crystal canyons erupt, inverting into glassy, shimmering plateaus; the Technicolor desert dissipates into nothingness, replaced by an icy tundra; and the jungles morph into eerie swamplands. Only the city at its center remains static.

"As you can see," Morpheus continues, "the central city, which we call Somnia, endures, as the surrounding area known as Oneiros transubstantiates from time to time."

"What does that mean?" Rasui asks, cocking his head and looking as puzzled as a faceless bedsheet ghost can look.

"Transfigure, mutate, convert," Endri answers coldly. "He means it changes."

"Exactly," Morpheus agrees. "The shifting of the Dreamscape is a regular occurrence. However, *how* it shifts is as puzzling to us old-timers as it is to newcomers. That also makes it dangerous. You do not want to catch yourself in the shifting landscape, lest the terrain open up and swallow you whole. In the best case, you'll lose yourself within the unstable topography for millennia. Worst, you'll spit out the other side and fall into the infinite void below—or whatever else is out there, I'd prefer not to find out. That's why, without an escort, no human spirit may leave the city of Somnia to wander the land of Oneiros."

"Couldn't we just fly back up like we are right now?" Yume asks with her squeaky whisper.

"No," Morpheus scowls. "We're not even really flying up here right now. It just *looks* like we are. We're still in that classroom back down below. If you get sucked down into that infinite void… Suffice it to say, nobody knows what happens, but it can't be good. Better not to find out, I say."

This time, it was Alora's turn to ask a question. "Why does it do that, transform or whatever?"

"Because the Dreamscape itself is a dream," Morpheus answers.

"Dreams within a dream," Rasui mutters. "That's pretty meta."

Ignoring the comment, Morpheus continues, "Vishnu is the being that rules over the Dreamscape and is also its creator. But all this only exists because of Vishnu's everlasting slumber.

"Like the dreams you might have had in the material world, Vishnu's dream is unstable and sometimes erratic. As such, it

19

lacks a static form. The only reason the city of Somnia doesn't shift each time the rest of the Dreamscape changes is because of our COO—and Somnia's chief administrator—Maya."

"The golden, four-armed lady from the video," Kanasu suggests.

"Correct," Morpheus confirms. "She is Vishnu's right hand and, effectively, serves to interpret and enact the god's will. She's also the source of the magic that has locked Somnia in its fixed state to keep us all safe. As such, we serve her who serves Vishnu. We kind of owe her."

"What happens if Vishnu wakes up?" Yume asks.

"*That*," Morpheus says with a shrug, "is a hotly debated subject. As long as I've been here, Vishnu has been asleep. And, as far as I know, the Dreamscape has existed for far longer— definitely longer than creation itself and perhaps longer than most of the rest of the Afterworld. If there ever comes a time that Vishnu wakes, there's a pretty good chance we all *poof* out of existence. Or maybe something much worse."

"We get sent to Hell," Kanasu giggles.

"There are worse fates," Morpheus retorts. Kanasu's eyes widen with fear—*or maybe fascination*, Alora thinks. "But no— not at least the way you mean it. Hell doesn't exist as you humans seem to believe it does. Most of your religions got the whole thing wrong. The Nordic folks got pretty close with the multiple realms, as did some of the Buddhists. Modern folks, not so much. A musician from around your time was really onto something before he Ascended. I think his name was…it was something royal. King? No, that's not it. Earl? No, not quite. Prince! Yes, that's it. Or was he formerly a prince? Whatever. It doesn't really matter.

"But that does bring up another issue you'll surely ask me

about sooner or later, so I'll just nip that right in the bud. Time doesn't work here in the same way as it does in the corporeal realm. Minutes, hours, days…they don't exist on this plane. Nor does the linear flow of time you were used to on Earth. We could be making dreams for humans who lived long before all of you were born or well into humanity's future. We won't, but we could."

Morpheus claps his hands, and, in a puff of smoke, the group returns to the musty old classroom. Standing at the front of the room once more, the well-dressed older man tugs on the pull-down screen, rolling it back into its spool and revealing the whiteboard behind it. On it, there's a sizeable circular diagram broken up by several branching paths, each with a small collection of cartoon ghosts drawn at their ends.

"Here in the Afterworld, time is circular." Morpheus points to the diagram. "Therefore, it is also infinite. There is no beginning and no end. As human spirits, you'll find this all but impossible to comprehend, and that's okay. To cope with this, we keep y'all in groups alongside other human spirits who, in the mortal realm, existed around the same time. That way, it ensures you'll better understand the dreams you'll be working on—dreams of people from your earthly time—and hopefully won't experience the drawbacks of working outside of that period. Plus, we nonhuman entities have discovered that it also offers you human spirits something else you need."

"Companionship," Endri interjects.

"Precisely," Morpheus smiles. "We used to have y'all inter-mingle, and it became a bit difficult to manage. Have you ever seen what happens when you place an Aztec warrior and a Spartan in the same room alongside Quakers and Hare Krishnas? Glorious, entirely unproductive chaos. But you should all have a similar understanding of the mortal realm and, therefore, will have plenty to chat about."

"What happens when people work outside of their understanding of time?" It was Yume again.

"Pure madness," Morpheus replies with a nod, still smiling—albeit genuinely and not with malice, Alora notices.

Alora raises her hand timidly.

"You, Polka Dot," Morpheus addresses her. "You have an inquiry." It was more a statement than a question.

"Why can't we remember anything?"

"Finally, a good question," Morpheus chuckles. "A while back, we didn't have that in place. But you humans just can't let things be. So many spirits tried to contact their loved ones back on Earth; it was chaos. And that made our counterparts in the mortal realm uneasy. It's one thing for the gods to meddle in y'all's affairs, but it's another thing entirely for deceased humans to go on haunting the living unchecked. So, the higher-ups put the kibosh on that. Specific memories—those that allow you to remember who you were—are suspended in the Dreamscape, as they're unimportant to the task at hand."

"That doesn't seem very fair," Rasui says.

"Hey, I don't make the rules." Morpheus shrugs.

"How is all of this even possible?" It was Alora again.

Morpheus looks at her, stunned. "Are you asking me to explain the intricacies of ancient, otherworldly, incomprehensible magics older than the universe itself?"

"I guess not," Alora answers, lowering her hand and head.

"I'm sorry, that was rude," Morpheus says with a furrowed brow. "Truth is, I have an almost infantile understanding of it myself, at least compared to some *higher*-higher-ups here in the Dreamscape. But I have a few words of advice: keep your heads down, do your job, and know better than to stare too deeply into the void lest you wish to discover what might be staring back. Before you know it, I presume you'll be out of here and on to bigger and better things."

"Bigger and better things," Alora repeats. "Wait, I have one more question. What's *Ascension*?"

"And we have a winner," Morpheus announces, throwing his hands into the air. "That's the eternal question, now, isn't it? Someone always asks, and rightfully so. If I were a mortal soul, I'd want to know the same damn thing. Do your job well, and you transcend. And if you don't do your job satisfactorily, you're reassigned to another realm.

"But here's the best bit," Morpheus continues. "Not even I know what that means in either case. As a nonhuman entity, I have no soul of which to speak, so I can neither transcend nor transfer to another realm. I'm stuck here forever. And souls who leave this plane never return, so I can't speak to where they go or what one might expect once it happens. As such, we really don't know what's in it for you—just broad assumptions. For instance, do a good job and reap the rewards, or do a bad job and suffer the punishments. I understand it's much the same on Earth, correct?"

The bedsheet ghosts nod defeatedly.

"I guess you just have to take it on faith, then, that there's anything in it for you at all," Morpheus giggles, clapping his hands. "Oh gods, that is always my favorite part."

Chapter Two

Dorm Assignments: Where to Go When You're Not Dreamweaving

After dropping his bombshell—and without clearing up so much as half the questions everyone had—Morpheus sends Alora and the rest of the bedsheet ghosts on their way, pointing them in the general direction of the human soul dormitories.

"Just follow the path. You can't miss it," the ghosts' mentor had said, handing each a small pamphlet. "Oh, and take these. Once you're all settled in, we'll reconvene."

Trying to keep pace with the rest of her companions, Alora now looks down at the little trifold piece of parchment.

The cover reads, *So, You're a Spirit; Now What?* It features a small drawing of a cartoon ghost draped in a bedsheet. It looks just like every human spirit Alora has seen so far.

Inside, Alora finds a collection of frequently asked questions with mostly vague, unhelpful answers.

The first reads: *Why Does Everyone Look Like They're Wearing a Bedsheet? Because the human mind cannot fathom the most authentic embodiment of a soul. After an eternity of tinkering, Dreamweavers, LLC found this arrangement to be the most bearable, comprehensible, and explicable to the formerly corporeal from all human eras.*

Another says: *Why Can't You Remember the Specifics of Who You Were? The Dreamscape is your new (after)life. Carrying memories of who you were back in the mortal realm may cloud your judgment and create unnecessary distractions in your work. Focus on your tasks; such trivial details will no longer bother you.*

"Pay no attention to the man behind the curtain," Rasui says, diverting Alora's attention by waving his pamphlet around like a magic wand in her face. "You reading this? I understand less about our situation now than when we first showed up in that classroom."

Alora hadn't noticed when they first left, but the area outside the classroom looked disappointingly unmagical— more like a studio back lot or a warehouse depot. The pathway below them looks and feels like run-of-the-mill asphalt and nondescript rectangular buildings of various sizes flank the path for roughly a half mile. For all the incredible things they had seen beyond the confines of Somnia, this part of the city looked an awful lot like Burbank, California. Alora glimpses a sign on one of the buildings. *Dream Stage 42*, it reads.

"If you're going to do something, do it right," Alora mutters to herself before addressing the rest of the group. "You heard that golden lady and the boss man—if we do what's asked of us, we'll get rewarded. *Ascension* or whatever. I think we might be better off just going along with everything."

"Dude called himself Morpheus," Rasui responds. "How do we know it's not a simulation or experiment or something? Like maybe we're all in a room plugged into a computer somewhere."

"The brain in a vat argument," Endri interjects, his plaid

sheet billowing around him.

"Huh?" Rasui blurts.

Alora shrugs.

"It's a philosophical concept. Essentially, there's no way for us to know if any of this is real or fake. Some would argue that we should treat it as though all of this is real since we cannot tell the difference. Real or not, this is our experience."

"So, we might as well play the game," Kanasu says. "At least until we know more."

"It makes perfect sense to me," Alora replies. "Yume?"

But Yume was distracted, staring off at something in the distance.

"We're not in Kansas anymore," Rasui whispers, looking down at his sci-fi bedsheet.

"There"—Yume points toward one of the buildings off to the side. "It's that black cat again."

The group turns to look, but there's no such cat in sight. Instead, they all see that the massive sliding door of one of the buildings—Dream Stage 42, the one Alora spied earlier—is slightly ajar. From inside, they hear a blood-curdling scream. On instinct, Alora floats toward the sound, slipping inside the gap in the door. Her companions, equally distressed, follow shortly behind.

The inside of the warehouse is dark, but Alora notices that it seems far more spacious than it did on the outside. Looking up, Alora can see a starry night sky peeking between what she tells herself can't possibly be clouds—*probably just clever staging, maybe loose-spun cotton in front of spotlights or something.*

And beyond that, she sees a dense evergreen forest.

"Even for a professional sound stage," Alora hears Rasui whispering behind her, "this is impressive."

The sci-fi-sheeted ghost glides past Alora, approaching one of the pine trees. He reaches out his hand to touch the bark.

"Whoa," he says. "Practical effects. Gotta love the dedication to the craft. This thing feels almost real."

The rest of the ghosts join Rasui, each touching the tree to see for themselves. Like everyone else, Alora is awed by how real the tree—and everything else in the warehouse—seems. And then they all hear the blood-curdling scream again.

"Should we really be doing this?" Alora asks.

"If we want to find out what's going on, it seems a good place to start," Endri answers.

"Sounds like it's coming from that way." Kanasu points farther into the forest. Because of their geometric bedsheet, Alora can't see Kanasu's expression, but she thinks they sound almost excited. Kanasu is the first to move deeper into the woods, followed by Rasui, Endri, Yume, and—realizing she's suddenly alone—Alora.

Weaving between the trees toward the intermittent screams, Alora sees they're approaching a light source. As they get closer, she sees the light illuminates a clearing in the middle of the woods. Upon noticing several silhouetted figures surrounding the clearing—and the horrible sight at its center— Alora freezes in place. Her companions similarly halt.

Lying in the middle of the clearing, spotlit by an unsteady orange-tinted streetlight, Alora sees an enormous, scaly snake-like creature in the midst of swallowing someone whole. Except the snake has almost human features—reminding Alora of an older woman. She also notices that the snake is wearing curlers in its hair and a floral, lace-lined nightgown covering the top half of its body. And its tail is constricted around the base of the streetlight.

Alora realizes the screaming is coming from the person trapped inside the snake-woman's jaws. It's another, much younger woman fighting for her life, trying to push herself up and out of the snake's mouth. But with each push—and each subsequent scream—the snake-woman swallows a bit more, climbing up her victim's body inch by inch.

"I told you all this was Hell," Kanasu says, the excitement drained from their voice.

The young woman screams again. The shadowy figures surrounding her continue to watch, unmoving.

"We should go," Alora whispers, "Right?"

"Seems like she needs help," Rasui asserts under his breath. "Except I haven't exactly brushed up on my basilisk-fighting skills."

"I have to say, I'm with Rasui on this one," Endri adds. "This seems dire."

"Same," Kanasu confirms.

Yume simply nods her head.

"If anything," Alora interjects, "we should get out of here before anyone notices us, get over to the dormitories like Morpheus said, and hope we don't get found out."

"Funny," Kanasu replies, "I could've guessed you'd be a teacher's pet."

"Uh-oh," Yume interjects.

Before them, the giant snake-woman finally reaches the young woman's head, swallowing her whole and confirming with a loud, repulsive burp.

In a blinding flash, like someone flipped a switch, the

forest shifts from night to day, and the once-shadowy figures surrounding the clearing—now revealed to be another, larger group of bedsheet ghosts—burst into uproarious applause. Another figure, joining the ghosts in their applause, moves into the center clearing toward the snake-woman, who Alora notices seems lifeless and stiff, almost like the theme-park animatronics of her childhood.

Despite the daylight-bright lights in the warehouse, the new figure remains cloaked in shadow and practically billows with darkness. But Alora, unable to avert her eyes, can make out the suggestion of shapes and a rough outline within those shadows. Like Morpheus, this being has devilish horns, wings, and a forked tail. Unlike Morpheus, it towers above the surrounding ghosts and fills Alora with a deep, almost palpable dread. She watches, frozen in place, as the creature stomps over to the now-lifeless snake-woman, reaches out a clawed finger, and pops it like a balloon, multicolored confetti exploding out of it.

"Congratulations, everyone," the creature exclaims in a deep bellow, its smile displaying a mouthful of jagged, snaggletooth fangs. "Spectacular work. Another great success."

Looking at the crowd gathered around it, the umbral beast narrows its deep crimson eyes and gazes directly at Alora and her companions.

"It appears we have spies in our midst," the monster says, pointing a clawed finger toward the intruders. "Show your-selves!"

The other bedsheet ghosts surrounding the clearing all turn to stare at Alora and the other newcomers.

Alora, Rasui, Endri, Yume, and Kanasu float into the clearing, unsure whether they move through their free will or if the great shadow beast compels them.

"Please don't kill us," Rasui finally blurts.

"Kill you?" The great demon bellows, its uproarious laughter shaking the forest around them. The other bedsheet ghosts join in the shadow-beast's amusement. "I can't kill you. You're already dead."

"Well," Yume interjects meekly, "please don't flay us or tear us to pieces or torture us, either."

Yume's request sends another wave of gleeful giggles through the crowd around them.

Alora finally speaks up. "We're sorry. We didn't mean to meddle; there was just a lot going on, and we got lost, and now—"

"You must be Morpheus's new brood," the towering demon interrupts. "Did you like the show?"

"I'd hardly call that a show," Endri says.

"More like an execution," Kanasu adds under their breath.

"Where's the body?" Yume asks, pointing to where the snake-woman once was, the younger woman it ate conspicuously missing from the pile of confetti.

"Back on Earth in bed sleeping soundly, I presume," the shadow-beast answers. "I think there's been a misunderstanding. Do you know where you are?"

Alora and company shake their heads.

"Leave it to Morpheus to eschew his most elementary of tasks," the creature says, rolling its eyes. Then, addressing the other ghosts in the warehouse, "This is exactly why our department thrives while his languishes and dawdles. Were it up to me, we'd redistribute their lot into our ranks. Then, perhaps these misguided, misinformed, misdirected miscreants might know what proper leadership looks like.

And with it, they'd know pride in their work."

The warehouse breaks into applause. The monster turns back to Alora and her companions.

"Lambaste aside, I believe introductions are in order," it says. "My name is Chernobog, and I am the God of Chaos, Misfortune, and Darkness. And I'm the head of the Department of Nightmares here at Dreamweavers. What you just witnessed was not Afterworld torture or execution but a victory of planning, preparation, and spirit! That, my friends, was a dream. A masterfully crafted one, I might add.

"And these good folks," Chernobog continues, gesturing to the surrounding group of ghosts, "represent the finest team of 'weavers among my ever-growing army of nightmare crafters. Work hard and display a particularly acute talent for 'weaving, and you might be lucky enough to count yourselves among them. Ask anyone—working in *my* department is the highest honor one can achieve at Dreamweavers."

The surrounding crowd bursts into a cacophony of *Hear! Hears!* and *Woo-hoos*. Chernobog lowers his voice, his emanating shadows growing even darker and his eyes burning a brighter red. Alora's sense of dread returns even more acutely.

"However, that day will never come until you've proven yourselves in both savvy and trustworthiness. And beginning your tenure here in the Dreamscape by spying on your competition is a piss-poor method of illustrating those values. Now, be on your way, and I'll see you all again at the proper, sanctioned time: during job shadowing. Give Morpheus my regards, the has-been."

Chernobog dismisses Alora and her companions with a wave, resuming the celebration of a job well done with his team.

☠

Alora and company slip back outside the warehouse the same way they came in and continue up the road toward the human soul dormitories, albeit all a bit more downtrodden than before.

"Anybody else get bad vibes from that guy?" Kanasu asks, breaking the tension.

"You mean the giant freaking demon?" Rasui asks. "Yeah, dude kind of sucks."

"To be fair," Endri adds, "we did intrude on their work. It seems like we might have been in the wrong."

"We're new! How were we supposed to know?" Rasui exclaims.

"The videos, the posters, the literature," Yume answers, waving her pamphlet like a paper fan. "Oh, and Morpheus told us so."

Ignoring the barb and gesturing to nothing in particular, Rasui continues, "Although, I guess the upshot is that it seems like this is all legit. Or at least it's not Hell."

"Still not sure that's a good thing," Kanasu mumbles.

"Kanasu is right," Alora says.

"That Hell would be better?" Endri puzzles, cocking his head.

"No, not that," Alora scoffs. "There's something off about...it was Chernobog, right?"

"Again, dude was a giant freaking demon," Rasui replies, extending his arms wide and shrugging his shoulders. "Of course, you got bad vibes. Wait, have you met demons before?

Are they usually nicer?"

"I hate to agree with him," Endri says, "but Rasui has a point. We have to leave human preconceptions at the door. This world is not like our own, so we cannot criticize it—or its denizens—as such."

"That's what I've been saying." Alora shakes her head. "We should just stay the course, keep our heads down, and do what's asked of us."

Kanasu rolls their head back and groans, "You would say that."

But before Alora can reply, Kanasu points upward at the facade of a skyscraper—a building Alora is sure wasn't there before.

"I think we're here," Endri says.

Above the opaque glass double doors that remind Alora of a corner convenience store, complete with bells tied to the handles, an almost insultingly drab sign reads Welcome, Human Souls. The bedsheet ghosts float inside.

To Alora, the human dormitory lobby might as well have been the ground floor of a New York City apartment building, complete with old brass mailboxes built into one wall, a corkboard on the opposite littered with old flyers, and a pair of elevators toward the back. There's just one glaring difference: at the center of the room, behind a cluttered reception desk, sits a bizarre creature with more arms than Alora can count dressed in a gray three-piece suit with black pinstripes.

As the ghosts approach the front desk, the well-dressed, hundred-handed being pays them no mind. Instead, with its many arms, it shuffles papers, takes notes, types data into some kind of archaic-looking computer console, thumbs through filing cabinets, stirs the dregs of an almost-empty cup of tea, and even flips through the pages of a worn-out book—the one task its eyes, peeking over a pair of wire-rim glasses, focus on.

After a few moments of gazing in awe at the creature, Yume is the first to break the silence by rapping her knuckles three times atop the reception desk.

Without looking up at the group, the busy being lifts a single finger from a single hand in front of them.

"Just one moment, please," it says before licking the finger it had raised and turning the page of its book. With a sigh and a smile, the creature closes the book and sets it down before pushing the glasses back up onto the bridge of its nose and greeting the ghosts with a smile.

"Many apologies, good folks. I'm always so busy I rarely have a moment to read. Hard to fit in with all this work, I'm afraid. The funny thing about time is that even when you have an infinite amount, it never seems enough, does it? Anyhoo, you must be Morpheus's latest recruits, yes? You're late. You're always late. But do not worry. We'll have you oriented in no time," he chuckles, "and you can get back to work. So much work, so little time. But you'll manage. You always do."

"I like you," Yume giggles, extending a hand. "I'm Yume. What's your name?"

The creature pauses, tilting its head before extending a hand in return. "How curious. How unexpected. How lovely. You may call me Cottus. It's a pleasure to make your acquaintance, Yume."

Taking Yume's cue, Alora also scoots forward, extending her hand. With another of its hundreds of hands, Cottus accepts Alora's greeting.

"Mind if we ask what you do here, Cottus?" Alora asks.

"Not at all. Be my guest," Cottus responds, staring back at

Alora silently.

Alora blinks, dumbfounded. Behind her, Rasui raises a hand to wave at Cottus, clearing his throat.

"Hi. Rasui, here. What *is* it you do here?"

"Administration," Cottus answers before adding, "facilities management, employee communications, data management, data *input*, data *dispersion*, temporal liaising, departmental and interplanar relations, all things related to the secretarial arts—I could keep going if you'd like."

"No, thank you," Kanasu blurts. "Uh, also hello. I'm Kanasu."

"Of course you are," Cottus responds.

"And I'm Endri," Endri says. "If you're Cottus, would that make you one of the Hecatoncheires?"

"Why, yes, it would!" Cottus lights up with genuine joy. "Impressive. Intriguing. Outstanding. You seem like a good batch of human souls, if you don't mind my saying so. Friendly and informed—such a rare pairing, even here in the Dreamscape."

"*Heca-tonka*-what?" Rasui exclaims.

"*Hecatoncheires*," Endri repeats. "The Hundred-Handers. They helped Zeus defeat the Titans. Do you not know your Greek mythology?"

"Hey, I know Zeus…and Hercules," Rasui huffs. "But that one seems like a deep cut."

"Ah, yes, Zeus," Cottus muses. "He, too, was confounded by my brothers and me. Although, he did find that we had our uses. Bloody work, that. A waste of our talents if you ask me. I don't miss it. Though there were bright spots, battling beside the gods. Anyhoo, not to worry. I take no offense. Endri, here, is correct. I am one of the three Hecatoncheires, alongside my brothers Briareus and Gyges. Or Aegaeon and Gyes, if you'd prefer. They certainly don't care either way, and neither do I."

"You're kind of a lot to handle," Kanasu mumbles.

"Don't be rude," Alora whispers, bumping Kanasu with an elbow.

Cottus laughs, his hundreds of hands continuing their busy work. "Think nothing of it. I understand my appearance and my capabilities are somewhat confounding to you mortals. But I assure you, there's a straightforward explanation. My brothers and I exist on multiple temporal planes at once. While you experience time as linear, we do not—much like the Dreamscape itself. We can exist in a single place and time or thousands at once, as I am doing right now.

"While you see me as a multi-limbed monstrosity, the simple truth is you're merely witnessing multiple instances of my existence simultaneously. It's not that I have thousands of arms, so much that thousands of my arms exist in this location simultaneously, so to speak. We can also exist simultaneously in multiple locations. Thus, we are uniquely well-suited to our jobs here at Dreamweavers. Rather than depending on a staff of hundreds or thousands of beings, my brothers and I can easily handle all the work ourselves. Unlike Zeus, Maya saw our true potential and employed us as her support staff here in the Dreamscape, for which I am eternally grateful. Although, my brothers have their own impish opinions on the matter."

Rasui whistles. "A simple explanation, he says."

"Before we came in," Alora interjects, "this building wasn't here. And then it was. But we were told the city of Somnia is static, unlike the surrounding lands of…"

"Oneiros," Yume says, twirling back and forth.

"Right, what she said," Alora continues. "What's the deal with that?"

"You're very observant." Cottus grins. "Like my brothers and myself, certain edifices in Somnia occupy a single space but can shift temporally. These human dormitories, for instance, are both here and not here, mostly depending upon the needs of those around them. The dormitories appeared because you approached them and were looking for them. There are several other facilities at this particular location, including a few empty lots, which may be what you observed. Maya could not decide what to erect in the lots, so they remain empty until new facilities are needed."

"I think I'm starting to get a headache," Kanasu says.

"Can ghosts or spirits or whatever even get headaches?" Rasui asks.

Endri shrugs.

"Anyhoo, onto the matter at hand," Cottus continues, turning to look where a pair of his hands shuffled through a stack of papers. "You need your room assignment. That way, you can rest your weary heads. Here it is, room…eleven. Or is it two-seventeen? No, wait, four-ninety-one. Doesn't matter. Take the elevator behind me, and you should arrive at your dormitory, barring any temporal anomalies or tears in space-time. But no, it should be fine. I'm sure it's fine. You'll be fine. You always are."

The ghosts all turn to look as a cheerful ding rings out behind Cottus. One of the elevators at the back wall is open and waiting for the group to enter. Alora turns back to ask Cottus another question, but the Hecatoncheire is already nose-deep in his book once more, his hundreds of hands just as busy as ever.

"Going up?" Rasui asks. Alora turns around to find her companions waiting for her in the elevator. She floats inside, squeezing between them as the elevator doors close with another cheerful ding.

Chapter Three

Icebreaker: Getting to Know Your Fellow Dreamweavers

After an uncomfortably silent, too-long ride, the elevator doors open again, sounding the same cheery chime as before. Alora and company float over the elevator's threshold and into a spacious, curious room that's as familiar as it is bizarre. It's full of furniture typical of human living spaces—sofas, love seats, a dining area, a coffee table, and even a diner-style counter—but everything is arranged against the back wall and faces the wall opposite—the one with the elevator door through which the group emerged.

"Oh my god," Rasui exclaims excitedly, gliding into the center of the room and plopping down on one of the couches. "It's a freaking sitcom set! This rules!"

Like a light switch flipping, Alora realizes that the sci-fi-sheeted ghost is right. The bizarre arrangement of the furniture—and even the style of the pieces therein—reminds her of the shows she watched growing up, especially during sick days when she stayed home from school. That's why it feels both comforting and confounding.

"So, this is what we're reduced to in the afterlife," Kanasu chuckles, "sitcom characters."

"Mythologically speaking," Endri says, floating over to the diner counter and sitting down on one of the chrome-plated stools, "there are far worse places we could have ended up."

Yume scurries toward the back of the room, leaning over with her hand outstretched and making a *pss-pss-pss* sound at a shadowy corner.

"Are we going to talk about all this or what?" Kanasu says, addressing the group. "We all wake up in a classroom where we meet a demon who tells us that he's not a demon at all and we're here to make dreams for people. Then there's another demon-looking guy who claims to be a god, and he's the one responsible for nightmares. Plus, there's a dude downstairs who seems like he has a thousand arms but is really some kind of time-traveling monster that used to pal around with Zeus. And now we're all trapped in a room that looks like a sitcom set without any windows, and the one doorway we had to the elevator is suddenly missing entirely!"

Kanasu points to the wall where the elevator used to be, but the doors—and their seams—are conspicuously missing.

"Whoa," Rasui gasps. "Super weird."

"Not to mention," Kanasu continues, ignoring Rasui, "we're all cartoonish bedsheet ghosts without any physical bodies, and none of us can remember a single specific thing about who we were before we got here. Does that about sum it up?"

The ghosts hesitantly nod in agreement.

"And we're all just okay with this?" Kanasu's arms drop, and they let out a deep sigh. Without giving their companions a chance to answer, they sulk over to one of the room's reading chairs and collapse into it.

When they look up again, Endri kneels before them, flanked by Rasui and Yume. Alora stays back, looking uncomfortable by herself in a corner.

"None of us are okay with this," Endri says.

"You wanna know who you are?" Rasui interjects. "So do we."

"We're all in this together," Yume adds with a tilt of her head. "Right? Like a team."

In the background, Alora raises a hand. "I'd like to know myself just as much as everyone. But I want it on the record that I still think we shouldn't meddle. Who knows? Maybe we'll get more privileges down the line."

"We should start with what each of us remembers," Kanasu says, ignoring Alora. "And we'll go from there."

For what felt like hours—*I'm never going to understand how time works here*, Alora thinks—the bedsheet ghosts went through what they could remember about their mortal lives. They started with the big stuff that stood out, like where they were from—Alora grew up in a big city; Endri came from a college town; Kanasu was from the suburbs; Rasui hails from a small rural village; and Yume moved from place to place her whole life—before trying to pin down the minutiae of their experiences.

While they still couldn't remember specifics, like their Earthly names—Alora wasn't the only one who felt weird about her name—or even how many people had been in their families, they discovered that they remembered much about what it felt like to be human. Each of them had something intimate, almost instinctual, that bubbled to the top of their minds. Moreover, they realized how much they all had in common, or at least how easy it was to relate to one another.

Rasui told jokes that, while cheesy, even got a chuckle out of eternal stoic Kanasu. Endri waxed almost poetic about the vastness of the physical universe and how waking up in the Afterworld forced him to question his basest understanding of it all. Yume danced—little more than bouncing and twirls—assuring the group that her performance would have been far better if she still had all her limbs, yet it elicited raucous applause all the same. Kanasu made it three-quarters of the way through a creepy ghost story before realizing they were all already ghosts and, therefore, the tale had lost its scare factor—ultimately garnering a bigger laugh than Rasui's jokes.

But when it came to Alora's turn, she mostly drew a blank. The only thing that had felt familiar, like something from her past, was the phrase she had used earlier: *if you're going to do something, do it right.* She could recall no unique talents, deep wells of knowledge, or hobbies or habits that stuck out. Alora felt like she didn't have anything in particular to share. So, she didn't, trying her best not to stick out as everyone else reveled.

While the rest of the bedsheet ghosts found comfort in what vague bits of their past they could remember, Alora felt hollow—as hollow as the space beneath the sheet over her head. In accepting her companions' attempts to remember—despite her gut feeling that they should all simply stay the course—she had found nothing. She was no closer to recalling who she was and had somehow managed to compound the emptiness she had felt since those first moments in the Afterworld.

For the first time since waking up in that classroom, Alora was glad nobody could see her face. It made it easier to hide how she was feeling. Besides, who was she to take away the glee she had roused in the rest of the bedsheet ghosts? Better to let them enjoy it while it lasts, she figured. Plus, it felt good that everyone enjoyed getting to know one another. Surely, something would come to her eventually. Maybe she just needed more time to acclimate. She hoped she just needed more time.

"Hey, you okay?" It was Kanasu, leaning over and whispering so only Alora could hear them.

"Yeah, totally," Alora replies. "Why do you ask?"

"I don't know. I haven't exactly been all that friendly. It's just, all of this…" Kanasu scoots a bit closer. "Maybe I shouldn't hold it against you that you're okay with everything as it is. You wanna go with the flow; that's your prerogative."

Alora can't tell if Kanasu is being snarky or genuine, so she deflects—just to be safe.

"Oh. Yeah. I'm fine, I think. I just… It's good to hear all these stories and laughter, and I don't want to interrupt."

"Right, gotcha. Well, if you ever do feel like interrupting, I'm here."

Alora wants to reassure Kanasu, to tell them that she appreciates the camaraderie around her and that everything is fine. But it isn't. She just wants to keep her head down and do what she's told. She wants everyone to want that.

Instead, she feels surrounded by people—or disembodied human souls, *whatever*—who wouldn't just let it go. It wasn't right. It's disorderly. And that makes her nervous, skittish, maybe a little angry. Somehow, Kanasu can tell, even through Alora's polka-dotted bedsheet. Alora feels both seen and exposed. And that makes her even more uncomfortable.

"Everything would be fine if you'd all just follow the rules," Alora finally snaps. "This is pointless."

Kanasu recoils, scooting away. "Right. Message received."

Alora regrets the words as soon as they leave her mouth, but it's too late. Yes, it's how she feels. Yes, she believes it. But now everyone is staring at her as if she spit in their faces. It's too loud a reaction, too obstinate. And if there is anything Alora dislikes more than breaking the rules, it's drawing unwanted attention to herself.

Kanasu gets up and wanders away, rejoining the rest of the group as they resume their conversations, interjecting in an argument between Rasui and Endri on the merits of time travel.

Alora curls up tight in the love seat she had crawled into, feeling even worse than before. Except now, she recalls something about herself, an intimate detail from when she was still alive, something that defined so much of her time spent on Earth. Alora remembers what it felt like to be alone.

Chapter Four

Departmental Training: An Essential Guide to Your Duties

"Good to see we're all getting along like fire and brimstone," Morpheus announces. So wrapped up in their conversations, the bedsheet ghosts don't even notice when their mentor—*Mentor? Caretaker? Professor? Supervisor?* Alora still isn't sure what to call him—enters the room. They can't even be certain if he came in through the elevator or manifested inside the dormitory.

Regardless, he had shown up in all his bombastic, self-indulgent, well-dressed glory. And for Alora, the timing couldn't have been better, as she had spent the better part of the past few hours stewing in self-pity. Morpheus's return meant he had something for them to do, and that would keep her mind occupied elsewhere—or so she hoped.

"I take it we've finally reached a level of acceptance that will allow us to continue our work, yes? Good," Morpheus says, not waiting for an answer. "Now that we've gotten orientation out of the way and those first-day jitters shaken off, it's time for you to see a bit of what we do in earnest."

Morpheus snaps his fingers, and, in that same instant, the ghosts return to the classroom where they first met. And once again, that old film projector on its metal cart is in the center of the room. With another flick of Morpheus's wrist, the lights dim, and the projector spins to life, a new video displayed on the screen. As the ghosts watch the image come to life, Morpheus sits down in his desk chair, kicks his feet up, and almost immediately starts to nod off.

"What an inspiring leader," Kanasu whispers sarcastically.

But only Alora reacts, shushing them as the on-screen animation begins. Kanasu shushes back mockingly. Embarrassed, Alora lowers her head.

The same blue-and-gold font from the Dreamweavers orientation video wipes across the screen, only this time it reads *Dare to Dream* and below that *A Beginner's Guide to Your Dreamweavers Department*. As the text fades, an image of the golden four-armed woman—Maya, Alora remembers—fades in. She is once again seated in her lotus chair, surrounded by the same animal-filled swamp.

"By now, you should be familiar with the bureaucratic structure and three-departmental organization of Dreamweavers, LLC," Maya says with a gentle smile.

"Hey, hold on," Rasui stammers. "What is she talking about?"

"Morpheus, sir," Alora interjects, raising her hand. "Sir? I think this might be the wrong video. We haven't gone over this."

Morpheus, his eyes still closed, answers. "Put your hand down and watch."

Alora lowers her hand slowly.

"If you're still unclear, fret not," Maya says as the video continues. "You'll soon have a chance to see it in action during interdepartmental job shadowing. For now, however, let's get to know the intricate duties and responsibilities you'll have here in the Dreamscape."

The image of Maya in her verdant swamp fades, and another line of text wipes across the screen. *Department of the Mundane: Where Even the Insignificant Is Essential*, it says. A voice-over kicks in. This time, it's not Maya's calm, soothing voice. Instead, it's Morpheus's—albeit with much more exuberance than any of the bedsheet ghosts have heard up to this point.

"Now? Is it recording now?" Morpheus stammers as a cartoon animation of a group of ghosts comes to life on the screen. "Hello, and welcome to the Department of the Mundane, where even the insignificant is essential. As you likely already know, I am your department head, Morpheus, and I'm here to walk you through your duties and response— what? Oh right, sorry. We've already gone over that bit. Okay. Where were we? Yes, right, what do we do here in the Department of the Mundane..."

The cartoon ghosts, bobbing up and down cheerfully, float across the screen into the doorway of a slightly uneven rectangular building with the words *Dream Stage* written across its side. Once inside, they take their places around an empty stage. The first one operates a little spotlight. The second floats over to a small (and crudely drawn) soundboard and fiddles with the knobs and levers. The third picks up a megaphone with the word *Director* scrawled across its side. And the last one picks up a small film slate, clapping the top down and eliciting a jagged little comic book-style word bubble that reads *Action!*

"While not as flashy as the Department of Nightmares or as wondrous as the Department of the Fantastic," Morpheus continues, "the Department of the Mundane is no less an integral part of what we do here in the Dreamscape. This is because every dream is crucial, even when they're not meaningful—Are we sure that's the phrasing we want to use? Oh right, sorry. Does the mic pick up everything? Right. Can we just edit it later? No? Oh okay, sorry."

On the screen, a tiny stick figure suddenly poofs onto the stage between the cartoon ghosts. The ghost manning the spotlight points it at the stick figure; the ghost at the soundboard fiddles with the switches and knobs; the little director ghost holds the megaphone up to its face; and the ghost that had been holding the slate now holds a small fishing pole with a carrot attached where the hook should have been, dangling it over the stage in front of the stick figure. Seeing the carrot, the stick figure reaches out for the vegetable but can't quite grasp it, as the cartoon ghost holding the fishing pole keeps yanking it just out of reach.

"As we all know, humans require sleep," Morpheus continues, finally back on track. "And when they sleep, their souls can astral project out of their mortal bodies and travel into the spiritual planes—or, as we know them, the constituent realms of the Afterworld. However, astral projection can be extremely dangerous for a mortal soul, especially those with the potential to get lost within the spiritual planes. To keep these souls safe and return them to their bodies before a given sleep cycle ends, we in the Dreamscape intercept astral projecting souls and redirect them to our dream stages. Here, we craft dreams to keep these souls occupied for the duration of their astral projections and, in many cases, to offer inspiration these spirits can take with them back into the mortal realm."

On the screen, the ghosts surrounding the little stick-figure human all disappear in little clouds of smoke, and the human flies out of the dream stage, across the Dreamscape, and back to the mortal realm, Earth. There, the stick-figure soars around the world, down into a neighborhood, and through the wall of a carelessly drawn little house—the kind a child might have sketched with a triangle-shaped roof, a pair of windows, and a rectangle door with a tiny circular knob. Inside, the flying stick figure gently lays down on a bed with closed eyes. A moment later, its eyes open, and it springs out of bed with one arm raised triumphantly and an illuminated lightbulb—which Alora assumes is meant to signify inspiration—popping up over its head.

The little cartoon on the screen fades to white again, and a new graphic wipes across. *On Earth as It Is in Heaven* it reads in the same blue-and-gold lettering as before. As it appears on the display, Morpheus continues speaking.

"Across locales, cultures, and even religions, living souls have collectively decided that the content of their dreams holds special meaning. And due to the Heaven-and-Earth Accord—an ancient and heretofore unbreakable agreement between the realms—our responsibility at Dreamweavers, LLC is to provide mortal souls with that meaning. A nightmare, for instance, may be designed to illustrate what might happen to a mortal soul should they shirk their worldly duties. Similarly, a dream crafted by the Department of the Fantastic may give someone the impetus to embark on a new venture."

The letters fade from the screen, and a new image fades in. This time, it's Morpheus, back to his impossibly dark blue winged form and reading clumsily from a teleprompter. The camera follows him as he passes before a series of dream stages—although these are far smaller than the one where Alora and company had encountered Chernobog. Other bedsheet ghosts mull about these small stages, setting up cheap-looking, unconvincing scenes made from hastily taped-together cardboard cutouts.

"But Dreamweavers simply does not have the resources and staff to make every single dream a consequential one. Still, mortal souls must be corralled during astral projection to keep them safe, sound, and away from the other realms of the Afterworld. This is where we come in here at the Department of the Mundane. It's our job to fill in the gaps, crafting the in-between dreams. These are, effectively, meaningless."

Morpheus frowns, addressing someone offscreen. "Are we sure that's how we want to word it? Yes, I know the script was already approved. It's just so repetitive. And it doesn't sound very good—"

The video cuts abruptly, now showing Morpheus standing outside between the warehouse-like dream stages, smiling once again.

"While our work might not bear the same meaning as the dreams crafted by the Department of Nightmares or the Department of the Fantastic, it is no less essential. We are shepherds of mortal souls, keeping them safe and sound in their time away from the waking world. Imbued with significance or not, our work in the Department of the Mundane is a necessary and crucial part of operations here at Dreamweavers, LLC, serving as the backbone of the entire organization. And I, for one, can't wait to start our work together in earnest!"

Morpheus gives the camera a wink and a thumbs-up, pausing for effect before addressing someone offscreen again.

"Yes, that was much better. Not so drab and depressing. For gods' sake, these people are already dead and haven't exactly arrived at the proverbial pearly gates." He motions to his surroundings. "We don't need to demoralize them further. What do you mean it's still rolling? Can't you edit it later? Well, cut the damned film, then—"

The screen goes white as the film on the projector runs out, flapping against the roll before slowing to a stop. The lights in the classroom come back on, but Morpheus remains reclined in his desk chair, feet up and eyes closed.

"The next step is interdepartmental job shadowing," Morpheus says. "You'll be split into two groups. The first will go to the Department of Nightmares, the second will visit the Department of the Fantastic, and then you'll switch. Got it? Endri, Rasui, and Yume will be group one, and Kanasu and Alora will constitute group two."

Alora winces at the assignment, but Kanasu leans over and whispers at her before she can protest. "Don't worry. We don't have to be friends. We just have to work together."

"Well," Morpheus continues, "get on with it, then."

Morpheus snaps his fingers, and the two groups teleport from the classroom to their respective assignments.

Dream Log #2

Courtesy of the Department of the Fantastic

Earth Date: Holocene Period, Age of Humankind, Twentieth Century, 1995 CE (Earth calendar)
Corporeal Location of Subject: Toledo, Ohio, USA (Earth)
Subject: Human, female-identifying, catering waiter, aged approximately twenty-three (Earth years)

Start log.

A young woman in a teal dress, white apron, and paper hat stands behind the counter of an idyllic diner, complete with freshly baked pies in the display fridge, chrome-lined counters, stools, and booths, and big, wide windows looking out to the semitruck-filled parking lot. A few patrons are hunched over the counter, some eating heaping plates of food and others tending only to cups of coffee.

The young woman tops off the coffee of one of the patrons as he—she thinks he's a man, but she can't make out his face beyond his trucker jacket's upturned collar and long-billed cap—slides a piece of paper across the counter.

She hesitates before picking up the paper, afraid of what it might say. But she steels herself and opens the folded parchment, finding a simple three-word phrase etched on it: *don't look down.*

She looks up and begins to ask, "What is this supposed to—"

But she's no longer in the diner. Instead, she's hundreds, if not thousands, of feet up in the air. And worse, her surroundings are not ones she recognizes. She sees the diner in the distance, but it isn't on the ground—it's centered on a floating island, hovering in the sky. And there are thousands of these little islands all around her.

And then she makes the mistake of looking down.

Like a rock, she plummets toward the ground below, picking up speed with the whooshing wind enveloping her. Her body tumbles, first head over feet, then twisting and turning before she finally stabilizes, doing her best to mimic the skydivers she remembers from an inspirational poster in the diner's back office.

She realizes suddenly, feeling her heart in her throat, that the ground is rising too quickly below her, and she isn't wearing a parachute. She'll hit the ground at full speed, and that will be the end of it. With a deep breath, she closes her eyes, exhales slowly, and waits for the inevitable impact.

But the impact never comes.

Instead, she realizes the whooshing wind is no longer coming up at her but instead coming laterally, like a warm summer breeze on her cheeks and through her hair. She opens her eyes and finds that she's no longer falling—she's soaring.

Imagining herself as a superhero, she puts her arms before her and straightens her legs, flying through the sky like a rocket. And the thrill is not lost on the young woman—she beams with excitement and even fails to stifle her giggles as she cuts around, over, and under the rocky floating islands and through the clouds.

She arcs high up in the sky before turning back downward, diving toward the ground with her arms tucked to her sides and her legs as straight as she can manage, doing her best torpedo impression. The young woman picks up speed, traveling even faster than she was when she fell, careening at almost supersonic speed toward the earth below.

At the last possible second, she slows herself, tilting her body backward so that her feet are once again below her, and alights on the ground as gently as a falling feather.

She takes a moment to catch her breath, still giddily giggling and grinning from ear to ear. Then, with a squat and jump, she launches back into the sky, sailing upward, faster and faster, up into the sky.

She flies so high that even the floating islands below her look like little more than specks. Then she dives once more back toward the ground below, reaching her hands out to run her fingers through the clouds and spinning her body like a top to avoid crashing into the floating islands.

And then she does it again. And again. And again.

On her final flight, she doesn't land on the ground below. Instead, she gracefully lands in the diner's truck-filled parking lot, casually strolls inside, walks to the back, and knocks on the manager's door.

"Whaddya want?" The voice that comes through the door is equally familiar and alien—as if the manager she'd worked for over the past decade had caught a bad cold.

"Jerry." She beams. "I quit."

End log.

Chapter Five

Interdepartmental Training: An Essential Guide to the
Duties of Others

Of all the strange and incredible things she had witnessed since arriving in the Dreamscape, seeing someone experiencing the joy of flight—even only as a stranger in a dream—was the one that made Alora feel the most like she was where she was meant to be, especially since her various snafus with Kanasu.

Witnessing this young woman's dream conjures the same excitement Alora recalls in giving someone the exact right birthday or holiday gift. For a brief moment, it feels perfect.

With the young woman's astral spirit projected back into her body on Earth, the Department of the Fantastic staff, accompanied by Alora and Kanasu, gathers toward the center of the expansive Dream Stage. In a semicircle, they surround the department's head—Mamu, the Mesopotamian goddess of dreams.

"Beautiful job," Mamu announces in her warm and welcoming, albeit rumbling voice. "A masterwork of inspiration. Perhaps now, in the waking world, that young woman will finally have the initiative to follow through on her aspirations of becoming a… What do the humans call it? Pilot? Yes, that sounds right. Shall we discuss?"

Earlier, Alora and Kanasu learned that Mamu was one of Dreamweavers' most senior employees and, throughout the company's existence, the only entity (nonhuman or otherwise) to lead the Department of the Fantastic. Yet, despite her literal eons of experience and expertise, Alora found the deity somehow relatable and approachable.

Her welcoming nature was especially astounding, considering how intimidatingly enormous and beautiful she was compared to Alora, Kanasu, and all the other bedsheet-wearing human souls.

By Alora's estimation, Mamu has to be at least twenty feet tall, if not taller, with long and graceful limbs, a slender neck that meets a razor-sharp jawline, and enchanting eyes that are almost pitch-black and speckled with points of light—more like encapsulated galaxies than eyeballs. She wears an elegant, slinky, floor-length gown—again, all the more impressive considering her stature—that looks like an otherworldly tailor had stitched it from twinkling stars and glittering spider-webs.

"You must be Morpheus's new brood," Mamu had said upon Kanasu and Alora's arrival at the Department of the Fantastic's dream stage. She knelt down and extended an enormous hand, attempting a customary human greeting. "It's a tremendous pleasure to meet you both. You may call me Mamu, Nyx, or Ratri—whichever denomination suits you is fine."

"Which do you prefer?" Alora asked.

"The need to name things is a distinctly human trait," Mamu

answered. "All of them are my name, and none encapsulate the whole of my existence. As such, I have no preference."

"Whoa," Kanasu laughed. "That's pretty badass."

"Badass," Mamu repeated with a tilt of her head, puzzling over the compliment. "Thank you."

The towering deity gave Alora and Kanasu a tour of the facility herself, introducing them to all the department's staff members along the way. She knew all of them by name, and they, in turn, showed Alora and Kanasu the same respect, stopping whatever they were doing to greet the pair. As the trio traversed the dream stage and its constituent annexes, Mamu even took the time to try to get to know the two new bedsheet ghosts, inquiring about their experiences in the Dreamscape—and the larger Afterworld—thus far.

"And how is Morpheus doing these days?" Mamu asked toward the end of the tour with curious urgency, giving Alora the impression that the deity had been waiting to ask this very question the entire time.

"Aloof," Kanasu had answered curtly.

"Honestly," Alora interjected, eliciting a scowl from Kanasu, "we haven't had much chance to talk to him ourselves. Mostly, he's been just playing videos and sending us off on errands. I don't think he likes us very much. Humans, I mean."

"Dreadful shame," Mamu agreed with a smile, but her tone betrayed her sadness. "But you shouldn't take it to heart. It's not you. I had such high hopes for him, you know. We eternal beings don't have families in the same way as humans, but I've always considered him a kind of son. Such a shame. But perhaps it is for the best. He's just not been the same since his brothers—perhaps it is not my place to say."

"His brothers?" Alora asked.

"My other sons," Mamu answers. "They work in the Department of Nightmares now."

"With Chernobog," Kanasu interjected with a grumble.

"Yes," Mamu replied. "Spectacular weaver of dreams, but perhaps too ambitious for his own good. Still, it seems he may get his way if Morpheus's work does not improve."

But an alarm sounded before Alora could ask Mamu what she meant, signaling that the Department of the Fantastic's staff had finished dream stage preparations and that the dream was about to commence. By the time it had ended, Alora had entirely forgotten to inquire further.

"What could we have done better?" Mamu asks the human souls surrounding her on the dream stage. "Or perhaps the question is better worded thusly: How could we have made this young woman's dream a more enjoyable and enlightening experience?"

As Mamu fields answers from several surrounding bedsheet-wearing human souls, Alora sidles up to Kanasu, determined to smooth out the wrinkle she had caused in their relationship.

"I always thought flying dreams were so scary, you know?" Alora whispers. "Do you remember that feeling?"

"Not really," Kanasu replies flatly.

"Plus, I think I was afraid of heights. Being up that high is just not for me. I would never feel like I was in control."

"Can we just watch and listen?" Kanasu snaps. "Isn't this what you wanted, anyhow? For us to all follow the rules."

"Yeah, sorry," Alora replies, lowering her head. "It's just that lack of control, you know? There's always that feeling in the back of my head that I could fall and—"

Kanasu raises their hand, waving it back and forth to draw Mamu's attention.

"Yes, Kanasu?" the deity calls on them.

"Alora has an idea. For how to improve this woman's dream, I mean."

"Wonderful," Mamu says with a smile. "Please share this idea with the rest of us."

"Uh…yeah, I was just…I thought," Alora stammers. Again, Kanasu managed to put the spotlight on Alora, and again, Alora is reminded of how much she dislikes being the center of attention. But she isn't going to let Kanasu win this time. "Control."

"I'm not sure I understand," Mamu says. "Can you elaborate?"

Alora hears Kanasu snickering beside her.

"What if we let the human souls, I don't know, participate in the dream? Like, let them control where they go and what they do. Let them decide for themselves."

"That is a lovely idea," Mamu says, momentarily sitting with it. "But I'm afraid that's just not how things work here. However, it does make for a great opportunity—a lesson, if you will."

Trying to shrink back into the crowd, Alora drops her shoulders and hangs her head. This is precisely why she prefers to stay quiet and blend in. You can't get singled out and made a fool of if you keep to yourself. Kanasu had gotten the better of her again, but it was her own fault this time.

Maybe Kanasu was right after all—they needn't be friends, only coworkers.

"Who can tell me why we do not cede any control of these

dreams over to the human souls partaking in them?" Mamu scans the crowd, picking out a bedsheet ghost on one of the far sides of the semicircle.

"Because human souls don't know what they want," the ghost answers.

"Very good," Mamu claps. "That is absolutely correct. We have a responsibility to help guide these souls toward an idea or decision. It is our burden to usher them toward solving their earthly dilemmas. If we let the souls decide how a dream plays out, it would be utter chaos. And worse, it would be pointless."

The conversation continues, with Mamu posing questions and ideas to the crowd and the Department of the Fantastic's staff addressing them. Once the debrief wraps up, Mamu thanks Alora and Kanasu for their participation and sends them on their way—instructing them on how to find the Department of Nightmare's live dream stage.

"Can't you just, like, snap your fingers and put us there?" Kanasu asked.

"Is that what Morpheus has been doing?" Mamu shakes her head. "No, it is not customary for those of us with the ability to teleport you from place to place. Gods, how does he expect you to become acquainted with your new reality if he won't allow you to find your way? He's far worse than I had thought, it seems. What a waste of potential. Such a shame."

And with that, Mamu leaves Alora and Kanasu, gesturing toward the exit and sending them off to Chernobog's Department of Nightmares.

☠

Outside the Department of the Fantastic's dream stage, Kanasu keeps their distance from Alora, pacing ahead and not even bothering to check to see if Alora is keeping up. But Alora, livid at being put on the spot in front of everyone, catches up with her coworker, intent on cutting them off and confronting them once and for all.

"What the hell was that?" Alora stammers, gliding into Kanasu's path and stopping them.

"You wouldn't leave me alone," Kanasu answers.

"I was only trying to be friendly."

"I already told you: we don't have to be friends; we just have to work together." Kanasu tries to scoot around Alora, but Alora cuts them off again.

"You made me look stupid. On purpose. In front of everyone."

"You made yourself look stupid."

"You know, there's a big difference between not being friends and you sabotaging me," Alora hisses.

"Well, maybe you'll learn a thing or two and just keep it to yourself next time," Kanasu says.

"I was just trying to smooth things over between us."

"Well, you did a bang-up job. Now look at us: the best of friends!"

"You're impossible," Alora snaps.

"And you're a selfish turd," Kanasu retorts.

"Well, maybe I should just transfer departments, then."

"Maybe you should."

Exasperated and out of comebacks, Alora feels so furious that she could cry—if that were even possible as a bedsheet ghost. But there's a part of her that knows Kanasu is right. Even now, she's only thinking of herself and how she feels.

Only at this precise moment does it occur to her that she never even bothered to apologize to Kanasu for snapping at them back at the dorms when their feud first started.

"This is so stupid," she mumbles to herself. "Can't even make friends in the afterlife."

"If you've got something to say to me, speak up and say it to my face," Kanasu replies, cocking their head.

For a moment, Alora considers apologizing in earnest. It wouldn't be hard to admit fault, put the spats behind them, and maybe foster a positive relationship. And maybe, just maybe, she could get Kanasu to understand her way of thinking. That it's better just to keep their head down, do what's asked of them, and stop causing trouble.

If you're going to do something, do it right, a voice chimes in Alora's head. She had tried to follow the same familiar refrain since waking up in the Afterworld—it was her guiding principle.

But this time, she ignores it.

"You suck," Alora snarls instead.

Kanasu says nothing in return, instead turning and resuming toward the Department of Nightmares.

Alora follows shortly behind.

"You're late," a towering beast—part lion, part bear but dressed in a fine suit rivaling Morpheus's—awaits Alora and Kanasu, blocking the entrance to Dream Stage 42—the very same stage they had stumbled upon when they first met Chernobog.

"We got lost," Kanasu replies coldly.

Alora, still fuming, remains silent.

"The boss has already started," the well-dressed lion-bear continues, ignoring Kanasu's tone. "We've got a schedule to keep. Can't make exceptions for more of Morpheus's flunkies. Keep quiet, keep your heads down, and stay out of the way."

The imposing beast steps aside, opening the door to the dream stage just wide enough for Alora and Kanasu to slip through before closing it again. Inside, the warehouse is dark—even darker than the first time they stumbled upon it—making it difficult for either bedsheet ghost to navigate toward the center of the room.

As the pair gets closer, they can finally make out the staging at the center of the immense space. A far cry from the spooky forest they had seen only a short time before, the stage is now set with an approximation of a rural American farmhouse, but one that has had addition after addition after addition tacked onto it haphazardly—like some kind of monolithic, labyrinthine fun house instead of a place a person might actually live.

While Alora and Kanasu—still locked in their tense silence—slowly approach the house, the whole structure shudders and shakes before shifting into a new configuration—looking to Alora like some kind of macabre Rubik's cube. To her left, Alora sees the low glow of screens just beyond the edge of the house's yard. Gently, she places a hand on Kanasu's shoulder, and Kanasu nearly jumps out of their bedsheet.

"Are you trying to give me a flipping heart attack?" Kanasu rasps, trying their best to keep quiet.

"Over there," Alora says, offering no apology for the scare. "I think there's some kind of monitors or a viewing station."

Together, they approach the workstation.

Aided by the glowing light, Alora can make out another

beastly creature sitting at a confusing and convoluted console marked by displays, buttons, knobs, switches, levers, and dials. Like its counterpart outside the dream stage, the monster is also dressed in a fine suit, its fabric hugging a body made from rocks, ore, and glimmering crystals. It sees Alora and Kanasu approach, lifting a finger to its lips—*they look like lips, at least*, Alora muses.

"If my brother let you pass," the creature whispers in a gravelly baritone, "you must be the newbies. Come, gather 'round. This nightmare is already well underway. Watch."

On the displays, in the green glow of night vision, Alora sees a potbellied man in his midforties dressed in shabby overalls and sporting an exceptionally long mullet running away from an older woman, her hair in curlers, bunny slippers on her feet, and a floral robe over her shoulders.

Except, her facial features aren't quite right—they look less like she has eyes, a nose, and a mouth and more like there's coloring on her skin or a pattern to give the impression she has facial features. And where her stomach should be, there's a gaping mouth filled with dozens and dozens of sharp, jagged, semitranslucent teeth instead—reminding Alora of some kind of deep-sea fish.

As the mullet man runs from the angler-woman, the Rubik's cube farmhouse shifts, separating them momentarily. On the display, Alora can see the relief on the man's face as he leans over, braces himself on his knees, and tries to catch his breath.

But then the farmhouse shifts again, creating a new path between the man and the monster. And the chase resumes once more.

The scene continues for some time until, as the farmhouse shifts, the angler-woman gets trapped, pinned between two walls closing in on one another. The mullet man sees the monster get stuck and starts to laugh, the fear gone from his face.

And then Alora hears a familiar booming voice fill the dream stage.

"End it," Chernobog says over the loudspeaker. "End it now!"

In an instant, the mullet man vanishes from the displays in a puff of smoke, and the lights in Dream Stage 42 come up. Finally, Alora can see the whole interior, noting the dozens of other ghosts operating half a dozen different stations around the off-kilter farmhouse.

Toward the center of the dream stage—between the monitoring station and the farmhouse's front door—the blackest of shadows begins to bubble up from the ground, spreading and expanding until a great, clawed hand reaches out of it.

The claw slams down on the ground, shaking the entire building. Then another emerges and slams down beside its sibling. Finally, like a whale breaching out of the ocean's surface, the rest of Chernobog's shadowy form rises.

"Uh-oh," the glimmering rock creature blurts. He wags a finger toward Alora and Kanasu, ushering them closer. The bedsheet ghosts lean in as the beast whispers, "This kind of showmanship is never a good sign. Someone's in serious trouble."

Stretching like a jungle cat waking from its slumber, Chernobog rises to his full height before addressing the room. Though unsure how it's possible, Alora thinks Chernobog's shadows look even darker than they did the first time they met.

"What in Muspelheim just happened?" The tone of Chernobog's voice would have sent shivers down Alora's spine if she still had one. Looking around the room, Alora can see that most of the other ghosts are either cowering or frozen in place. But when no one answers, Chernobog asks another question, louder this time.

"Will no one come forward and explain to me what I just witnessed?"

Still no answer.

In the silence, Alora gets an idea. If they're so intent on not playing nice—not playing by the rules—she can teach Kanasu a lesson. She'll pull the same move on Kanasu they had pulled on her at the Department of the Fantastic. She turns to her partner and leans in.

"Now it's your turn," Alora says, ready to throw her hand in the air.

Panicked, Kanasu tugs at Alora's bedsheet. "Don't do this," they say, reaching up to pull Alora's hand down. "Please, stop."

"Why not?" Alora tries to sneer at Kanasu, remembering too late that her face—if she even still has one—is hidden beneath her polka-dotted bedsheet. "You deserve it."

While this kind of infighting isn't something Alora loves, it also isn't technically against her internal rule book or anything they've learned about their dreamweaving jobs so far. Still, she can't bring herself to raise her hand and return Kanasu's earlier "favor."

Chernobog turns to see the pair quibbling, his crimson eyes burning like wildfire. But he does not call on them. Instead, he turns to one of the other workstations.

"Sector three, come forward," the umbral god bellows.

Three bedsheet ghosts—one in stripes, another dotted with stars, and the third in plain gray—float around their console. They close the gap between them and Chernobog, who addresses them loud enough for everyone in the room to hear.

"Which one of you activated the shift too early?"

The plain gray ghost and the one in stripes turn to look at the third ghost, the one in stars. The star-sheeted ghost floats forward, bowing their head.

"Me, s-s-sir," they stutter. "It was my fault. I take full responsibility."

"Very good," Chernobog says, his temper seemingly quelled. "It's admirable that you would stand up for your team and shoulder the burden."

With a giant claw, Chernobog pats the ghost on the head before addressing the rest of the room.

"Precision is of the utmost importance when we craft these nightmares. Everything and everyone must work in perfect harmony, lest we make a mockery of our profession. The difference between a nightmare and a comedy is in the timing. Today, we failed in our chief endeavor. The terror we were meant to convey was muted by imprecision. These are mistakes we simply cannot make. Thankfully, this is but one nightmare. We will learn, and we will move forward."

The enormous, shadow-billowing beast turns back to the star-sheeted ghost standing before him.

"But you will not join us in that undertaking."

Chernobog slams a giant hand down on the ghost, and the whole dream stage shudders with the impact. When he raises his hand, the ghost is gone, sheet and all.

"And you two," the God of Chaos, Misfortune, and Darkness howls. "Not only did you allow this imprecision to infringe upon your work, but you did not stand with your compatriot and accept the blame yourselves. You, too, are unworthy of employment here in the Department of Nightmares."

Chernobog lifts both hands this time, smashing them down on the two remaining ghosts. And once again, when he raises his hands, there is no trace of either of them.

Chernobog clasps his hands together with a ghastly smile and addresses the whole group again.

"Time to set up the staging for the next nightmare. Chop-chop. We've got work to do!"

With that, half of the remaining ghosts start breaking down the set, pulling apart pieces of the farmhouse and the surrounding staging with incredible speed and moving them out of the way, while the other half begins setting up the next nightmare.

Chernobog struts over to the monitoring station where Alora and Kanasu, gobsmacked by what they had just witnessed, still stand.

"Hey, boss," the well-dressed rock creature sitting at the station says.

"Phantasus," Chernobog answers, "I presume these are our tardy trainees."

"That they are," Phantasus confirms.

"Well," Chernobog says, addressing Alora and Kanasu, "did you like what you saw? It seems we have some openings here in the Department of Nightmares after that trio of regretful but necessary transfers. And I have it on good authority that our department is the one to join. Big things are ahead for us. But you'll have to clean up your act if you want to be a part of the winning team. Tardiness simply will not do."

All Alora and Kanasu can do is nod their heads.

"Good, good." Chernobog smiles. "Now, scurry back to Morpheus. Oh, and do tell him hello from me."

Chapter Six

Human Resources: How to File a Complaint

Alora and Kanasu don't talk for a long time.

In silence, they leave Dream Stage 42 and drift back toward the human soul dormitories, floating between and around other groups of bedsheet ghosts going about their business.

They glide through the dorm lobby, past Cottus—already nose-deep in a new book with his hundreds of hands busy as ever—and into the elevator.

Only then does Alora finally break the silence.

"We have to do something, right?" She asks. "He...can't just do that and get away with it."

"Oh, so now you're interested in figuring all this out? Wouldn't you rather just stay silent and do as you're told, like a good rule-follower?" Kanasu's voice is calm and measured despite the barb. "Besides, he's a god. What exactly do we do?"

"I don't know." Panic begins to creep into Alora's voice. "But that could have been us. It could be us next."

"I know. It was almost me."

"I didn't—"

"You wanted to—" Kanasu starts.

"Not like that," Alora interrupts. "What's the point of following the rules if they don't apply to everyone?"

"Even the gods who can blink us out of existence at any moment?"

"Especially them."

Kanasu thinks momentarily before reciting Alora's mantra, "If you're going to do something, do it right."

"Bingo."

"You actually believe all that, don't you?" The anger is gone from Kanasu's voice. And Alora almost thinks she hears a tinge of respect in the question, however small.

"I do," Alora confirms. "And I think we might really have to do something about it."

"Like what?"

"We should start with Morpheus. He's our direct superior, right? He probably already knows all about Chernobog. He should have told us. Should have warned us or something."

"You heard Mamu," Kanasu says, calm once again. "He doesn't care about anything, least of all us. And we don't need his mommy to tell us that. We've already seen it. Dude is checked out."

"Okay, then we go higher." Alora perks up. "If our so-called boss doesn't care, we find someone above him who does."

"To another god," Kanasu reminds Alora.

"Yeah, so?"

"So, after what we've witnessed so far, what makes you think any of them will care about what a couple of human souls in the *flunky* department have to say?"

"It's gotta be bad for business, right? The rules and regulations exist for everyone working here—or at least that's the idea. I say we go see that golden four-armed lady. The one in charge. Maya. If anyone will care about…mismanagement, it'll be her, yeah?"

"I don't know what you'd call a death wish when you're already in the afterlife, but you've got one."

"So, that's it, then?" Alora begins to raise her voice. "Now you're gonna be the one who keeps your head down and stays quiet?"

"If you think I'm going to hop on the expressway to getting slapped into oblivion or whatever for you, you're cuckoo bananas. We just left the Nightmare Department. If Maya comes to talk to him about it, he'll know it was us. Even if she wants to help us, he could get rid of us long before facing the consequences."

"And if we don't do anything, he'll just keep abusing his power. You saw all the other ghosts in there. Nobody is going to say anything."

"I think I like this color on you," Kanasu chuckles. "But maybe we should see what the rest of the group thinks before we make any drastic moves that'll get us *transferred* or whatever."

The elevator doors finally open, attracting the attention of Endri, Rasui, and Yume in the dorm beyond. Eagerly, they move toward the elevator as Kanasu floats off, but Alora remains.

"Fine. You tell them. In the meantime, I'm going to Maya. If I don't see you again, I guess you were right, and this was a terrible idea."

Before Kanasu or any of the other ghosts can protest, Alora pushes the lobby button, and the doors close again.

The elevator ride back down to the lobby is long enough for Alora to realize she has no idea where Maya's office might be. She and her companions have been so busy with on-the-job training that there hasn't even been a moment to wander the city of Somnia. Alora hadn't even been outside the confines of the dream stage lot since her arrival in the Afterworld.

But she knows someone who would know where to go.

"Cottus," Alora chimes as the elevator doors open to the lobby. "I have a favor to ask."

"Alora," the Hecatoncheire answers in kind, not so much as glancing up from his book. "I was wondering when we'd have this conversation. Let's see. I believe it is at this point you explain to me what a *favor* is. Oh wait. No. That's not quite right. First, I have to tell you that, in the Afterworld, favor is what we refer to when a human soul curries the support of a god or other nonhuman entity. Yes, that sounds right. Then I ask you, is that what you mean?"

Alora laughs. In just the two short conversations they'd had, she'd already grown to like Cottus, as strange as he was. He was an oddball, a misfit like her, and talking to him now momentarily eased the discomfort in her gut—the fear and uncertainty of what she was on her way to do.

"Okay, I'll play along," she says. "For humans, a favor is when we do something for one another above and beyond what we might normally do. Usually, it's something we ask of a friend."

"Are we friends, Alora?" Cottus inquires, but his tone suggests he already knows—he's simply playing out the conversation.

"If we are," Alora says, the cheer dissipating from her tone, "then I think you might be my first."

"For now, perhaps," Cottus replies. "Wait. There's more, I

73

think. Yes, yes. This is the part where you tell me—"

"That I suppose one friend is better than none," Alora interrupts.

"Yes." Cottus smiles. "That's right. Okay. So, about this favor…"

"Right. I think I need directions. Can you tell me where I might find Maya?"

"Yes."

"Yes, you can?"

"No. I mean, yes. But, no."

Alora stares blankly at the hundred-handed secretary.

"I can tell you where you need to go to find Maya. That's the *yes*. But you're going to get lost along the way anyhow."

Cottus dog-ears the page of his book, closes the cover, and sets it down on the desk, finally looking up at Alora.

"Oh shoot. I always do this. I tell you human souls things you're not yet meant to know. Or things you've already come to understand. Either way. Both? The point is, you'll find your way there on your own, eventually. I really shouldn't say more. Must get back to my book. Yes, that's right."

Cottus looks at Alora momentarily, giving her a sympathetic nod before picking up his novel again.

Alora sighs. "Well, thanks, I guess."

"Anytime," Cottus says, glancing up from the book with a wink. "That's a bit of Hecatoncheires humor for you, dear. See, because time works differently for—"

"Yeah, I get it, Cottus. Thank you."

The Hecatoncheire smiles, and Alora nods in return before leaving the human dormitories, searching for the Dreamweavers, LLC COO's office.

☠

"Excuse me," Alora says, interrupting a conversation between a pair of bedsheet ghosts outside the human dormitories. "Can you tell me where I might find Maya?"

One of the ghosts shrugs while the other shakes their head.

"Do you know where Maya's office is?" she asks another human soul and gets another shrug.

And then another.

And then another.

Finally, someone stops to consider her question. "I heard she stays off campus, somewhere in the city." The ghost points away from the dream stages, deeper into the city of Somnia.

That's odd, Alora thinks. *Shouldn't the COO of the dream-making company stay near where she's supposed to work? Why would she be stationed so far away?*

She thanks the ghost but decides to get a second opinion. After several more tries, she finally encounters another human soul who relays the same sentiment.

"Honestly," the ghost says, "I'm not sure I've ever seen her around here. Just those videos they make us watch. Now that I think about it, it's kind of weird, right? But I guess she's the boss. She'd know better than any of us."

Perplexed and frustrated, Alora decides to take the risk and wanders deeper into Somnia.

Alora quickly discovers that Cottus's prediction that she'd get lost trying to find Maya's whereabouts is spot-on. While the dream stages and surrounding facilities have a relatively straightforward, single-street format, the surrounding city of Somnia is more akin to a labyrinth.

Seems appropriate for a city of dreams, Alora muses.

But while the spaces between the dream stages and the human dormitories are awash with human soul activity—bedsheet ghosts wandering to and fro and, at times, congregating among themselves—the rest of Somnia is practically devoid of human souls entirely.

Instead, Alora finds herself standing out like a sore thumb among the hordes of what she recognizes as mythical creatures. Worse, they don't seem keen on seeing a human soul wandering about. And they're entirely unconcerned with whether she can hear their opinions on her or not.

"I wish these humans would stay where they belong," a hunched-over, wart-addled, hag-like creature mutters to an enormous dog as Alora turns a corner.

"Filthy, strange little creatures," a grotesque horse-goblin snaps at her as she floats by.

"Stay away from me, disgusting beast," a bony, long-clawed, red-eyed woman shrieks, jumping away from Alora after her bedsheet grazed the woman's elbow.

"Don't listen to them," a booming voice announces across a courtyard. Alora turns to see an enormous creature with the body of a lion, a serpent's tail, and a human's head adorned with an ornate headdress sprawled out under a Technicolor tree. "They don't know of what they speak."

"Thank goodness," Alora says, looking up at the colossal creature. "I'm extremely lost and was hoping I might find someone friendly enough to point me in the right direction. But it seems folks around here don't care much for my kind. Say, are you a—"

"A sphinx? Yes."

"You're beautiful." Alora practically spits out the compliment.

"Why, thank you, little one. I like your polka dots."

"Thank you," Alora says with a shimmy. "Why does everyone around here seem to hate humans?"

"I thought I was the one meant to ask riddles," the sphinx chuckles, but Alora just stares at them. "Oh, you're serious. Well, I suppose it's the same reason your people don't much care for one another. Misunderstanding."

"Fair point," Alora says, puzzling the sphinx's answer.

"They just don't grasp that you still serve a purpose despite your myriad flaws and exceptional ugliness."

Alora scowls at the creature, again realizing too late that she has no face with which to express disdain. "That's a little rude."

"It's the truth."

"If I ask you where I might find Maya, will you give me a straightforward answer or make me solve some stupid puzzle or riddle or something?"

Now it was the sphinx's turn to frown. "I should have known better than to try to help a wretched little monster like you. My mother always told me I was too kind and forgiving."

"Hey, you started it."

"Typical human. You expect so much and give so little."

Alora spins and glides away, angrier than ever at her inability to storm off.

It seems to her that the Afterworld, or at least the Dream-scape, wasn't all it was cracked up to be. While Morpheus's indifference was frustrating, at least it was palpable. But this? Almost every nonhuman entity she had interacted with regarded her with, at best, a curious disgust. At worst, they were actively insulting and threatening her.

But her sense of unwelcome only furthers her resolve. Alora

would find Maya, report Chernobog's behavior, and then have her vindication.

She continues her hunt, scouring the streets for any sign of Maya's office and ignoring the jeers of the mythical creatures filling the streets.

But after what must have been hours (at least back on Earth) of traversing the roads, passageways, and alleys of the sleeping city as deliberately as she can manage, she's no closer to tracking down where Maya might be. Nor does she even feel like she has a better understanding of Somnia.

Morpheus had told Alora and her dreamweaving companions that the city didn't shift—it was one of the only static parts of the whole Dreamscape. But it sure didn't feel like that to Alora.

As far as she could tell, the layout made no sense. Some streets veered off in seemingly random directions. Others abruptly halted in dead ends. And some doubled back on themselves. To Alora, Somnia was less a metropolis and more a tangled ball of yarn.

Eventually, she found a random stoop on a quiet avenue and plopped down, defeated. She would have tried to find her way back to the dream stages, but she wasn't even sure she could manage that without some help.

Instead, she sits, huffing and puffing and generally feeling sorry for herself. She had failed. And now she would have to trek all the way back to the human dormitories. And since Kanasu had almost definitely told the other ghosts about everything that transpired with Chernobog and the Nightmare Department, Alora's return would make her the center of attention. She'd have to confirm what Kanasu told everyone and tell them where she had gone and why and what happened. It all sounds exhausting.

But then she hears a familiar voice.

"Do you really think he can pull it off, Ikelos?" It's Phantasus, the stone creature Alora and Kanasu had met during their Nightmare interdepartmental training. And he's talking to the lion-bear who guarded the door to Dream Stage 42. The pair sits at a table outside some kind of rundown café. *Otherworldly Eats*, the flickering sign says.

"How many times are you going to ask me that?" The lion-bear, Ikelos, is hunched over a bowl of slithery, undulating, bright green glowworms, popping one after another into his mouth. As he speaks, bits of the worms spill from between his teeth.

Alora jolts back behind the building, leaning her head as close to the corner as she can to better eavesdrop on their conversation.

"Would you mind not spewing those things all over the table? It's disgusting," Phantasus responds before slurping a spoonful of steaming mud from his own bowl.

"Look," Ikelos says, "a hostile takeover is all well and good, but it's not practical. Absorbing the other departments will take time. You gotta be more patient. The boss knows what he's doing. Maya isn't just gonna hand over the keys to the company, you know? Once he has enough support, he'll overthrow that golden hag, and we'll be in charge of everything. It's foolproof. What are you so scared of?"

"I don't know. I don't want to get demoted to human cleanup duty or something," Phantasus answers, grazing a crystalline cheek with the back of a rocky hand. "I don't think my complexion can take that kind of filth."

"It's not gonna happen, trust me."

"You keep saying that, but I don't think you know any better than I do. You're just more confident, though I can't figure out why."

"Hey," Ikelos says, shoveling another handful of worms into his mouth, "my confidence is what got us this gig in the first place. We weren't gonna move up the corporate ladder if we stayed working for you-know-who."

"Yeah, maybe you're right. I just—"

"You just what? You miss the thankless gruntwork? You miss being mommy's little angel? You miss spending eternity going nowhere? Or maybe you're regretting going turncoat on you-know-who,"

"Hey, there's no need for that."

Alora leans her head just a bit farther, peeking an eye around the corner.

"Look, Phantasus, things are pretty good now, right?"

"Right."

"And before they were…"

"Less good?"

"Bingo. If everything goes according to plan, things will get even better for us. No more glowworms and swamp mud. We'll be calling the shots and living large. Stay the course, brother."

Phantasus turns his head toward Alora, and she jerks back behind the corner.

"Hey, did you see that?" the rock creature starts to rise from the table.

"See what?"

"I think someone's watching us. Looked like a human."

"Sit back down. Ain't no humans in this part of the city. You're just paranoid."

"Yeah, maybe," Phantasus sits back down and slurps another spoonful of muck into his mouth.

"Besides, what are they gonna do? Rat us out? To whom?"

Phantasus rises once again. "I think I'd just feel better if I checked."

"Yeah, whatever." Ikelos turns his attention back to his bowl of worms.

Phantasus, as carefully and quietly as a rock monster can manage, slinks up to the corner, pressing his body against the wall. With a start, he jumps around, throwing his hands up and shouting, "Roar!"

But the alleyway is empty.

☠

Floating as fast as she can away from the Dreamscape café and Chernobog's loose-lipped lackeys, Alora frantically resumes her search for Maya's office.

Her sense of duty and justice—or at least her desire for order—reignited, she presses onward. Now, she had an inalienable claim to Chernobog's wrongdoing. She was certain that Maya would have to act. And then, when she returned to work, everything would be tidy once more. Alora wouldn't even mind being the center of attention for such an occasion. She'd be the hero who restored order to the Dreamscape. That would look great on her résumé.

She careens through the streets, dodging groups of mythical creatures—most alarmed enough at seeing a human soul darting around to hop out of the way of their own accord—and desperately looking for any sign mentioning Dreamweavers, LLC on it.

Then, smack-dab in the middle of one of Somnia's widest and busiest streets, she halts.

There before her, towering high above most other buildings in the area and decorated with glittering, iridescent crystal, stands an enormous tower with a gigantic lotus flower billboard three-quarters up its height.

And on a small sign outside, she recognizes the same blue-and-gold font from all those videos Morpheus had her and her coworkers watch. *Dreamweavers, LLC Corporate Offices*, it reads.

Alora feels stupid for not noticing the giant building before. But she steels herself and floats through the revolving doors into the lobby.

Inside, the building is even more ostentatious. The iridescent crystal lines the interior and, on almost every surface, including the ceiling, are elaborate paintings, like the verdant, floral swamp from the Dreamweavers introductory video.

Alora floats up to one of the paintings closest to the door and realizes it's not a painting at all—it's moving. The animals graze, the water undulates, and a breeze blows through the trees and grasses.

In the center of the hallway, there's a long walkway leading back toward a reception desk. It's flanked on both sides by ponds filled with lotus flowers. Below the flowers, fish as iridescent as the building's crystal swim in the ponds.

The expansive lobby is so entrancing that Alora doesn't even realize who sits behind the reception desk until he greets her.

"Alora," Cottus titters excitedly, "You made it. See, I told you that you'd find your way here. Or wait, have I told you yet? I must've. Yes, certainly. If you're here, I must have told you by now."

"Cottus?" Alora tilts her head, puzzled. "You're here, too?"

"I'm everywhere, my dear. And nowhere. I'm only joking. I'm the Dreamscape's resident secretary. It helps that time doesn't quite work for me as it does for you. I can be in numerous places at once, remember? Right now, I am here and in a few hundred other places. It's quite a challenge to explain in terms of your linear temporal experience. I can't imagine how bland that must be, only experiencing time in one direction. So tragic. Such is the plight of mortals, I presume. But back to the matter at hand..."

"I'm here to see Maya."

"Yes, right. I took the initiative and let her know you were on your way. Glad to see I got that timing right. She's already expecting you. Top floor. Through the elevator back there." Cottus points to the wall behind him with one of his hundreds of hands as the rest stay busy filing papers, typing on his keyboard, and carrying out dozens of other tasks. "And good luck, not that you need it."

"Thanks," Alora says as she floats past the reception desk, into one of the elevators, and presses the button for the top floor.

The ride up is long enough that it gives Alora time to calm her nerves and practice what she'll say when she's finally face-to-face with Maya, the second highest-ranking god among the whole of Dreamweavers, LLC's staff.

First, Chernobog, she recites in her head. *Then, the hostile takeover. And finally, if there's time, I can file a complaint about Morpheus. Okay, Alora, you got this. You got this. You've definitely got this.*

Then, the doors to Maya's office open at the glimmering, crystalline tower's pinnacle.

Massive cathedral-style windows surround the top-floor suite, revealing the entire city of Somnia outside (and even the wild lands of Oneiros beyond). As far as she can remember, it's the most beautiful and confounding view Alora had ever seen.

The room within the windows isn't too shabby, either. It's lined with plush sofas of varying shapes and sizes, all styled to look like lotus flowers. The floors beneath are covered in ornate rugs, all stitched with images resembling lush, verdant swamps—just like Maya's background in the Dreamweavers training videos. Dozens of gorgeously engraved bronze bells hung from the ceiling on chains of varying lengths.

And the smell. The whole room smells of earth, wood, and citrus. Alora breathes in deep and feels a calmness wash over her.

"You like the frankincense, I take it," a voice calls from the far side of the office. "I hear tell humans are quite fond of it."

Maya, the golden goddess, wears the same sharp suit and sits in the same lotus-styled chair from the training videos. She waits behind an enormous, filigreed bronze desk. Two of her hands rest atop the desk, their fingers interlaced. A third holds a long ivory pipe, wisps of smoke rising from its bowl. The fourth ushers Alora forward.

"Please, come in and have a seat. "I understand you have something you wish to discuss."

☠

"...and I think that's everything," Alora says, catching her breath. She sits across from the golden, four-armed goddess, feeling like she'd been yammering for hours. But she did it.

She told Maya everything.

Maya scowls, turning the information the polka-dotted bedsheet ghost just shared with her over in her head.

"To summarize," the golden goddess finally says, "You believe that Chernobog, head of the Department of Nightmares, is abusing his power, ruthlessly removing human souls from our realm, while secretly conspiring with at least two of his top underlings to absorb the other Dreamweavers departments in a bid to overthrow me and take control of the whole company?"

"Yes." Alora nods. "Oh, and Morpheus, you know, my boss or whatever, either doesn't know this is happening or doesn't care."

"Yes, that does seem rather concerning," Maya says, rising from her lotus chair and turning to look out the window. She crosses two arms behind her back, holds her pipe with the third, and strokes her chin with the fourth. "And you have proof of all of this, of course?"

"Well, no…"

"How about a corroborating witness or two?"

Alora hangs her head. "Well, everyone in the dream stage saw Chernobog take out his anger on those human souls, including my coworker, Kanasu."

"But did anyone else hear what Ikelos and Phantasus discussed at the café?"

"No. I was alone."

"Understood."

"But it happened. I'm not just making this stuff up." Alora starts to panic, realizing this conversation is not going as planned.

"It's alright, dear." Maya turns around, a sympathetic look

in her eyes. "I know you've only recently arrived here, and everything seems so *big* and *scary*. It's a lot for a human soul to handle. You're all so prone to drama and exaggeration. But you will get used to it, I promise you."

"I'm not making this up!" The bedsheet ghost rises from her chair and smacks her hands down on Maya's desk, too late to realize just how much she's overstepped. She recoils her hands, sits back down, and lowers her head. "You—you have to believe me."

"I believe that you misunderstand your circumstances," Maya says calmly, the sympathy gone from her eyes. "I believe you're afraid you are unqualified to work for Dreamweavers, LLC. I believe you are frightened you might lose your job and be transferred to another realm. And I believe you're doing your damnedest to ensure you curry my favor to avoid that outcome."

"No! I'm telling you, I heard them—"

"Quiet, human!" Maya's voice fills the room, vibrating the crystalline walls, and her eyes ignite with white-hot fire. "You do not know your place. Chernobog is a department head. He is well within his rights to measure the performance of his employees and extend or cut short their tenure as he sees fit. He is a loyal and valuable part of this company and has proven that for eons."

Maya takes a deep breath, regains her composure, and sits back in her lotus chair. She takes a puff from her pipe before continuing.

"As for the rest of it, I can handle murmurs of insurrection myself, thank you. I do not require the assistance of some *human* to help me expose those hungry for power. You think me so naïve as to suggest I am unaware of Chernobog's comings and goings, especially when his idiot lackeys discuss their plans so nonchalantly? And out in public, no less. I am the chief operations officer of Dreamweavers, LLC and one of the most powerful beings in the Dreamscape. I know *everything* that happens here!"

"I'm sorry," Alora says, defeated. "I just thought—"

"You thought wrong. Chernobog's insatiable hunger is a part of what makes him so good at his job. I allow it because it gives him hope and something to strive for. It has been this way since the dawn of this company. You think you're the first human to come forth with such information? You think you're somehow special? You're all so arrogant, you mortals."

For a moment, Maya allows the silence to punctuate her statements. Finally, she continues.

"Let me give you a bit of advice: humans souls who don't know when to quit tend to end up among the Haunted. Remain on your prescribed path. Do not stray. You might just make something of yourself."

"You're not going to...*transfer* me?"

Maya laughs a bit too long for Alora to think it's genuine.

"No. Of course not. You're foolish and pompous, but you're *only* human. Consider this a lesson...and a warning. Step out of line again and our next conversation will go very differently."

Maya snaps with one of her golden hands, and Alora is immediately transported out of the office and back to the Dreamweavers campus.

Chapter Seven

Congratulations, You Made It to Your First Performance Review!

For a long time, Alora hovers outside the human dormitories, trying to convince herself to go inside, float past Cottus, ride the elevator up, and rejoin her coworkers. But she just can't get herself to move forward.

It hadn't been as long as she had spent lost in the streets of Somnia—at least, it didn't feel like it—but she had been hovering out there long enough to watch a few dozen other bedsheet ghosts come and go. It was getting a little ridiculous.

And the longer she waited, the worse she felt.

Alora's do-gooder attempts at adhering to the rules (and expecting others to do the same) had done her no favors. Instead, they had only served to alienate her from her closest acquaintances, especially Kanasu. She wasn't sure if she could salvage those relationships or if she was simply destined to be as lonely in the afterlife as she had felt back on Earth.

Worse, she was now on the wrong side of the one person—or god—who ultimately controls her fate. All things considered, it was a pretty upsetting start to her afterlife.

"Come on," Alora whispers to herself. "You got this. Just

get it over with and move forward. If you're going to do something, do it right. You're the one who keeps saying that, yeah? Now do it."

"Do what?"

Alora jumps, jerking her head to see another bedsheet ghost approaching her.

"Did you say something to me?" The ghost cocks their head.

"What? No. Nothing. Sorry."

Shaking their head, the ghost continues.

Great, Alora thinks. *Add another person to the list of those who think I'm a total weirdo.*

She looks up at the entryway to the human dormitories, steeling herself, and immediately turns back around.

Embarrassed and utterly disappointed in herself and her inability to get over her anxiety, Alora meanders back past the dream stages, not headed anywhere in particular.

Alora had clearly overstayed her welcome at Dreamweavers HQ, plus Maya had specifically teleported her back in front of the human dormitories. She already knew she couldn't depend on Morpheus, who didn't seem to care about anything at all—that left reporting to him out of the question. And she couldn't seem to make herself go back to that weird television set-turned-dorm-room where the other ghosts were.

She didn't know where to go. She had nowhere to go.

Out of the corner of her eye, she sees something small and black dart behind one of the dream stage buildings. Letting her curiosity get the better of her, and with no other prospects anyhow, Alora follows it.

Seeing its back half dart around another corner, Alora can tell it's a black cat—presumably the same one that Yume had pointed out earlier.

Unless multiple black cats are wandering around this part of Somnia, Alora muses.

Not that it matters to her. The cat is just an excuse, something to do to keep her busy and get her mind off things. So, she continues to follow it all the way to the city's outskirts.

In a clearing right at the edge of Somnia—where the city ceases and the wilderness of Oneiros takes over—the cat stops and looks back at Alora, waiting.

Alora approaches cautiously, careful not to make any sudden movements that might spook the beautiful black feline. The cat's tail flicks back and forth as it stares at her with glinting golden eyes.

As she gets closer, Alora extends a hand and bends over, reaching for the cat's head. But just as she's about to touch it, the cat darts away, another foot or two, just out of reach.

"Got it, no head pats," she says. "Mind if I stay here with you for a bit?"

The cat sits back down, eyeing the pink polka-dotted bedsheet ghost. As Alora floats to the ground, she notices a small pool toward the center of the clearing. And next to it, there's a sign that reads *Narcissus's Pond*. It reminds her of the city parks back on Earth—a beautiful bastion of nature in an otherwise cold, concrete landscape.

In the pond's calm surface, she sees the reflection of the beautiful sky above.

Right, Alora reminds herself. *It's the only reflective surface in the whole of the Dreamscape.*

To get a better look, Alora leans back and stretches out, lying in the lush grass and staring at the impossible, infinite celestial expanse above.

In the parts of the sky that resemble daytime, she sees

Technicolor clouds and rainbow ribbons that are more vibrant than anything she can remember. And in the parts that look like night, there are more stars and constellations than she ever thought possible.

Alora notices a pod of the enormous, bizarre elephant-whale creatures they had seen in class flying high above Somnia and Oneiros. Most of them float listlessly across the sky, but Alora sees two smaller calves taking turns chasing one another across the sky, bumping into the other, larger creatures in their pursuit. They're playing.

"It's beautiful here," she says. "Is this what you wanted to show me?" But when she looks back down, the black cat is gone. She sighs. "Great. Scared off another potential friend."

Suddenly, a voice rings out behind her. "Excuse me, what are you doing here?"

Alora scrambles back upright and shakes herself off.

"I'm sorry," she says without looking at who the voice came from. "I was just... Well, I was wandering, and then I saw this black cat, so I followed it here. I can go somewhere else. Don't mind me."

"Oh. It's you."

Alora turns to see Morpheus, back in his dark blue winged form, walking toward her. He frowns at her.

"Oh. It's you," Alora parrots back.

"Found the pond, then?" Morpheus asks. "You humans are so strange. You all look the same, yet you can't help but come here to gaze at your own reflections. It baffles me. Though, I suppose the folly of Narcissus isn't strictly relegated to humans, him being a demigod and all."

"So, you're not here to chew me out?"

Morpheus shrugs, his wings flapping reflexively. "I'm not

sure what you mean."

"Lecture me," Alora reiterates. "Give me a stern talking-to."

"Why would I want to do that?"

"Chernobog. Maya. My going behind your back to tattle—"

Morpheus interrupts. "Do you know what the concept of *giving someone an out* is? Fascinating human conversational tactic I learned about some time ago."

Alora stares blankly at the blue demon.

"I didn't think you needed another lecture," Morpheus continues. "Would you like to sit with me for a bit?"

Morpheus lowers himself down in the clearing next to Alora, joining her in looking out across the wilds of Oneiros. They sit quietly for a moment before Morpheus breaks the silence.

"Honestly, I didn't know you'd be here. And I wasn't looking for you. This is just a place I go to from time to time. When I'm not failing miserably at my job of ushering a group of flunkies through basic training, that is."

"So, you did hear about everything," Alora replies defeatedly. "Look, I'm sorry—"

Morpheus raises a hand, stopping her.

"Word travels fast around here. You think humans love gossip? Gods invented it. I suspect the story of the *arrogant little human* who confronted Maya in her office has probably already made it to some other realms by now."

"Great." Alora's shoulders slump, and she hangs her head. "So, everyone in the Afterworld knows how bad I screwed up."

"Well, not *everyone* everyone. Just everyone who matters."

Alora groans. "Not helping."

"I have to prod you a little," Morpheus chuckles. "You did go behind my back, after all."

"Yeah, that's fair. I did. But I didn't know it was going to turn into all this. I thought I was doing the right thing."

"Preaching to the choir," Morpheus extends his arms wide. "That's a human phrase. Am I using it right?"

"I don't know. Maybe?"

"Perhaps you need some context. Then you can tell me if I used it correctly. Sound good?"

Alora nods.

"I was a busybody like you once—"

"Not off to a great start." Alora shifts uncomfortably.

"Just give it a minute; you'll see where I'm going." Morpheus clears his throat before continuing.

"A very long time ago, before Somnia extended quite this far into Oneiros, back when Dreamweavers was little more than a fledgling operation, I was one of our organization's brightest stars. I know—hard to believe. But it's true.

"A true devotee, I was sprightly and approached each and every dream with vigor and aplomb. Back then, we had only two departments: Nightmares and Fantastic. In those days, Chernobog still headed the D-o-N. But I worked under my mother, Nyx, whom you've met at the Department of the Fantastic. But my favorite part of dreamweaving was working alongside my brothers.

"For the most part, everything ran smoothly. We had a few hiccups here and there: human souls going astray, dreams not quite measuring up to our expectations, that sort of thing. But they were nothing more than occasional kinks and—*what do you humans call them?*—speed bumps.

"For a time, everything was good.

"Then, Maya called the whole of Dreamweavers into an all-hands meeting. Along with the usual stat and performance reports, she declared a huge, Dreamscape-changing announcement: a new department was to be created.

"Billed as the connective tissue between the two preexisting departments, the Department of the Mundane was explicitly designed to handle all the extra human souls astral projecting into the Dreamscape, which the other two departments were unequipped to handle.

"It was a huge opportunity, and somehow, I was tapped to lead. Apparently, Maya had taken notice of my enthusiasm and aptitudes. She had even gone so far as to discuss it with my mother well before the announcement. It was an unexpected honor—not one I could pass up. I had only one request, one requirement before I could accept: I wanted to bring my brothers along with me.

"Maya had anticipated my request, and she had even already mocked up the transfer paperwork. I was to become the head of the Department of the Mundane, and my brothers would be my chief support staff, along with a swath of new human souls.

"Again, everything was good...for a time.

"As the eons passed, it became apparent that this new department was not given the same resources and aid as the original two departments. Our dream stages paled in comparison to those under the umbrella of the Department of Nightmares, and our staging assets were laughable compared to those at the Department of the Fantastic.

"We were an afterthought. We weren't treated equally and were unappreciated and underfunded. We were peons.

"My brothers came to me numerous times, begging me to

use my influence to improve our conditions. I told them time and time again that I had no more power over the situation than either of them.

"I asked them to help me prove our worth—to overperform despite our department's shortcomings.

"And we tried our damnedest. But no matter how much we did and how successful we were at maintaining our integrity and high performance, the frustration and disgruntlement only festered.

"I grew weary, so exhausted by realizing that my first leadership role, what should have been a dream job—pardon the expression—was slipping through my fingers like sands in the hourglass.

"And the dissatisfaction grew in my brothers' hearts, too.

"Until, one day, they came to me again. Only this time, they were not confiding in me or asking me for help. They were turning in their resignations.

"So, it seemed Chernobog had been whispering in their ears and sowing their discontent, as the God of Chaos, Misfortune, and Darkness is wont to do. He promised them everything they wanted, especially their own positions of leadership in a department that wanted for nothing. And, eventually, they had accepted.

"I could have refused. I could have argued. I could have confronted Chernobog himself. But I had no fight left in me. The ages had drained from me all I had to give. I was defeated. I accepted their resignation.

"Give or take a few hundred eons since then, and that about brings us up to now."

☠

Alora and Morpheus sit together, looking out at Oneiros and the elephant-whales floating high above. This time, it's Alora's turn to break the silence.

"I'm really sorry all that happened to you."

Morpheus chuckles. "Why would you apologize for something you had no hand in?"

"I don't mean it like that. It's a human thing. Like I feel bad."

"Oh. So, it's pity, then?"

Alora groans. "No... That's not... I'm just saying—"

"It's okay," he says. "You're pretty tightly wound, even for a human."

"Your brothers," Alora says, ignoring the barb. "Do they—"

"They still work for Chernobog, yes. Ikelos and Phantasus, whom you have also met."

Alora nods. "Can I ask you something?"

"Please."

"Was that story supposed to make me feel better?"

Morpheus chokes on his laughter. "Oh gods, no. I'm not even sure how I would go about something like that. Your predicament is wholly unique. I can genuinely say I've never met a human who has so magnificently self-destructed—and so quickly, too."

This time, it's Alora's turn to laugh. Once her giggle fit peters off, Morpheus continues.

"I can also say I've never seen a human display such drive and purpose. I know things seem pretty bad—and they are— but your single-minded pursuit of doing what you thought was right is, frankly, extraordinary. Some might even call it inspiring. I think, I'm trying to say, I see you, human."

With a colossal claw, Morpheus pats Alora on the head. And Alora begins to sob.

"Oh no," Morpheus says with genuine concern. "Did I say something rude?"

Alora shakes her head and leans in, resting her shoulder on Morpheus's side as the big blue winged creature rests his arm over her shoulder.

"Thank you," she finally says. "I was starting to think I didn't belong here."

"I think you're exactly where you need to be." Morpheus pats Alora on the shoulder and begins to rise. "Come, I have something I want to show you."

As Alora rises upright, Morpheus marches forward, crossing Somnia's border into Oneiros. But Alora doesn't follow. Instead, she waves her hands in a panic—a useless gesture, she realizes, since Morpheus doesn't turn around to see it.

"Hey, wait," she shouts. "I thought we weren't allowed out there!"

"Only if you don't have an official guide," Morpheus shouts without looking back. "Pretty sure your department head counts."

"Right, okay. I guess we're doing this." Alora takes a deep breath, brushes off her bedsheet, and follows her mentor.

☠

Morpheus leads Alora through the wilds of Oneiros along a long and winding yet deliberate path. As they travel, Alora notices that the surrounding landscape shifts, but the trail they follow appears to remain intact—she can even see it behind them the few times she takes a moment to glance back.

Her mentor's pace is quick but not so fast that she struggles to keep up. And it allows her to take in the sights and sounds of the fascinating, threatening land of Oneiros.

To her left, she watches a crystal canyon—twinkling with light and echoing like a thousand wind chimes—collapse into itself to become red-and-purple dunes.

To her right, she sees a verdant bog erupt into a mountainous, jagged cliffside, a mist of still-wet soil raining down upon her head.

The whole journey is as magnificent as it is terrifying. But Alora has other things on her mind. Though she trusts Morpheus, the trek had already taken them what must have been miles and miles from the city of Somnia. And the big blue winged demon had yet to show any signs of slowing.

"Where are we going?" Alora finally asks.

"Just a bit farther," Morpheus calls back, veering to the side to avoid a thick forest as it collapses into a lake. He looks up into the sky. "Should be just ahead."

Alora looks up, too, noticing that the number of colossal flying beasts has increased. And they seem to be following Morpheus and her.

"Those things…they're not dangerous, are they?"

"No, of course not," Morpheus replies. "Not to us. Come, now, we're almost there."

No sooner had Morpheus spoken than the pair marched over a ridge overlooking a great valley. A perfectly bowled crater, the valley was lined with jagged peaks that sloped downward into lush fields of flowers in more colors than Alora thought possible. And at its center grew a solitary tree.

As Morpheus leads Alora into the valley, Alora notices that the tree has a twisted, craggy trunk that splits into thousands of equally twisted and craggy branches. And on those branches grow jade green leaves and bright red fruit.

The closer the pair gets to the tree, the more Alora has to crane her neck to look up at it. She imagines she couldn't reach halfway around its trunk, even with her arms fully outstretched.

"Here we are," Morpheus says.

"What is this place?" Alora twirls, taking in the oddly familiar valley with the enormous tree at its center. Then, she looks up at the branches, squinting to better see the fruit hanging from them. "Are those pomegranates?"

"Indeed they are." Standing a few feet taller than Alora, Morpheus reaches up and plucks one. With a squeeze of his hand, he cracks it open and pours the seeds into his mouth.

"You know, you humans have all these bizarre assumptions about the gods and what we like to do—even with food," he says between chomps. "Your poets and musicians talk of ambrosia, the so-called food of the gods, as if it's some big secret we were keeping from you, hoarding for ourselves. But it was always just pomegranates."

With the fruit empty of its seeds, Morpheus drops the husk onto the ground and licks his fingers. "Simply delectable. I would have offered you some, but..." He motions to Alora's bedsheet.

"Right," she replies. "No mouth hole. Can't eat. Don't get hungry."

"Bingo." He winks. "Anyhow, this is one of the few parts of Oneiros that doesn't shift. And before you ask, I don't know why or how it got here. But I've been coming here for ages. It's very special to me."

"I can see why," Alora stammers, the stunning, flourishing valley still keeping her entranced.

"You don't know the half of it." Morpheus grins, reaching

up to pluck another pomegranate. And then another. And another.

He cracks one open and hands it to Alora. Then he motions for her to follow him.

The pair moves out from under the tree's shade, and Alora sees dozens of great, flying elephant-whales gathered in the sky above. Morpheus whistles, raising his pomegranates in the air, and the pod of creatures descends toward them.

Frightened by the enormous animals, Alora instinctually floats backward toward the shade of the tree.

"Get back out here," Morpheus urges. "There's nothing to be scared of. They won't hurt you."

The first creature to arrive is even larger than some of the dream stages back in Somnia. Its trunk alone, which it gingerly reaches toward Morpheus, is longer than the dark blue demon is tall. Alora notices the creature is covered in thick, greenish-brown fur, has two small tusks sticking out from below its trunk, and has a quartet of tiger-striped flippers lazily flapping along its side. As it plucks half a pomegranate from Morpheus's hand, she sees its huge, glassy eye trained on her.

"These are Baku," Alora's mentor says as he pets the creature's trunk. "They've been here in the Dreamscape longer than any of us. So the legend goes, they eat nightmares. But I've found that they're quite fond of pomegranates. Then again, who isn't?"

One of the smaller Baku—about the size of a city bus, Alora estimates—floats down toward Alora. The creature gently rests the tip of its trunk atop the pomegranate half in her hand and deftly slurps up the seeds. With her free hand, Alora pets the Baku's proboscis.

"After everything that happened with my brothers and Chernobog, I found this place. Not on purpose, mind you." Morpheus walks back over to the tree, grabs a few more pomegranates, and continues to feed the Baku. "I felt particularly reckless and thought a walkabout through Oneiros might do the trick. And if I got swallowed up by the landscape, so be it."

"Morpheus…" Alora sighs.

"I know, I know." The big blue demon bats his wings and shakes his head. "It wasn't my best moment. But I didn't get swallowed up. In my aimless wandering, I stumbled upon this valley and met the Baku instead. Kismet, you might call it. Almost like it was here just for me."

The pair continues to feed the Baku. Morpheus plucks and breaks open the pomegranates, and Alora—becoming more comfortable with the gentle enormous flying creatures—hands the fruit off.

"But why did you bring me here?" Alora finally asks.

"The loneliness. The defeat. The purposelessness. This place helped me retain a bit of myself from before all that. It kept me here. Kept me from giving up."

Finished with their pomegranate snack, the Baku float back into the sky. Alora waves at a smaller one as it eyes her one last time. Morpheus wipes off his hand and holds open one of his palms.

A small flame erupts from his palm and extinguishes just as quickly. In its place, the cloud of smoke coalesces into a plain manila folder haphazardly stuffed with papers.

"I can't give you back your memories. But I do have some access to the dream records. I did a bit of digging, and here's what I found."

He hands the folder to Alora. She flips it open, thumbing through the pages. Each one outlines a different dream, but yellow highlighter accents certain parts, and thick black marker covers others. At a glance, Alora can't make sense of any of it.

"The thing is, the complete, unredacted reports on each of you are sealed in the records room beneath Dreamweavers HQ. They can't be removed. Trust me, I've tried plenty of times in the past. Step out the door with them, and—*poof*—they vanish and recombobulate back in their respective cabinets. It's quite frustrating, actually. These documents are the best I could do."

"How did you—"

"Kanasu came to me while you were off gallivanting around Somnia, believe it or not. They told me everything—said it was your idea, actually. How else did you think I gleaned all that's transpired?"

Alora cocks her head. "Aren't you a god? I thought maybe you were all-seeing and all-knowing or something."

Morpheus smiles. "As far as I know, the only omniscient being in the Dreamscape is Vishnu, and they're taking a long nap. I should probably also tell you that this folder isn't just yours. It has information that might pertain to all of you newbies. Sharing it with them could go a long way toward rebuilding that goodwill you so deftly shattered."

"I get the feeling this could get you into a lot of trouble if anyone finds out," Alora says, closing the folder.

Morpheus smiles. "Meddling in the affairs of other gods is a long-standing tradition among us immortals. And I'm a bit overdue for some stirring of the proverbial pot. However, if I were you, I'd be more concerned about my own meddling."

Alora cocks her head. Morpheus bows his head before

continuing, breaking eye contact with the pink polka-dotted bedsheet ghost and lowering his voice to a whisper.

"I know you've only been here for a brief moment, but has anyone told you about the Haunted?"

"Haunted?" Alora coughs. "Maya said something about that to me. I thought it was like a metaphor or something."

"It's quite real, so I've been told," Morpheus continues, clearing his throat. "I've seen human souls come through with a nearly uncanny recollection of their past selves. Nothing too specific, of course, but they do have some unbreakable tie to the world of the living regarding who they were. It manifests as a kind of self-assuredness.

"Others seem incapable of recalling even their basest instincts, and these souls are usually quite contented. And therein lies their confidence—an acceptance of their fate, so to speak.

"Those who can neither remember nor accept this lack of self...usually don't last very long here. These folks can't wrap their head around it, which interferes with our work. They generally end up transferred to another realm.

"The only thing worse, as far as I can tell, is those who somehow remember everything."

"Is that even possible?" Alora asks. "I thought all of this was controlled by...what did you call it? Shouldn't that prevent stuff like this?"

"Ancient, otherworldly, incomprehensible magics, yeah. It's rare, but it does happen, at least according to our records. Those who remember everything are said to be driven mad in the pursuit of returning to the world of the living."

Morpheus pauses, and Alora seizes the opportunity.

"But you've never met someone like that? A Haunted?"

Morpheus searches his memory. "I can't say that I have. I've only ever seen it referenced in documentation. I've had a few pupils who turned out to be Haunted, but I never witnessed their transgressions for myself."

"That seems odd. What happened to them?"

"Again, I can't say with absolute certainty, but I've heard that getting transferred is the least of one's worries once they become Haunted. Something about their souls being *unmade*."

"Well, that sounds horrible."

"Indeed it does. Then again, the gods are known to twist the truth to their favor from time to time. Who is to say whether the Haunted are even real or if they're just an excuse conjured up by jealous immortals? I suppose you'd have to get into that records room to find out for certain." Morpheus smiles and winks. "I really should break this habit of mine, always saying a bit too much."

Carefully measuring Morpheus's words, Alora nods. "Why me?"

"Because you remind me of what things used to be like." The big blue winged demon pats Alora on the head and turns around, heading back toward the valley's edge.

"And I think it might finally be time for a change," he shouts, waving for Alora to follow him. Together, they walk the path out of Oneiros and back into Somnia.

Act Two

Chapter Eight

Dreamweaving in Action: Getting the Job Done

W ith no need for sleep or food (and thus, no semblance of a circadian rhythm) and a bafflingly inconsistent work schedule, Alora has difficulty figuring out how long she's been in the Afterworld.

Between being a relatively recent arrival and a mortal soul, it's hard for her to think of the Dreamscape's time as static—or rather, existing all simultaneously—so she desperately clings to a vague twenty-four-ish-hour-day cycle. She doesn't know how else to track the passing (or non-passing) of time.

It certainly doesn't help that the sky is in a perpetual state of both day and night, the two swirling together but never truly blending—like oil and vinegar. Or that her coworkers all seem to have a slightly different way of marking the time.

If she had to guess, she'd say it has been about six months since her arrival.

While her first few days were turbulent, to say the least, the months following have been, comparatively, pretty humdrum.

Alora is very thankful for the tranquility.

On this particular day, Alora and her colleagues, Rasui and Yume, are helping her set up one of the Department of the

Mundane's stages for a remarkably tame dream.

"Cardboard. I can't believe they're making us use cardboard," Rasui says, erecting a green spray-painted bush in the stage's background. "This whole afterlife place runs on *ancient unknowable magics*, and we're stuck doing arts and crafts."

"I kind of like it," Yume replies, poking at a different, smaller cardboard bush and watching it spring back and forth. "It's cute."

"At least this feels real," Alora grunts as she drags a wrought-iron bench with worn wooden planks toward center stage.

Rasui, finished with setting up his cardboard bushes, floats back over offstage to grab the final pieces of the dream setup hidden inside a small burlap sack. He reaches inside and pulls one out.

"You gotta be kidding me." He sighs, holding a small sock puppet high enough for Alora and Yume to see. It resembles a bluebird, crafted with felt wings, button eyes, and a yellow foam beak. He pours three more out of the sack and onto the floor, each with a different color pattern. "What are we supposed to do with these?"

"The instructions say we gotta hide behind the bushes and, you know, puppet them," Yume chimes in.

Rasui tosses his head back and lets out an exasperated groan. Yume giggles and floats toward him, picking two bird puppets up off the ground. With giddy excitement, she slips her hands inside them and puppets them at one another, making small chirping noises.

"I think that about wraps it up," Alora says, tapping a billowy cotton cloud above her head. The cloud, tied to the dream stage's rafters high above, sways back and forth on its string. "You sure you've both got this one covered?"

Still giggling, Yume shoots one of her hands into the air, nodding the bird puppet's head up and down.

"Hide behind the bushes and pretend our hands are birds? Yeah, I think we can handle it," Rasui confirms.

"Alrighty, I won't be long," Alora says. "Just gotta check on Endri and Kanasu, and then I'll come right back, promise."

"You got it, dude!" Yume hops up and down, her bedsheet billowing like a jellyfish. "And say hi to Dublin for me!"

Alora exits the dream stage with a nod and a wave and heads back toward the human dormitories. It must have been around a shift change, as the streets between the stages are unusually crowded with human souls heading to and fro. Alora glides between them, excusing herself while dodging some and nodding hello at others.

Eventually, she turns down an alley between stages and finds herself on a much emptier stretch of road that butts up against the wilds of Oneiros. It isn't exactly on the way, but she made it a part of her path every time she traveled between the dorms and the stages, as it was where she usually found Dublin.

Dublin is the name she has given the black cat that's been following her and her coworkers since their arrival. She isn't sure why she picked the name; it just feels right, and the cat doesn't seem to mind.

Right on cue, the black cat scampers from behind a tree and sidles up to Alora, rubbing its head against her pink polka-dotted bedsheet. Alora leans down and scratches Dublin behind its ear. Tilting its head, Dublin purrs.

"Hey, Dubs, how're you doing today?"

The cat pulls away, walking in a small figure eight before returning to Alora's outstretched hand.

"Yume says hello," Alora continues.

Dublin purrs again.

Rising upright, Alora wipes her hands on her sheet and continues toward the dorms. "Gotta go, buddy. I'll see you on my way back."

From there, it was just a short jaunt back to the dorms.

Alora stops in the lobby to greet Cottus. The Hecatoncheire is as busy as ever while still managing to keep most of his focus on an old paperback book—the one he's reading now, which Alora finds strangely familiar, has a pair of hands holding a red apple on its cover. Alora keeps the conversation short so she can slip into the elevator and ride it up to her team's floor.

With a cheerful chime and a whoosh of the doors, Alora exits the elevator and floats into the dorm. Endri and Kanasu sit cross-legged in the center of the room, poring over a collection of documents strewn across the floor. Alora sees the manila folder Morpheus had given her tossed in the seat of an angular color-blocked chair.

With her hands on her hips, she addresses the pair. "Find anything yet?"

☠

After getting the dream log folder from Morpheus, Alora considers keeping it for herself—just for a little while. It might be a lot to drop on her coworkers all at once, especially the stuff about the Haunted and what a huge risk it might be to dig too deep into who they used to be, so she thinks of it as doing them a small favor.

But she remembers Morpheus's words—that this folder is not hers and hers alone; she is to share it with her companions. These dream logs are not her property. They belong to everyone.

So, she returns to the dorms and tells her fellow bedsheet ghosts everything she can remember: about her trip out into Oneiros with Morpheus, about the manila folder haphazardly stuffed with dream logs, about the dangers of becoming Haunted, and the potential to have their souls unmade. Even the records room where the files supposedly came from.

While the info dump is a lot to take in, Alora is relieved that everyone, even Kanasu, seems grateful she chose to share it. Of course, the big blue demon was right.

Together, they agree to keep the folder a secret and work in shifts going through it—which turns out to be a larger task than anyone expected, as the magical folder seems to refill at the bottom with each dream log they take off the top.

"You didn't think it would be that easy," Alora imagines Morpheus saying to them with a chuckle.

Still, the bedsheet ghosts dedicate themselves to the work. And the task has one unexpected, albeit welcome, side effect: it has mostly smoothed things over between Alora and her coworkers.

☠

"We've got a few more here and there," Endri says, motioning to the dream journals. "But the folder has no end in sight."

"Seems like Rasui is on a bit of a tear," Kanasu says, gesturing to a stack of papers far taller than any others. "Nearly every third dream log he looks at has something in it he recognizes. I saw one about a plumber fighting a gorilla, space wizards with laser swords, a guy who rides giant worms through the desert, and even a big pink ball that eats people to gain their power."

"Kind of sounds like he spent more time asleep than awake," Alora says.

"That's what I said," Kanasu replies. "How are things going on the dream stage?"

"Pretty good. Rasui and Yume are holding down the fort, but we should probably get back soon. The next dream is gonna require more of us, so we can't just sneak off like this."

"Probably for the best," Endri says. "Wouldn't want to get caught here when we're supposed to be working, especially if any of Chernobog's henchmen come poking their nose into things."

"You sure you don't want to look through some of these, Alora?" Kanasu asks.

"Nah, I'm alright," Alora answers. "We should probably just get going."

Kanasu frowns. "We can cover the dream. It's not gonna need all five of us. You should take a little time to go through some more of these."

"I said I'm alright," Alora asserts with a huff.

In truth, even after all this time, Alora has yet to find a single report in the dream folder that looks even remotely familiar. While Kanasu and the others have stacks of their own, Alora is still empty-handed. And while everyone can tell it's taking a toll on her, Alora insists everything is fine.

"I'm sorry," Alora finally says. "It's just frustrating, you know. I mean, look at Rasui's pile. That's ridiculous."

"Yeah, we know," Kanasu replies. "But it's not like any of these are actual confirmations of who we were or anything."

Alora cocks her head. "What do you mean?"

"Well." Kanasu clears their throat, tossing a stack of papers across the ground. "We've all found stuff we recognize, right? But all the important info—where these dreams came from, who dreamed them, *yada yada*—is all redacted. I'm starting to think Rasui just has a lot of pop culture knowledge stored up in his cranium and that all of this is purely circumstantial."

Alora realizes Kanasu may have a point. As months of thumbing through the papers have proven, anything too personal is redacted from all the files. None of the details are specific enough to confirm or restore any of the bedsheet ghosts' earthen memories.

"What if these dream logs aren't really what Morpheus was giving us," Alora says, scratching her head.

"What?" Endri lifts his head. "Can you elaborate?"

"Well, maybe the whole point of this is to frustrate us. There's enough to give us a taste of who we were—most of us, at least—but not enough to clear up our brain fog or whatever it is that stops us from remembering."

"And what are we supposed to do about that?" Kanasu asks, rising to their feet.

"He told me something else when he gave me the files."

"The records room," Endri remembers.

"Bingo," Alora chimes, pointing a finger at Endri. "Morpheus said the files are complete and unredacted in the records room, just that he couldn't physically remove them. If we can get in there, we can see them all for ourselves. Right?"

"Trying to break into Dreamweavers HQ seems like a suicide mission," Endri says.

"Doing something like that would give Maya plenty of reason to label us…what did you call it? Hunted?"

"*Haunted*," Alora confirms.

"And then we run the risk of, what, being unmade? What

does that even mean?" Kanasu scratches their head.

"I don't know, but it doesn't sound good," Endri replies.

"And that's if we even make it that far," Kanasu finishes.

"Something about how Morpheus worded it…" Alora lowers her voice. "He didn't seem very worried about it. It was too casual."

"Well, he's an immortal," Endri says. "He doesn't have anything of which to be afraid."

"No, it's not that," Alora continues. "I don't think he buys that it's real. He's never even seen a Haunted for himself. I guess whenever it happens, all the immortals just kind of take Maya's word for it. She's the big boss-god, after all."

"So, what does that mean?" Endri asks. "They're either turning a blind eye because they don't care, or they're afraid of what might happen if they question her. The gods themselves won't even look into it, let alone intervene. I can't be the only one who sees that as a huge red flag."

"It does seem extra sketchy," Kanasu says.

"Right?" Alora shouts. "He said the only way we'd know for sure is by getting into that records room and finding out for ourselves. I think that was his plan all along. He's asking us to look into it in his own weird way."

"That is exceptionally flimsy logic," Endri groans. "Even if you're right, what's the endgame for us? We're mortals, and they're gods. They could just blink us out of existence."

"He's got a point," Kanasu says.

"Yeah," Alora sighs. "Maybe we should just get back to the dream stage to help out Rasui and Yume."

"Finally, a plan that isn't going to get us all erased from existence," Endri replies.

☠

Still engrossed in his book in the lobby, Cottus raises his head when he sees Alora with Endri and Kanasu in tow.

"You made it!" the hundred-handed secretary exclaims.

"From the dorm to the lobby?" Kanasu ponders. "Wasn't exactly a long trip."

"Oh no," Cottus grumbles. "I'm afraid I've gotten my moments mixed up again. Say, have you met either of my brothers yet?"

"Can't say we have," Endri replies.

"Ugh," Cottus groans. "I'm way off, then. You still have a long way to go."

"Can we get a hint?" Alora asks.

"I'm not sure what you mean," says Cottus. "A hint of what?"

"Where it is you think we're returning from. Would it happen to be the records room under Dreamweavers HQ?"

Cottus looks surprised, but a sly smile quickly replaces his bewilderment. "You know, I just can't say. Maintaining the correct timeline is a delicate and dangerous art. A slip of the tongue such as that and I'd be… Well, let's just say it wouldn't bode well for any of us."

"Can't blame a girl for trying." Alora smiles.

"Of course not, my dear." The Hecatoncheire pushes his glasses up to the bridge of his nose and turns back to his book. As Alora, Kanasu, and Endri head for the lobby doors, Cottus bids them farewell. "Wherever it is you're headed now, I'm sure you'll figure things out."

Alora stops. "I'll catch up with you at the dream stage," she says to Kanasu and Endri. Kanasu shrugs, and Endri nods.

Alora twirls, and, as her companions slip out the double

doors, she floats back over to Cottus.

"Have you ever heard of the Haunted?" she asks.

All of Cottus's hands stop. Slowly, he puts his book down, leans forward, and looks up at her. "How did you hear about that?"

"Morpheus told me. He said they're humans who know too much, and that once someone becomes Haunted, they have to be unmade. Is that true?"

Cottus shakes his head. "I can't say."

Alora leans forward and whispers, "I think you know something. What aren't you telling me?"

Cottus stares at her, a coldness in his eyes.

"You can trust me. I'm good at keeping secrets between friends."

Cottus shakes his head again. "You don't understand."

"No," Alora agrees, "but I'm trying to."

The Hecatoncheire's mood shifts, his voice growing more serious. "This is a dark path you're headed down, *human*."

Alora recoils.

"Can I tell you something, as a friend?" Cottus asks, but he doesn't wait for an answer. "Trust is earned. Not everyone deserves it."

Realizing she's touched on something she maybe shouldn't have, Alora backs up toward the front doors. "I…think I'd better get going."

"Of course!" Cottus leans back, his serious demeanor melting back into his usual friendliness. "Just so we're clear, I *do* trust you, which is probably a good thing, considering you still have so much work to do."

☠

Outside, Kanasu and Endri wait for Alora. And once again, she's glad they can't see the terrified look that would have been on her face—if she had a face.

"Hey, you okay?" Of course, Kanasu can still tell something's off, even without being able to read Alora's expression.

"Oh yeah," she responds in a fumbled attempt to play it off. "It's nothing."

"Okay…" Endri says. "We should probably get back. We've wasted so much time already. Yume and Rasui are probably about done with the dream. They may even already be setting up for the next one."

Alora nods, unable to muster any more words.

Together, they travel back through the dream stages of Somnia, taking a detour to go check on Dublin, the black cat, but he's nowhere to be found, which doesn't help to settle Alora's nerves.

Finally, they arrive back at their stage. Slipping inside, the trio sees that Rasui and Yume are still at work, and the dream is currently active.

In the center of the room, a middle-aged woman with curly dark hair sits on the wrought-iron bench. She wears jeans and a T-shirt. A pair of headphones—plugged into a small yellow box-shaped device sticking out of one of her jeans' pockets—cover her ears. And she's drinking something out of a disposable white cup.

Endri and Kanasu gently float into the room and off to the side, by the dream stage's primary control station—a more rudimentary version of the ones used by the Department of Nightmares.

But Alora, still in a stupor from her brief conversation with Cottus, floats closer to the stage.

As she nears the edge, right where the thick green carpet meant to be grass begins, she stops in her tracks.

The young woman—the human soul who should be too distracted by the staging around her to see beyond the stage—is staring directly at Alora.

She rises to her feet and drops her drink, the foam cup cracking open on the ground and sending its thick icy blue contents spraying across it.

"Is it really you?" she asks, pulling the headphones off her ears and reaching a hand out toward Alora.

Alora reaches back, and their hands touch. The tips of Alora's fingers are separated from the young woman's only by a thin pink polka-dotted bedsheet.

And then the woman disappears in a puff of smoke.

Dream Log #3

Courtesy of the Department of the Mundane

Earth Date: Holocene Period, Age of Humankind, Twentieth Century, 1999 CE (Earth calendar)
Corporeal Location of Subject: London, England, UK (Earth)
Subject: Human, female-identifying, florist, aged approximately forty-four (Earth years)

Start log.

A middle-aged woman with curly dark hair sits on a park bench on a warm, sunny day. She's dressed in jeans and a plain T-shirt and has a headset over her ears. The headset connects to a small yellow Walkman—a kind of tape player—that sticks out of her pocket.

She looks down at the tape player curiously. She reaches down and presses the play button. One of her favorite songs—a repetitive pop melody about sunshine theft—plays through the headphones.

A foam cup with a plastic lid and a bright red straw sits on the bench beside her. She picks up the cup and takes a sip.

It's a frozen, sugary-sweet, blue raspberry-flavored drink. It reminds her of her childhood.

She looks around the park but doesn't notice much. There are a few bushes, a couple of trees, and several birds chirping about. Despite the sun high in the sky above her head—it's unseasonally hot, she notices—the wrought-iron park bench still feels cold to the touch.

The woman listens more closely to the song playing through her headphones and notices that the same part is playing repeatedly. She pushes a button on the Walkman to stop it and then starts it over. Still, the song is stuck on the same roughly thirty-second loop.

She looks around again. The park seems smaller than it should be. Too small. She can't see beyond just a few bushes and trees, but she feels that there's nothing else beyond them. And now the birds look more like puppets than real animals.

And then she sees something just beyond the park's border. It looks like a bedsheet—a pink polka-dotted bedsheet—except it's thrown over something—or someone. And it has eye holes cut into it, like a cheap Halloween costume.

But the woman knows that bedsheet. She's seen it before, though she can't quite place where. And then it hits her.

She rises from the bench, drops her frozen blue raspberry drink, and spills it all over the ground at her feet, covering the concrete. The park seems so small and artificial—like a movie set instead of a real place.

The woman steps forward, taking off her headphones and reaching out a hand.

"Is it really you?" she asks.

The pink polka-dotted bedsheet ghost says nothing but reaches out a hand in return. The ghost and the woman's fingers touch.

End log.

Chapter Nine

What to Do in Case of an Emergency

A s the dream stage's lights come up, Alora stands in the center of the room, still dumbfounded by what had just transpired.

"She knew me," she says. "She recognized me."

Alora turns to see Endri floating by the control console, his hand still pressed against the emergency stop button. Kanasu, standing next to Endri, stares at him, flabbergasted.

"What did you do?" Alora shouts, floating toward her fellow ghosts. "She knew who I was, and you...you—" She's too upset to find the words.

"I stopped the dream," Endri protests. "It's protocol! You know that. Everyone knows that."

"Forget protocol!" Rasui shouts from behind one of the cardboard bushes, his hands still stuffed inside the bird puppets. "You know how important this is to her, to all of us."

"And then what?" Endri shouts back. "Think about this logically. In the best-case scenario, we all get transferred. In the worst-case scenario, we get our souls unraveled or whatever the heck it is that happens to the Haunted. I don't

121

want that for me or any of us. Do you?"

"You could have given me a moment to just ask her how she knew me," Alora screams, shoving Endri away from the console. "You could have let me ask."

Endri raises his hands. "I don't know what you want from me. It's done. That's it. Dream over."

Alora balls up her fists, raising one toward Endri, before dropping her arms to her sides and storming off.

"Pretty uncool, man," Rasui says, pulling the bird puppets off his hand. Yume stands next to him, shaking her head and the heads of her bird hand puppets.

"It's protocol," Endri repeats with a halfhearted shrug.

Alora flies out of the dream stage, bumping into another group of ghosts and shoving them aside as she passes.

"Hey," one of them shouts at her, "What's your problem?"

"She's just having a bad day." Kanasu waves to the group of ghosts before following Alora. "Botched dream, you know how it goes."

The ghosts shake their heads and continue on their way.

Alora cuts through the alley out to the edge of Oneiros—the same spot she always went to—and drops to the ground in a heap.

Dublin, the black cat, eyes her from the edge of the Oneiros wilds, keeping his distance.

The pink polka-dotted bedsheet ghost heaves and sobs, her body wrenching between fury and agony. She finally found something—a thread, however small—that might lead her to understand who she was. And Endri, without so much as a thought as to how it might affect her (or any of them, for that matter), ripped it from her grasp with the simple push of a button.

The worst part was that she knew Endri was right to do what he did. No good could come from interacting with an astral-projected human soul, not if she wanted to remain in the Afterworld.

The dream logs record everything that happens in the dream stages during a dream. And all it would take is a single audit for this one to get them all into even more serious trouble. If Maya kept close tabs on their activities, waiting for a slipup, it might already be enough to draw her wrath.

As Endri said, it was protocol to end any dream where it seemed like the subject was becoming too aware of their surroundings or the fact that they were anywhere other than inside a dream. It didn't matter if there was no explanation as to why this was the case. The rules are the rules; Alora knows this.

Even Chernobog, with his sinister aspirations of a hostile takeover of Dreamweavers, followed that one unbreakable rule.

Who was Alora to think she was any exception?

Still, having been so close to finding out something—anything—about herself only to have it ripped away just as quickly was gut-wrenching torture.

Alora didn't even know it was possible to feel so physically ill without actually having a physical body.

She heaves and writhes on the ground, screaming in despair. And when she can scream no longer, she sobs.

Eventually, she rolls over to stare at the endless, impossible sky above. Except Kanasu is standing over her instead.

Without so much as a word, Kanasu lies down next to her. They don't say anything for a long while—just stare at the endless swirling expanse above.

Finally, Alora breaks the silence.

"You'd think there wouldn't be this much crying in the afterlife," she says.

Kanasu chuckles. "I'm still not sure all of this is even real. Who's to say this isn't all a dream itself?"

Alora shrugs. "A group delusion?"

Kanasu shrugs back.

Alora starts to sob again. "I just don't understand why I can't be okay with this. Why *we* can't be. Is there something wrong with us? Or do all the other humans feel like this but are just better at hiding it?"

"I don't know," Kanasu answers.

"We should just be happy, right? It should be enough that we're here and not somewhere else, like the *actual* fire-and-brimstone Hell with a capital *H*. But it's not, and I just can't figure out why."

Kanasu's voice steadies. "I think we have to figure out how to break into the records room under Dreamweavers HQ."

"Endri was right. That's a suicide mission," Alora answers. "I have to just let this go. Let all of it go. There's no point. What am I even trying to do here?"

"You want to know who you were," Kanasu says. "Just like we all do. It's not just you who can't stand not knowing. It's all of us."

"I know, but what for?" Alora moans. "What's the point of any of it? Say we find out—we learn everything there is to know about ourselves and who we used to be. What good does that do us? We're still dead. We're still stuck here. We still have to just go back to doing our jobs, right? So, what does it matter?"

"It matters," Kanasu says.

"Give me one good reason."

Kanasu stares up at the sky with its swirling patterns—cloudy blues entangled with starry blacks—and takes a deep breath.

"It's what makes us human."

Alora props herself on her elbows and turns to look at Kanasu.

"I never really thought that much about it before," Kanasu continues, still staring up at the sky. "But it's who we are as people. Without our memories and experiences, we're all pretty much the same—especially here. We're just souls draped in bedsheets. If we don't have any of that stuff that makes us who we are, we're not really anything at all. There's something not right about keeping that from us."

Kanasu sits up, turning to Alora and crossing their legs. They extend their hands, palms up. Alora places her hands in Kanasu's.

"This is bigger than us," Kanasu says. "But we're the ones with the chance to figure it all out. Maybe we can make it better."

Alora nods. Then she shakes her head. "Where do we even start?"

"Pretty sure we both know the sad answer to that one."

"You know," Morpheus sighs, "The whole point of giving you that folder was so you'd leave me out of it and go handle all of this yourselves. You might be the most exhausting group of recruits I've ever had to deal with, you know that?"

Alora, Kanasu, Yume, Rasui, and Endri—hovering in the

background with his head down—float in front of Morpheus's desk in the drab college classroom where they all first met.

"By the way," their mentor—now back to his gray-haired, suave older man form—continues, one of his eyebrows raised, "if you're all here, who's operating your dream stage?"

"Nonlinear time," Rasui pipes in. "They can wait."

"Fair point," Morpheus concedes with a raised eyebrow. "Okay, so run it by me again. What is it you want?"

"We're going to break into the records room," Kanasu says.

"Well, I can't help you with that." Morpheus shrugs. He leans back in his chair, putting his feet up on the desk and his hands behind his head. "The moment I walk through those Dreamweavers HQ doors, Maya will know about it. She has eyes and ears all over that building. Plus, it's kind of hard to hide the goings-on of one of the company's most *distinguished* employees. She probably knows we're all here talking right now."

"So, what, like she's got you bugged?" Rasui asks. "Like a spy movie?"

Morpheus scoffs. "Bugs are too unreliable to make good spies," he says. "Always buzzing about and such short attention spans."

Kanasu rolls their eyes. "That's not what he means. Is she listening in on us?"

"Oh, I see," Morpheus answers. "No, she's not. It's one thing to keep tabs on our locations. It's another to try to keep cued in to our private conversations. That'd leave a magical signature. You might not notice it, but I certainly would."

"I know you want to help us," Alora says, leaning forward. "Or maybe you want us to help you. Either. Both. Why else would you have given me that folder?"

"See"—Morpheus points to Alora—"this is why I like you. You're the clever one."

"That's not an answer," Kanasu cuts in.

Morpheus lowers his feet from the desk and sits up. "I can't help you *directly*," he says.

"Well, what can you do?" Alora asks.

"I can give you—what is it you humans call it?—intel." Morpheus winks at Rasui.

"Just like a spy movie," Rasui whispers.

"Well, that'll have to do," Kanasu says.

"It's better than anything else we've got so far," Alora adds.

Morpheus draws the group of bedsheet ghosts forward with a beckoning hand. "Here's what I can tell you."

☠

"Dreamweavers HQ isn't exactly a fortress—nothing stops anyone from walking right through those doors—but that comes with some significant caveats.

"When I say Maya has eyes and ears all over that building, I mean that more as a turn of phrase. It would be more accurate to say that Maya *is* the building. Or rather, they're closely tied. Since she conjured it with her own magics, it functions almost like an extension of her body. Thus, she can sense what's happening inside at any given moment.

"However, that doesn't mean she's always paying attention. We were talking about bugs earlier, right? You can think of human souls as flies, and Dreamweavers HQ is like a horse. Got it? The flies can land on the horse's backside without the horse even knowing their existence. But the second one of those flies takes a bite, the horse notices.

"Your job is to be the flies *without* the bite. My magics would immediately draw Maya's attention if I walked through those doors. But y'all are practically invisible unless you do something big and flashy. Alora knows this firsthand.

"But because of Alora's prior antics, Maya has probably been watching for y'all, specifically. So, the trick will be getting into that building without drawing her initial attention. If y'all can figure out some way to distract Maya, at least long enough for one or two of you to slip into the records room, she probably won't ever notice you're there at all.

"That's hurdle number one.

"Hurdle number two is the custodian of the records room itself.

"By now, you're all familiar with Cottus, the Hecatoncheire—the gentlemen with the hundreds of arms, yes? Well, he has two brothers. And the three of them are all in Maya's service—something to do with an inter-realm work exchange with the Olympians. Cottus, as you know, is Dreamweavers's resident secretary. His brother, Briareus, is the records room custodian, meaning he's responsible for keeping it in order and watching over it.

"That includes keeping human souls out of and away from the restricted section. As such, his desk sits between the dream logs room—the section human souls are allowed freely in and out of—and the personnel files—where you wish to go.

"Lucky for you, that's a fairly Herculean task itself, leaving Briareus with little spare attention for anything else—which is saying a lot, considering his predisposition to exist simultaneously in multiple times and places. I'd wager that one particularly irksome human soul could keep Briareus busy enough that he wouldn't even register a second slipping past him.

"That leaves one more hurdle.

"Remember that work exchange with the Olympians I mentioned? Well, the restricted section of the records room has one other employee of sorts: the Minotaur.

"Supposedly, if the rumors are true, Maya got him on loan directly from Hades. And while I don't think the Minotaur can permanently damage human souls, it's horrific enough to scare off most mortals. If that doesn't do the trick, it's also undoubtedly capable of ejecting them from the records room.

"Lucky for y'all, the Minotaur is anything but subtle. As it wanders the stacks of restricted records, you'll be able to hear its footsteps and heaving breath and bellows long before you find yourself face-to-face with it. Keep a bead on the Minotaur, and you should be able to get into the files and back out of the records room before anyone is the wiser.

"Oh, and I almost forgot.

"I know I mentioned this before, but it bears repeating: removing the files from the restricted section is impossible. They're magically bound to that location. Take a file through the doorway between the restricted and nonrestricted sections, and you'll find yourself quite literally grasping at smoke. So, anything you hope to glean, you'll have to simply memorize for yourself.

"And I think that about covers it. Questions?"

Yume counts on her fingers and mumbles aloud, "First, distract Maya. Second, squeeze past Briareus. Third, avoid the Minotaur. Fourth, make a clean getaway."

"There's no other way into or out of the records room?" Rasui asks. "This just seems like a lot of chances to get caught. If there was a back door, maybe we could get in and out before anyone knows. That's how they do it in heist movies, sometimes, right? Sneaky-sneaky style."

"Technically, yes," Morpheus answers. "There is another way into and out of the records room through Dreamweavers HQ's subbasement."

"Well, that's great news," Alora pipes in. "Why don't we just do that?"

"I agree," Kanasu adds. "Seems much simpler. Or at least less risky than—"

"I really wouldn't recommend it," Morpheus interjects. "For starters, it's an unholy labyrinth of tunnels down there. Then, there's the added difficulty of the fact that the subbasement isn't actually a part of the city of Somnia."

"Oneiros," Yume gasps.

"Bingo." Morpheus points at the small bedsheet ghost. "Somnia only covers the city's limits and the land's surface. Go far enough below ground, and there's a border there, too. If it were just tunnels, I could easily draw you up a map. But the tunnels aren't static. They change. Often. And at random."

"But the pomegranate grove," Alora says. "You took me there. You can navigate Oneiros, you said so."

"I have a fixed point of reference," Morpheus answers. "The pomegranate grove doesn't change. I can find it because I'm familiar with its magical signature. I have no such fixed point in the labyrinth below Somnia. If you wander into those tunnels and they shift before you can escape, you might never find your way back out." Morpheus lowers his voice. "And I'd be powerless to save you."

"Well, that's ominous," Endri says.

"Let's start with problem number one," Rasui chimes in. "We tackle these steps one at a time, and I'm sure we can come up with at least a serviceable plan, right?"

"How do we distract a practically all-powerful god who finds humans to be a minor annoyance?" Kanasu says.

The room goes quiet.

"*Hyakki Yagyō*," Yume finally says.

"What now?" Rasui responds.

Yume turns to Morpheus. "Are we allowed to throw a parade?"

Chapter Ten

Dreamweavers Respects and Recognizes All Cultures,
Immortal and Mortal Alike

Sitting at his station in the human dormitories, Cottus finally moved on to a new book—this time one with a dinosaur skeleton on the cover. And while he typically keeps busy with his normal tasks, he's fairly engrossed in the story—so much so that he doesn't notice when the bedsheet ghosts approach his desk.

"Excuse me," Yume says, rapping her fingers on the counter, "Mr. Cottus?"

"Oh hello, child," he says, flustered. "So sorry. I thought you'd be here later. Or earlier. Not this particular moment, either way."

"New book?" Alora asks.

Cottus smiles. "Indeed. Quite engrossing, as you might've guessed. It's got everything: monsters, mayhem, genetic engineering, and children!"

"Just wait until you see the movie," Rasui says.

"What's a movie?" Cottus responds.

"Oh man," Rasui says. "You and me gotta have a talk sometime. I think you're gonna love 'em."

Alora interrupts, slapping a manila folder onto the desktop, "Right now, we have something else we need to discuss."

Cottus picks up the folder and opens it, thumbing through the pages inside and mumbling to himself. "Permit 33b... request for traffic reduction for roadway event...special dispensation for an event of cultural significance...signed supervisory approval...bypass rush supplemental for short turnaround... Are you folks throwing a parade?"

"We are!" Yume bounces up and down excitedly. "A Parade of Human Souls."

"We believe you'll find everything in proper order," Endri interrupts.

"Yes, quite thorough," Cottus says, looking up over his glasses. "Just one small issue: this request must be submitted directly through Dreamweavers headquarters—the main office. I'm afraid you can't file your request through the human dormitories' secretarial station."

Cottus sets down the folder and pushes it back toward the bedsheet ghosts.

Kanasu places a hand on the folder and scoots it back across the desk toward Cottus. "We were hoping you'd do us a small favor in that regard. You see, we're all just so busy. You know how it is. So many dreams, so little time. And we don't have the benefit of having a hundred arms like you do, Cottus."

With an eyebrow raised, Cottus picks the folder back up.

"What they're trying to say," Alora says, leaning forward, "is that it would really help us out if you could make an exception this one time. It would just be such trouble for us to have to find the time to get away from the dream stages, travel through Somnia, and submit these forms in person at HQ. We just thought, since you're here and there at the same time, maybe you could—"

"Some might say this constitutes a tremendous breach of standard operating procedures," Cottus interrupts, scowling. "You know, we have these systems in place for a reason. Bureaucracy is not something you can simply bypass for your own personal convenience. It ensures that everything runs like a well-oiled machine."

Alora stands upright, floats backward, and raises her hands defensively. "I just thought…"

Cottus sets his book down on the desk and rises to his feet. For the first time, the bedsheet ghosts discover just how gargantuan a creature he is, standing so high that the top of his head nearly scrapes against the vaulted ceiling of the dormitory lobby.

"You thought what?" he says, spreading his hundreds of arms wide. "That I am some fool you can manipulate to your will? That I should be complicit in your attempts to skirt the rules? To think you'd take advantage of our rapport for something so sinister as this…"

Alora and company scramble backward, unable to take their eyes off the towering monster before them.

And then he smiles. "I merely jest."

"Not cool," Kanasu says.

Endri scoffs.

"Dude, what the heck," Rasui says.

Yume giggles.

And Alora lets out a sigh of relief.

Cottus lets out a belly laugh and sits back down. The bedsheet ghosts approach the desk once more.

"Oh my," Cottus says, wiping a tear from his eye as he continues to chuckle. "So rarely do I get to indulge myself in a bit of drama. What a wonderful concept. You know, everyone thinks the gods made up the idea of drama. Your ancient civilizations tell so many stories about the goings-on of the gods and all the tragedy and comedy that results. But most of them are actually quite boring and stiff. It was our kind, the Titans, who created and perfected drama. And you humans—you'd think there would be more excitement around here, always surrounded by human souls. But you're all so worried about doing your jobs. Too rarely do I get to indulge myself. Thank you. That was wonderful."

"Does that mean you're going to help us?" Alora asks.

"Funny thing, that," Cottus responds. "There's actually no rule that says you can't submit those forms here in the dormitories. The rule merely states that all form submissions must travel directly through the Dreamweavers HQ secretary, i.e. myself. Since I am both here and there at all times, this is a perfectly acceptable means of submittal. Very clever work-around, my human friends. Request approved."

Cottus pulls out a huge rubber stamp and smashes it onto the forms, one by one. When he's finished, the folder and its contents disappear into thin air with a puff of smoke.

"You know," the Hecatoncheire continues, "I thought we'd get to this point a lot sooner. But it seems you humans are wont to take the scenic route whenever possible. Then again, who am I to judge? I get to take all routes at once."

"Thank you, Cottus," Alora says. "You don't know what a big help you've been."

"I know precisely what a big help I've been," Cottus replies with a wink. "I have been to the end and back already, you know. In any case, I'm very much looking forward to your parade."

☠

With their parade request approved, the bedsheet ghosts get to work on the next step: making flyers for the big event. It's mostly a cut-and-paste job, the intention being to make the notice look festive and fun. But once they have it all put together, Alora thinks it comes across more like a ransom note.

Still, the promise of a big event for all the human souls in the Dreamscape is an immediate hit. Even the ghosts who had never heard of such a parade—not that they should; Yume based the fictional holiday procession on Japanese folklore—are excited to partake.

As it turns out, nearly every human soul in the Dreamscape has yearned to partake in some measure of festivity. Unlike life on Earth, the Afterworld has no changing seasons or even the passing of days, so it's hard to pinpoint when people might celebrate or what milestones would call for a jubilee—let alone what kind.

The gods never gave much thought to what human souls might need to feel a sense of normalcy. To them, the infinite stretch of never-ending time *was* normalcy. While human souls, especially on Earth, were wont to celebrate in the names of the gods they served, it appeared the gods themselves never cared for such events in any meaningful way.

Though it made her feel bad for the human souls who had been in the Afterworld far longer than her, Alora was thankful that it was working in her favor. Based on her numerous interactions with the souls from other departments, the parade was shaping up to be a smashing success.

That meant it was time to iron out the rest of the details for the next part of the plan, which Alora and her companions did surreptitiously in the comfort and privacy of their dorm room.

"So, we're in agreement that Yume will lead the parade, yes?" Alora says.

Kanasu, Rasui, and Endri nod in agreement.

"Endri can bring up the rear," Alora continues.

"That leaves one of us to run interference when Maya inevitably comes poking around," Kanasu says. "And two more to sneak into HQ—one to actually do the snooping and the other to keep Briareus busy. I think it makes sense that we put Rasui on interference, and then Alora and I will sneak inside."

"Actually," Endri interrupts, "I was thinking I might be better suited to keeping Briareus company while Alora sneaks into the restricted section."

The room goes quiet.

Endri takes a deep breath. "I want to make up for what I did. Make things right. We can talk about thought experiments, paradoxes, and theoretical physics—the kinds of things that have kept human scholars and philosophers stumped for generations. If Briareus is anything like his brother, he's going to be curious about the human mind, too."

"Well, then, why not have Rasui do it?" Kanasu says. "He's full of pop culture knowledge and references. Then you can take up the rear of the parade, and I'll—"

"I don't know about that," Rasui interrupts. "I don't even think I could handle dealing with Maya. I don't do well under pressure. I'd rather be on parade duty."

"Okay, then I'll take Maya," Kanasu says. "Endri can lead the parade, and Yume will distract the Hecatoncheire."

"Can I trust you?" Alora says, addressing Endri directly.

Endri stares at her for a moment and nods. "I can do this. I need to do this."

"Are you sure?" Kanasu asks Alora, eyeing Endri.

"Yes," Alora answers. "I trust him."

Kanasu shakes their head but does not object. "Fine."

"Then it's settled," Alora says. "Yume leads the parade. Rasui takes up the rear. Kanasu runs interference. Endri will handle Briareus. And I'll sneak into the restricted section."

Rasui sticks a hand into the center of the group. "Heist on three?" he asks.

One by one, the rest of the ghosts put their hands atop his.

With giddiness in his voice, Rasui chants, "One, two, three!"

"Heist!" they all shout, raising their hands in the air.

☠

The wide street outside the human soul dormitories was the obvious rallying point for the beginning of the human souls parade. But it remained to be seen if other bedsheet ghosts besides Alora and her companions would join them for the event.

"What do we do if nobody shows up?" Rasui is the first to ask.

They have only just arrived at the assigned meeting place, but the tension is palpable. Too much hinges on the parade's success, and they all know it.

"Then we figure something else out," Kanasu responds. "And then we try again."

It sounds confident, but Alora notices Kanasu fidgeting more than normal. Still, the rest of the crew nods in agreement—even Endri.

But as the moments roll by, Alora becomes increasingly concerned that the parade gambit—the most integral part of the bedsheet ghosts' plan—might fall through entirely. Then, after everything, they'd be left just as empty-handed as when they first got to the Afterworld. And it might not be so easy to bring morale back up. Then what?

The quandary would have made Alora's stomach churn if she had one.

That's when the first group of human souls emerges from the dormitories. And then another. And then another.

Soon, dozens upon dozens of like-minded bedsheet ghosts surround Alora and the gang, excited by the prospect of marching through the streets of Somnia together.

Some—apparently confusing a parade with a protest—even bring signs and posters.

Humans Are People, Too, Alora reads on one.

Dream Job? More Like a Nightmare, says another.

Toward the back of the crowd, Alora sees a group of ghosts holding up a huge banner with the phrase Mortal Rights Are Immortal Rights scrawled across it.

She even notices a few nonhumans—lesser immortals and other mythical creatures who regularly work with human souls across the Dreamweavers departments—gathering among the bedsheet ghosts. There are some impossibly black horselike creatures, a few vaguely humanoid djinns, and even a smattering of smaller winged gargoyles.

Kanasu nudges Alora with an elbow. "Pretty good turnout, huh?"

"Yeah," Alora titters. "This…is a lot bigger than I expected."

"At least a few hundred," Endri adds. "Could easily be more, I think."

"Dudes," Rasui interjects. "I guess word spread pretty quickly throughout the company. There are ghosts here from all the departments, even Nightmares. These folks were just telling me"—he gestures with his thumb at a random group of ghosts he had been speaking with—"most of the departments petitioned to join us. And since we had all the proper permits and it's a cultural event, the department heads had to let them."

"Chernobog isn't going to like that," Yume says with a giggle.

"Chernobog can eat turds. This is awesome!" Rasui responds. Then, with a whisper, "Maybe don't tell him I said that, though."

"One of us should probably say something, right?" Alora says, looking to Kanasu.

"Yeah, right," Kanasu agrees. "Gotta let everyone know what to expect and the parade route. You wanna do the honors?"

"Me?" Alora says. "I wouldn't even know what to say. What about Rasui?"

"No, thank you," Rasui says, raising his hands in protest. "I'm not the parade leader—hey, wait." He turns his head back and forth. "Where's Yume?"

Alora, Kanasu, and Endri also look around, but no one can spot Yume's fruit-patterned bedsheet.

What they can see is that the surrounding crowd is beginning to get antsy. Many of the bedsheet ghosts gathered in front of the dormitories are looking around, shifting impatiently. And the ambient volume of the crowd is rising.

"When's this march kicking off?" one ghost shouts.

"Let's get this show on the road!" hollers another.

And just before Alora speaks up, the doors to the dormitory open.

An enormous creature with hundreds of arms, a finely

tailored suit, and a pair of spectacles emerges from the dorms. It's Cottus. And Yume is standing on his shoulder.

Cottus rises above the crowd, stretching his arms out and fanning them downward, encouraging the hundreds of human souls to quiet themselves. This works to spectacular effect, and a hush falls across the square.

With the crowd calmed and quieted, Yume speaks.

"Greetings, mortals and mortal allies! Welcome to the inaugural Parade of Human Souls!"

The crowd erupts in applause.

After a few moments, Cottus fans his hands again, calming the crowd once more. Yume continues.

"Let me be the first, on behalf of our steadfast parade organizers, to say thank you for joining us. We hope this exceptional turnout means we'll be able to continue mortal cultural events such as this one into the future here in the Dreamscape.

"But that all depends on our own conduct as we march through Somnia. While I know we're all pent-up, remember that this is a gathering of togetherness—not division.

"We are here to prove to our immortal hosts that we deserve dedicated time for ourselves, to honor our human heritage, and to celebrate our mortal culture. And that means we need to treat the streets of our host city with respect, even if the immortals of that city do not treat us with the same level of respect."

This time, a wave of boos travel through the throng of human souls.

Yume taps Cottus on the head, and once more, he quiets the congregation.

"I know," Yume says in a measured tone. "It's not fair to ask a higher level of conduct than that showed to us by the powers that be, but it is of the utmost importance that we don't step on too many toes—especially with all the dancing we're going to do!"

Yume shimmies her hips and twirls atop Cottus's shoulder. Laughter rips through the crowd, and several ghosts whistle loudly.

"With this in mind, I have only one more question for you…"

Yume throws her hands up into the air.

"Who's ready to party?"

The crowd erupts in applause.

Cottus leans down, letting Yume rejoin her companions. She nods at the Hecatoncheire, and he smiles before reentering the dormitories. Then, Yume turns to her friends.

"How was that?"

Kanasu, Rasui, and Endri stare at her, gobsmacked.

"It was perfect," Alora says.

Chapter Eleven

*Mortal Access to the Dreamweavers Restricted Records Room
Is Strictly Prohibited*

While numerous lesser immortals and mythical beings joined the human souls parade at its outset, the other residents of Somnia are decidedly less enthusiastic about the horde of bedsheet ghosts meandering through the city streets.

Many of them jeer from the safety of their homes—hollering out their windows—while others line the streets to shake their fists, claws, wings, and tentacles at the passing mob.

Some even go so far as to throw garbage and food waste.

But the negative reactions of Somnia's more bigoted residents don't sway the crowd. In fact, it has the opposite effect. The humans and their allies march louder, prouder, and with even more enthusiasm. Their quiet chants flourish into rhythmic songs that reverberate through the city's streets, drawing even more attention from Somnia's residents.

The commotion is so great that by the time the congregation makes its way to Dreamweavers HQ, Maya is already outside and waiting for them, blocking their path forward.

"What's the meaning of this?" she asks, all four of her hands resting on her hips and a scowl across her face.

As planned, Rasui is at the back of the crowd, Yume is at its head, Alora and Endri hide in the middle, and Kanasu is ready to tackle the Maya problem.

Folder in hand, Kanasu marches up to Maya and flips the folder open. "I assure you, we have all the proper documents in order. This is a peaceful celebration of human culture, and we've already got approval from our supervisors and the secretary of Dreamweavers himself."

Kanasu flips through the forms in front of Maya before stacking them together and handing them to her. The golden goddess takes the papers in hand, glances at them briefly, and tosses them into the air. As they rain down, she places her hands back on her hips.

"I don't care how many forms you filled out or whose approval you've gotten. You're making a mockery of me and my city. I demand that this gathering disperses." Then, she addresses the crowd, throwing her hands into the air. "Don't you all have work to do? The dreams aren't going to make themselves. Get back to your assigned stations before I transfer every last one of you."

But instead of compliance, Maya is met with a chorus of boos. The humans (and immortals) holding signs raise them even higher, bouncing them up and down as the crowd resumes its protest chants.

Maya steps forward, grabs a poster from someone's hands— the one that reads Humans Are People, Too—and rips it in half before throwing it down on the ground and stomping on it.

Another round of boos erupts from the procession.

With both the goddess and the crowd distracted, Alora and

Endri take the chance to slip away and slide in through the front doors of Dreamweavers HQ.

Inside, Cottus is sitting at his desk, waiting patiently. "Good, you're finally here," he says. "The elevators are ready and waiting. They'll take you down to the subbasement."

"Thank you, Cottus," Alora says with a wave as she and Endri float by.

"Good luck with my brother," the Hecatoncheire responds. "Just remember, he's bound by the terms of his employment as both the records room's security and its librarian."

"Okay..." Alora says.

But Endri nods more enthusiastically. "Very helpful," he shouts.

The ghosts wave as the elevator chimes and its doors close.

The elevator chimes a second time, and its doors slide open, revealing a cavernous chamber that looks like it was carved out of the earth itself—or whatever the Dreamscape's landmass was made of. As Alora and Endri exit the elevator, they gaze upon the grandeur of the records room.

The walls stretch upward to a domed ceiling, from which several gargantuan chandeliers hang, each illuminated by dozens of candles. Alora squints up at them. Though they appear to be dripping with wax, none of them are getting any shorter. The same goes for the dozens of sconces lining the walls.

All these magical applications, Alora thinks, *and they couldn't automate anything in the dream stages.*

Beyond the entryway, the bedsheet ghosts can see the

towering shelves that fill the room (although none of them reach even halfway up to the room's domed ceiling), all crammed full of books, scrolls, and even stone tablets. Some are placed upright, while others are stacked on their sides, and others still seem to be just shoved wherever they might fit.

Finally, situated between the shelves and the entryway, there's a wide, curved wooden reference desk. And seated at its center, a Hecatoncheire—dressed in a tailored suit and wearing a pair of wire-rim glasses—hunches over a mess of binders, folders, and loose papers.

"You ready?" Endri whispers.

Alora takes a deep breath. "As ready as I'm gonna be."

With a nod, Alora and Endri approach the desk.

"Excuse me," Endri says, "Can you help us?"

The Hecatoncheire holds up a single finger on one of his hundreds of hands as he collects several huge stacks of paper and shuffles them together like a deck of cards. Then, once they're in order, he shoves them into a folder and sets it aside.

"Pray tell, why else would I be here?" he finally says. "What do you want? Not that I don't already know. But you're going to tell me anyhow, yes? It's not enough that I know what it is you're here for. You're all so self-important you have to tell me what it is you want yourselves."

"I'm sorry," Alora interjects. "Have we done something to offend you?"

Briareus finally looks up, and his scowl shifts to a look of surprise. "My goodness," he says as he pushes his spectacles up to the bridge of his nose, "I seem to have gotten a bit mixed up. I'm so sorry. I thought you were one of those dreadful gods that always comes down here, like that shadowy fellow with the bad attitude. The trouble with existing in so many places at once is that it can be a little difficult to remember the order. Remind me, this is the first time we've met, yes?"

Alora notices that Briareus looks almost exactly like Cottus. His suit, glasses, and general demeanor are all the same. The only difference she can see is that Briareus has a thin mustache.

"It is," Endri says. "I'm Endri, and this is Alora."

Alora waves a hand. "Big fans of your brother, Cottus. And I certainly see the family resemblance."

"What resemblance?" Briareus replies, stroking the end of his mustache. "We look nothing alike."

"Right," Alora says with a nod. "I must be imagining things."

"Yes, must be," the Hecatoncheire continues. "Okay. If I remember correctly, and this is indeed our first meeting—or you think it's our first meeting—then I believe you're here for some dream logs. Is that correct?"

"Uhh, yes?" Endri says.

"You seem a bit unsure," Briareus says, squinting. "Are you not here for logs? Let me see." The Hecatoncheire opens one of the folders on his desk, flipping through the pages as he speaks: "Four hundred seventy-eight, six thousand two hundred eighty-two, fifteen million forty-four, and"—he flips back to the first page—"Seven?"

"I don't remember—"

"Yes!" Alora interrupts. "That is exactly why we're here."

"Wonderful!" Briareus answers. "This may take a while, I'm afraid. If one of you wouldn't mind coming with me while the other waits here in the lobby area, that would be exceptionally adequate."

"I'd be happy to tag along," Endri says, looking at Alora with a shrug.

"Spectacular," Briareus says, rising from his chair to his

full, towering height. "And you wouldn't mind waiting here?" he asks Alora. "We Hecatoncheires can experience so many moments simultaneously, but we simply can't be everywhere at once, I'm afraid."

"Yes, happy to wait here," she answers.

"I just must ask you not to go wandering," Briareus continues. "Especially not to the restricted section, through the center and off to the back right. Humans are definitely not allowed to wander there. Again, that's through the center and to the right." Then, addressing Endri, "If you'd just follow me…"

Briareus winks at Alora, and she thinks she sees him mouthing the phrase "Good luck" as he and Endri disappear behind one of the shelves. As they go, she can hear their conversation fading away.

"If you don't mind me asking," Endri says, "how is this place organized? Do you use the Dewey decimal system?"

"What's a Dewey decimal?" Briareus replies.

Alora stands in the lobby for a few minutes, the conversation between Endri and Briareus fading deep into the records room before she makes her move.

As the Hecatoncheire shared, she scoots around the reference desk and marches straight down the middle toward the back. Once she reaches the rear wall, she follows it right until she finds a massive ornate entryway carved out of what looks like solid marble.

Alora stares at it in awe, entranced by its baroque carvings. Though she's no expert in mythology, the stone reliefs seem to tell the story of the Dreamscape's founding—from Vishnu's initial creation (and their subsequent slumber) straight on through to the establishment and continued operation of Dreamweavers, LLC.

At the top, in a bold and jarringly juxtaposed Times New Roman font, a huge off-kilter sign hanging by a golden string reads Restricted Section. And, below that, No Mortals Permitted.

Peeking through the portal, Alora discovers a huge spiral staircase leading down to the next level. Along its walls are more ornate carvings, ones whose story Alora does not recognize—perhaps everything that came before the creation of the Dreamscape, she muses. With a deep breath—an unnecessary performative reflex Alora had still not broken— she floats through the archway.

The staircase is much longer than Alora expected. Were she still flesh and bone, the descent would have exhausted her. Not growing tired was one of the few upsides of no longer having a physical body.

But as the stairs keep going deeper and deeper, Alora wonders if she's still headed in the right direction—or maybe the staircase is actually endless, and this is all just a clever trap to catch any human souls who have grown a bit too curious.

Several times, she stops to consider if she should turn around and head back up. But remembering all the effort she and her companions have gone through to get to this point, she pushes onward. And after a few more spirals, her patience pays off.

Through another archway—mimicking the ornate style of the one at the top of the stairs—she floats out to the edge of another massive staircase and finally gazes upon the restricted records room below. Alora didn't know what she was expecting, but it wasn't this.

Situated in a gargantuan cave that dwarfs the primary records room above, the restricted section looks less like a library and more like a labyrinth.

Alora surmises that the shelves stand at least twice as tall as a Hecatoncheire (having recently seen Cottus at his full height and then his brother, Alora thinks the comparison is both apt and accurate). And they're not arranged in a grid pattern like most earthly libraries. Instead, they form a great maze that, to Alora's eyes, seems impossible to navigate.

The only help she can ascertain comes in the form of several enormous signs dangling from absurdly long chains attached to the ceiling high above. Or at least Alora presumes they're attached to the ceiling—it's too high for her to tell.

She has to squint to make them out, but she sees one in a far back corner that reads Personnel Records. As best as she can manage, she tries to memorize a pathway through the maze that leads to that corner before making her way down into the restricted records room.

And then she hears it: a great bellow so loud and deep that it vibrates the chains of the humongous signs hanging above.

Alora shivers, remembering Morpheus's warning.

"Listen for the footsteps and the breathing, and you'll be fine," she reassures herself. "You're going to be fine. You're definitely not going to get eaten by a Minotaur."

Alora shakes her head, shrugs her shoulders, wiggles her fingers, and descends into the labyrinth.

Chapter Twelve

Beware: Local Dreamscape Fauna May Be Hostile to Mortal
Souls

The restricted records labyrinth is far more daunting than Alora initially thinks. Sure, standing atop the entrance, she had a general idea of which direction to head in—thanks largely to the massive signs hanging overhead. But navigating the pathways in the right direction is another story entirely.

It doesn't help that the sheer scale of the maze baffles her, either. The bookshelves tower nauseatingly high above, and even the rolling ladders are comically enormous—perfect for a gargantuan god or Titan but completely unmanageable for a human soul.

The only thing stopping her from getting completely lost—besides orienting herself to the signs hanging overhead—is that she remembers to leave herself a trail of breadcrumbs. Only they're not breadcrumbs. They're books.

Every few steps, she pulls one of the books from the shelf and lays it on the ground, helping her keep track of which paths she's already been down and giving her a quick escape should she come face-to-face with the other, much more terrifying creature wandering the labyrinth.

Right on cue, Alora hears the Minotaur let out a loud bellow. For a moment, she thinks it sounds like the beast is trying to say something. But she shakes her head, clearing the thought and continuing forward.

As she meanders down one corridor, turning the corner down another, she realizes she's doubled back on her own pathway. She finds a familiar corridor with several books already set down on the ground. She follows the path backward to the previous junction and heads down the other way.

She hears the Minotaur again but can't tell if it seems closer or farther away. And again, Alora can't shake the feeling that it's trying to speak but that it just can't seem to get the words out.

For what feels like hours, she wanders the maze, cautiously roaming the corridors and

keeping on track toward the back corner with the personnel records. She runs into dead ends or circular paths several times, discovering too late that she's headed in the wrong direction. But, using her breadcrumb books, she sets herself back down what she thinks is the right path—all while trying to pay close attention to the location of the Minotaur.

"You got this," she reassures herself with a whisper. "Just stay on track."

Alora thinks about her companions back aboveground, hoping they're doing okay. Going toe-to-toe with Maya, even in what you think is a casual conversation, can be intimidating—she would know. But going out of their way to draw her ire is downright dangerous. She hopes they're all okay and that they are back in the dorms waiting for her.

Thinking about her friends acts as a good distraction, right up until she hears the Minotaur bellow once more. This time, it's much, much closer. Alora wonders if it knows she's in the labyrinth, too. Maybe it can smell her. Perhaps it's hunting her.

The fear pushes her forward, and she traverses the maze a bit faster, leaving fewer books behind to mark her path. She finds herself trying to keep track of the turns: a right, then a left, then two rights, followed by a long straight, a left, another left—

Then she notices that the books on the shelves look different from before. Instead of the mess of tomes in various sizes, colors, and styles, they look much more uniform. In fact, they all look practically identical, save for the print on their spines. And they're not books anymore. They're binders.

She's arrived. Looking up, she can see the personnel records sign hanging high above her head. She made it. She found them.

She sees that the sections are labeled on the shelves, too. The one she stands in front of reads *Department of the Fantastic, Employees Be-Bh*. The next shelf over reads *Department of the Fantastic, Employees Bia-Bio*.

"Oh thank goodness," she says with a sigh of relief. "They're in alphabetical order."

All Alora has to do now is follow the shelves until she finds the ones for the Department of the Mundane. Then, she can find the books with her records and the records of her coworkers. But she'll have to be quick about it.

The Minotaur bellows again. It's closer this time. Much closer.

She'll have to be very, very quick. Alora pushes onward.

☠

Alora seeks out Yume's file first, reasoning that it's the farthest from the restricted records section's entrance, alphabetically speaking. After Yume's, she'd find Rasui's, Kanasu's, Endri's, and finally her own.

She tells herself that it's the logical order to find the files and that she's not just doing it that way because she's scared of what she'll find in her binder.

They had worked so hard to get this far, so it's silly for her to get cold feet at this point, right? Besides, there are bigger, louder, meaner things for her to be afraid of right now. She's just a little nervous, is all. That's right; it's just nerves. Now, get back to work.

Alora finds the end of the Department of the Mundane's personnel records a couple of rows and a few stacks down. And there, in the *Yi-Yu* section on a shelf just above her eyeline, she finds a thin three-ring binder labeled Human Soul: Yume.

Alora had thought the file might also include Yume's sur-name, as she remembers that's pretty typical of most humans who weren't pop star celebrities back on Earth, but maybe that isn't as big a concern here in the Afterworld.

To make certain, Alora plucks the binder from the shelf and flips it open. The first page is mostly white but has a few lines of text reading Yume, Species: Human, and Origin: Earth. There's also a small Polaroid of a ghost stapled to the upper right-hand corner. The ghost's bedsheet has a repeating pattern made up of tiny drawings of fruit. It's Yume, all right.

Alora flips to the next page and starts reading. But as she skims the page, a deep sense of despair begins to fill her.

The information is spotty and inconsistent, comprised

largely of things that could apply to almost everyone. And while some of it does appear to apply to Yume—like how she's a dancer, that she's easily distracted, and that she can sometimes be quite shrewd—it reads less like a personnel file and more like a poorly constructed Mad Libs.

"Yume likes to eat food with her friends," Alora reads to herself. Then, skipping to the next paragraph, "She's known for partaking in human activities, such as sleeping and breathing." And finally, "Yume may or may not have parents and siblings."

Alora closes the binder, baffled by what she's just read. It doesn't make any sense. The whole file is bogus, made-up, falsified.

She follows the stacks until she finds Rasui's.

This time, it's on a shelf down toward the bottom. And again, the Polaroid on the first page—this time depicting a ghost with a sci-fi design on its bedsheet—confirms that Alora has found the right file.

But a flip of the page elicits the same result. Sure, some of the information in the first few sentences applies to Rasui—his affinity for pop culture and bad jokes—but the rest is as good as randomly generated nonsense.

She drops Rasui's binder to the ground and finds Kanasu's next. And it's more of the same.

Alora can't make sense of what she's seeing. It *doesn't* make sense. She presses her hands to her head, trying to fathom what she's just discovered.

She decides that the only way to be certain is to find her own file. If she can pluck hers from the shelf and look at it, it may awaken her memories or confirm, once and for all, that this is all phony.

She rushes back to the Department of the Mundane's *Ai-Al* section and spots her binder up on a high shelf. Too high to reach. She glances around and sees one of the gargantuan rolling ladders down the aisle a few shelves over.

She rushes over to it and, with all her might, pushes it toward the section with her folder. It takes everything that she has, but the ladder moves, inch by inch, in the right direction.

With the ladder finally in place, she ascends.

Once she reaches the proper height, she extends a hand toward her file and plucks it from the shelf. Without even climbing down the ladder, she opens it up. And her heart sinks.

Her file, like all the others, is made-up gobbledygook.

Crestfallen, Alora descends the ladder and slumps onto the floor, surrounded by counterfeit personnel files. She looks up at the shelves and around at all the hundreds—no, thousands—of files surrounding her, and her mind begins to churn.

Why would Dreamweavers even keep personnel files if they're all fake?

Humans aren't even allowed in this room, so what's the point?

If these files are so clearly fake when looked at by a human soul, who are they even for?

Who would fall for such a ruse?

And then it hits her: the files aren't for the humans' benefit. The only beings who have access to this room—the only ones who would be fooled by such clearly fictitious information and not think anything of it—are the gods themselves.

But if this entire room is simply one big misdirection—one designed to pull the wool over the eyes of immortals—what is it hiding? And who is hiding it?

Alora isn't sure if deceased mortal souls can feel sick to their stomachs, but she's certain that how she's feeling is about as close as it gets.

And now, after all this—the organizing of the parade, the distracting of Maya, and the "sneaking" into the restricted records room—she has to go back to her friends empty-handed. Not that she could have taken the files with her anyhow. Like Morpheus said, they'd disappear as soon as they crossed the threshold.

Alora had felt bad enough when that woman had recognized her. When, before they could even talk, Endri had—

Right, Endri. Alora still hadn't found Endri's file. Not that it really mattered. If anything, she would find it just to be thorough, just so she could say for certain that she had done all she could.

She rises from the ground and follows the stacks back to the Department of the Mundane's *En-Eo* personnel records section. Alora traces her finger along the files, trying to find the right one: *Ena, Enalia, Enaya, Endia, Ender, Endrik, Endriel—*

She goes back and checks again. And again.

There's no binder for anyone named Endri.

A new feeling fills Alora, not of the hopelessness that had overtaken her but of panic.

If there's no file for Endri here...

She follows the stacks until she finds the section for the Department of Nightmares. Then, she finds the shelves for names that start with the letter *E*. And sure enough, right at her eyeline, she stumbles upon a folder entitled Human Soul: Endri.

Trembling, Alora pulls the folder from the shelf and opens

it up. There's no mistaking it. The Polaroid photo shows a ghost wearing a black-and-white plaid bedsheet. It's Endri.

Alora drops the folder.

"I can explain," a voice rings out from down the aisle.

Alora spins to face Endri, the ghost she thought was her friend. The one who had stopped her from speaking to the woman who recognized her. The imposter who had been working for Chernobog this entire time.

A rage rises inside her—a wave of anger so palpable she feels like she might burst into flames.

But before she can say anything to the deceiver standing before her, a small object rolls between them from an adjoining aisle.

Still fuming, Alora has a hard time making it out. It's small, circular, bright green, and has white lines. She leans over and picks it up.

It's a tennis ball.

She rubs her thumb on the ball's feltlike surface and notices it has some strangely slimy spots.

And then she hears the bellow of the Minotaur.

Only this time, it's much, much closer—close enough that she can feel the heat of its breath.

☠

Alora knows what a Minotaur is supposed to look like. Or at least she thought she did. Half man, half bull—simple enough. But seeing the creature with her own eyes is an entirely different, far more terrifying experience.

It stands head and shoulders above her, even hunched over between the restricted records room's enormous shelves.

And its body looks wholly unnatural—some spots covered with thick dark matted fur, and others nearly entirely bald, displaying the bulging, veiny muscles that stretch and contract with each movement.

The great creature stomps forward, its massive cloven hooves shaking both the ground beneath it and the fur on its haunches with each step. And Alora can see its long tail, which has another tuft of fur at its end, whipping back and forth behind it.

Its head is mostly that of a bull's, with enormous steer-like horns that protrude horizontally from the top of its skull before turning forward and tapering into two sharp points. Its jaws, lined with huge molars—which Alora assumes are adept at grinding flesh and bone alike—hang open, and saliva drips down its chin. And its eyes…its eyes frighten Alora the most, not because they are beastly or monstrous, but because they are unquestionably, undoubtedly human. And they look almost sad.

Until the monstrous creature looks over at Alora, and its eyes widen with excitement.

When the beast bellows this time, Alora is certain that it isn't merely moaning. It's speaking.

"PRAAAAY," it howls.

Alora turns as fast as she can and darts in the other direction.

☠

With nothing but sheer terror pushing her forward, Alora blitzes through the restricted records labyrinth as fast as she can.

She isn't concerned with finding her way out, which direction she's headed, or even the fact that she left Endri—*that snake*—behind.

None of it even crosses her mind.

She cares only about getting away from the towering, frothing, charging beast chasing after her.

"PRAAAAY," the Minotaur wails as it pursues Alora, crashing into shelves with enough force to send the books and binders raining down around it.

Alora turns another corner, narrowly dodging one of the records room's giant rolling ladders as she heads down another aisle.

The Minotaur, far less nimble than the bedsheet ghost it pursues, can't dodge the ladder in time. Instead, the monster smashes headlong into it, shattering it to pieces and sending the splintered lumber flying in every direction.

But the collision doesn't even faze the rabid beast. It simply shakes the wood dust from its shoulders and continues its pursuit.

It occurs to Alora that she needs some sort of plan. She can run from the Minotaur all she wants, but the labyrinth is its domain. She's the visitor here. And that means it's only a matter of time before she ends up completely turned around or, worse, finds herself in a dead end.

She considers climbing up one of the rolling ladders before remembering how easily the Minotaur destroyed the one it ran into. So that's out.

She could try to hide on one of the shelves, slipping behind some of the books and waiting for the Minotaur to pass her by. But that would take time, which she simply doesn't have.

If only she knew what it wanted.

"PRAAAAY," the Minotaur screams again.

Her mind is consumed with terror, and she can't figure it out. All she knows is that whatever she's gonna do, she has to figure it out quickly.

And then she sees something sitting in the aisle ahead of her. A small black shadow that seems somehow familiar.

As she gets closer, doing her best to keep ahead of the Minotaur chomping at her heels, she notices the shadowy shape isn't a shadow at all. It has eyes—two big yellow eyes.

"Dublin!" she shouts.

On cue, the cat stands up, does a little twirl, and starts running, glancing over his shoulder as if to say, "This way!"

With no other ideas or options, Alora decides to put her faith in her little feline friend. After all, he hasn't let her down yet.

She follows Dublin from corridor to corridor, making tight cuts around corners and dodging the occasional ladder.

But the Minotaur isn't far behind, howling and charging, shaking the ground beneath its massive hooves.

Before long, she realizes Dublin isn't leading her toward the exit. If the signs above are any indication—and Alora can steal only the quickest of glances—they've delved even deeper into the labyrinth.

I hope you know where you're going, little guy, she thinks.

Almost on cue, the black cat turns down another corridor. And Alora follows.

Except this time, it's a dead end. Worse, there's not even a shelf at the end that Alora can use for cover. It's one of the sheer rock faces at the edge of the expansive restricted records room.

Dublin slows to a trot before plopping down in front of the rock wall. And Alora skitters to a stop not far behind.

"No, no, no, no," she shouts. "What am I supposed to do now? That, that, that *thing* is coming, and we're trapped here! It's gonna gobble us both up or smash us to pieces or who knows what."

But the cat, staring up at her with its big yellow eyes, seems wholly unconcerned.

And then the Minotaur rounds the corner.

Alora steals a glance at the beast just as it rounds the corner. It sees the bedsheet ghost, and its eyes widen once more. Its mouth opens, and saliva spills from its jaws as it moans once again, more clearly this time, "PLAAAAY!"

At that moment, Alora realizes she's still holding the tennis ball. She'd been carrying it with her the whole time, not even thinking about it.

That's what the monster wants. That's why it keeps howling. It was telling Alora the whole time. She was just too frightened to realize it. The Minotaur wasn't saying "pray" at all. It only wanted someone to play fetch with it.

She winds up and, with as much power as she can muster, she hurls the tennis ball up and over the Minotaur and down the corridor behind it.

The beast watches the ball fly overhead and into the adjoining hallway before it resumes its chase. It clumsily lopes down the aisle, knocking books off the shelves and crashing into the enormous rolling ladders.

A few moments later, it comes barreling back with the ball held between its jaws. It drops the orb at Alora's feet. Alora picks it back up and throws it again. And again. And again.

Finally (and utterly relieved), Alora turns back around.

"Well, I feel a little dumb," she says to Dublin before realizing that the rock wall dead end is no longer a dead end at all.

In its place, she sees a golden door slotted inside a white marble archway—architectural notes that remind her of the Dreamweavers COO's office at the top of the tower above her.

Dublin meows at her feet, turning in a tight figure eight and rubbing his head on her shins—or where her shins would be, had she any—with each pass.

Alora leans down and scratches the black cat behind his ears. "I'm sorry I yelled at you," she says. "So, this is what you wanted to show me, huh?"

The cat purrs.

"Only one way to find out, I suppose," Alora says as she turns the knob and gives the door a push. "Let's see what's behind door number one. What do you say?"

Alora and Dublin get ready to step through the portal but not before the bedsheet ghost tosses the tennis ball for the Minotaur one last time.

Chapter Thirteen

Dreamweavers Hot Tip: When in Doubt, Remember Never to Peek Behind the Curtain

B eyond the golden door, Alora finds herself in a confusingly bland hallway—one with taupe walls, flickering fluorescent lights overhead, and little decoration.

There are a few paintings—at least that's what Alora thinks they're supposed to be—but they look like little more than some splashes of color on canvas. They're the kind of "art" found in a strip mall doctor's office, industrial park storefront, or three-star hotel.

But Dublin continues ahead, so Alora follows him.

However, the bedsheet ghost has started to feel a little strange. It's a familiar feeling—the kind Alora hasn't had since she was alive.

Gliding forward, Alora inhales deeply and instinctively raises her hand to where her mouth should have been.

But the black cat is still headed down the hallway, so Alora follows close behind. Or as best she can, considering her wooziness.

At the end of the hall, there's a pair of swinging double doors.

Dublin paws at one before pushing it open and slipping inside. A few steps behind him, Alora does the same.

Inside, the bedsheet ghost and her feline companion find another oddly banal space, only this time it's a waiting room, with a couple of rows of cloth-upholstered wooden chairs, a few end tables, and a pair of potted plants, (which, on closer inspection, appear to be fake).

There's also a window with a reception desk behind it, but no creature—mortal or immortal—sits at the desk.

Alora inhales deeply again, which strikes her as odd since she hasn't needed to breathe since waking up in the Dreamscape.

No, that's not right, she thinks. *It's not just deep breathing. It's yawning. Why am I yawning?*

She rubs her eyes and decides to sit down in one of the tacky, uncomfortable waiting room chairs. If she just rests for a moment, maybe she can shake this strange feeling and keep going.

As soon as her butt hits the seat, she closes her eyes and slumps backward.

After a time, she feels something heavy in her lap and something else—something soft—patting her face.

She opens her eyes to find that Dublin has hopped into her lap and is swatting at her with one of his front paws.

"Hey, buddy," she says. "Sorry, I don't know what's come over me. I'm just so tired all of a sudden."

No sooner do the words leave her mouth than she realizes their absurdity. Why would she be tired now? In all her time in the Dreamscape, she's not once felt so much as an inkling of these kinds of mortal, physical feelings. Not hunger. Not thirst. And definitely not exhaustion.

Dublin hops off her lap, meowing loudly and doing his little figure eights.

She shakes her head, rubs her eyes, and rises once more.

"Okay, okay," she says. "I'm coming."

Dublin leads her to the only other door in the room, just beside the empty reception desk. Only this one has a big gold placard with black lettering that reads Employees Only.

But the cat persists, pawing at the door. So, Alora ignores the sign, turns the door's golden knob, and pushes it open.

Beyond the door, the room opens to another massive space—not quite as large as the restricted records labyrinth but far larger than the first records room above it.

As soon as she crosses the threshold into the cave, Alora feels another wave of exhaustion—one so powerful she has to place a hand on the wall beside her. That's when she realizes that what she thought were stone walls surrounding her—the ones that encapsulate the entire room—are actually made of glittering gold.

The realization—nay, the awe and spectacle—shakes Alora from her fatigue.

She glides forward, traversing deeper into the bizarre, gilded cavern.

Surrounding the center of the room, Alora spies four golden pillars equidistant from one another. Though it's hard to tell, she thinks they're roughly her height, if not a little smaller. And each has an object hovering just above it—likely made possible by some sort of magic she imagines Morpheus would tell her she couldn't possibly comprehend.

The first on her left is a familiar shape: a lotus flower—just like the pin Maya wears on her lapel, Alora remembers, as well as the office chair in which she sits.

The second, in the far left corner, looks like a seashell—the kind that might be blown into and played like a horn. She vaguely remembers it being called a conch.

The third, in the far right corner, is an ornate disc. It reminds Alora of a CD because of the hole in its center, although it looks to have sharp edges and a design carved into its surface.

And the last looks to her like some kind of medieval weapon with a long handle and a hefty orb attached at its end—a mace, she remembers. Except it's opulent and gilded, just like the other objects in the room.

Alora sees a deep pit between the four pillars—too deep to see what's at the bottom from her perspective. But high above it, suspended by enormous golden chains, there's what she can only describe as the largest platform bed she's ever seen, complete with a plush gold-lined blue comforter and an assortment of matching pillows hanging precariously over its edge.

And it looks like there's a figure resting upon it, although Alora can't quite make it out because surrounding the figure is a vortex of what looks like thousands upon thousands of illuminated, almost ghastly shapes—orbs of light leaving trails of aura behind them—flowing around and up and down like a whirlpool.

She feels drawn to it, as though the swirling mass of light is ushering her forward. And her fatigue starts to return. The closer she gets, the more tired she becomes.

But there's something else she notices, too: a machine built into the ceiling of the room with a bevy of power cables stretching back toward the room's entrance. It has a long, tentacle-like, transparent tube arm that reaches forward toward the swirling vortex of ghastly orbs and sucks one into it. As Alora gets closer, she watches the orb travel up the tube and into the machine.

"I wouldn't get too close if I were you," a voice booms from behind her.

Alora whips around, shaken from her trance. She had been so awed by the spectacle at the room's center that she hadn't even noticed the extensive collection of computer terminals beside the room's entrance. Nor had she noticed the being operating it: the third, final Hecatoncheire.

"Correct me if I'm wrong, but you're Alora, yes?" he says. The hundred-armed Titan, busy typing on what looks to Alora like dozens of separate keyboards, pushes his glasses up to the bridge of his nose with a free hand. "Name's Gyges. But, having met both of my brothers, I think you already know that. It's good to meet you for the first time finally. This is the first time, right? I've been waiting for you."

☠

Gyges wears a finely tailored gray suit and wire-rimmed glasses like his brothers. But something else differentiates him from them: he looks tired—unnaturally so.

Maybe whatever it is that makes Alora feel so drowsy affects immortals, too. Or perhaps he's just been kept too busy.

Alora remembers that Cottus is always doing something with dozens of his hundred hands—usually some kind of file reorganization or other secretarial activity. Yet he still finds distraction in his books.

His brother, Briareus, seems to have a similar disposition: busy but not *too* busy to step away from his desk and indulge a pair of human souls, if only for a short time.

But Gyges is another story entirely. Clearly, he knows Alora is standing in the room before him, but—at least as far as she can tell—he's not once looked up at her. He simply hunches over his desk, typing away at his dozens of keyboards.

"You're not supposed to be down here, you know," he says. "Not that that has ever stopped you before. But I suppose you're here now, so I may as well answer your questions. You are going to ask me an exhausting number of questions, aren't you? You always do."

"Uh, yeah, hi," Alora stammers, still entranced by the scope of the strange chamber. "What is this place?"

"It's a bedroom," Gyges groans. "I thought that was obvious. It's a room. There's a bed in it. Bedroom."

"Right," Alora replies. "But it's not a normal bedroom."

"Oh, most certainly not," Gyges says, finally glancing at Alora—if only for a moment. "Not by mortal standards, at least. It's not quite up to immortal standards, either, if you ask me. But it's hardly my place to say so."

"So, whose room is it?"

"Maya's," Gyges grunts. "Ask obvious questions, and you'll get obvious answers. Can we speed this along, please? I am infinitely busy, and keeping you entertained isn't going to make my job any easier. It never has. It never will. Next question."

Alora frowns. "You're not as kind as your brothers..." But her frustration is quickly replaced by guilt. How would she feel were she in his position? Bitter, probably. Then again, she can always ask. "Are you okay?"

Gyges stops typing and glares at the tiny bedsheet ghost before him. And then his eyes soften. "You're right. I'm sorry. I've been so busy for so long, and I'm trapped in this godforsaken cave. I can't even tell you the last time I saw the stars.

"On top of that, my posture is ruined. We Hecatoncheires aren't meant for this kind of existence, to be plopped in front of a desk and made to peck at keyboards for a millennium. We are made to stand tall and proud, battling beneath an endless sky…"

Alora wants to tell him she's sorry, that her time in the Afterworld has been similarly frustrating. But, thinking better of it, she stops herself—choosing to just listen to him instead.

"And my brothers," Gyges continues. "Yes, they're locked into their contracts, as well—Maya is nothing if not thorough—but their imprisonment is Elysium compared to this. I know that's not their fault. And I know they're trying to help. I'm just so tired all the time. All I want is to stop this damned cycle and rest. I just want it to end."

Alora tilts her head and nods in a gesture she hopes looks more like understanding and not pity.

The Hecatoncheire takes a deep breath, and Alora realizes she sees tears in his eyes. He wipes his cheeks, pushes his glasses back up onto his nose, and gets back to typing. "Thank you for asking. Nobody ever asks—not that I get much company down here. Just them up there, Maya, and you haunted human souls."

"What did you just say?" Alora practically barks. "Did you say the Haunted are sent down here?"

"Oh goodness. I assumed you'd already know that by now. Guess my timing is a bit off," Gyges says, pointing up at the orbs circling the platform bed. "Tell me, what did you think those little sprites were up there?"

"I have no idea," Alora gasps. "Are they…being undone?"

"They're fine, promise. Just sleeping soundly."

"But the gods… They want us to believe they erase the Haunted from existence."

"Yes, that's correct."

Astonished by the Hecatoncheire's cavalierness, Alora's voice rises involuntarily. "But you just said they're fine!"

"I did. And they are."

"How can they be fine if they've been erased?"

"Because they're not. I agree that the gods would have you believe that. But it turns out erasing a human soul isn't so simple. Titans, gods, and immortals of all walks have been trying to figure that out for centuries—the dastardly ones, at least. But as far as I know, nobody has managed it quite yet. Although I must admit, this is a fairly elegant—if temporary—solution."

"What, exactly, is happening up there?" Alora stares up at the swirling vortex of sprites, which she has to remind herself are apparently actually human souls and not sprites at all.

"Funny anomaly, that. It turns out that close proximity to Them, Deep in Their Slumber"—Gyges gestures toward the figure asleep in the bed—"makes you folks fall right asleep, too. Not a normal sleep, either. More like an erasure of self? Yes, that's the best way to explain it, I think. That's why you're feeling so tired. But if you stay here for too long, you might start to forget."

"Forget what?"

"Everything."

"Who is it?"

"That is a rather expansive question. They're the Lord of Past, Present, and Future. The Creator of All Creatures. The Pillar of Immovable Truth. They Who Cannot Be Perceived. And a thousand other names. Take your pick."

Alora floats away from Gyges's station, closer to the center of the room. "I don't understand."

"I wouldn't go over there if I were you," the Hecatoncheire warns.

But Alora can't stop herself. Just like before, she feels drawn to the center of the room. As she floats, her head begins to bob up and down, and her eyes become so heavy.

"Hey!" the Hecatoncheire rises from his chair. "Come back here! Where are you going? I just said not to go over there!"

But Alora ignores him. She ignores everything. It all seems so trivial, so unimportant now. None of it matters. There is only exhaustion—only the need to rest. To lay down her head and fall into a deep slumber. Yes, that's it; she just needs to sleep.

She approaches the edge of the pit and looks down. At the bottom, she sees thousands upon thousands of pieces of fabric, each unique in its color and design. And beneath that, something massive undulating, breathing. She can see a part of the scaled mass peeking out from under all the myriad fabrics. It's a great serpent coiled around, under, and over itself.

Alora leans forward, just a touch too far, and she feels herself about to fall. But something holds her back. Something tugs at her bedsheet from behind.

She rights herself and turns around to find Dublin, the black cat, keeping her from falling into the pit.

"Oh hey, buddy," she mumbles. "You tired, too? You wanna come with me? It looks so comfy…"

But before she can reach down to pick up the cat, two enormous clouds of smoke burst before her.

As the smoke dissipates, she sees two familiar figures, one with skin made of glittering stone and crystal and the other covered in impossibly thick fur. It's Ikelos and Phantasus, Chernobog's henchmen and Morpheus's wayward brothers.

They lurch forward and grab her. And just as quickly as they manifest, they vanish, with Alora held tightly in their grasp.

☠

Her head still foggy, Alora tries to make sense of her surroundings. It's dark all around her, apart from a bright spotlight above.

She looks down and sees colorful tape smattered across the floor. They're markings used for staging dreams. She's in one of the dream stages. One of the big ones. One operated by the Department of Nightmares.

The bedsheet ghost shakes her head, trying to clear her mental cobwebs. She spies Ikelos and Phantasus at her sides, still holding her in place. And before her, on the ground, a deep, dark shadow begins to well up.

A great black figure with glowing crimson eyes, sharp claws, and enormous wings emerges from the billowing shadow.

Chernobog.

Suddenly, Alora remembers what she had discovered in Dreamweavers restricted records room. Endri was a plant. And Chernobog was the one who planted him.

The God of Chaos, Misfortune, and Darkness had been keen on their plans all along. And now he had Alora, a thorn in his and Maya's side, well within his grasp.

"Hello, human," he seethes, black smoke pouring from his jaws. "Nowhere to run now."

Act Three

Chapter Fourteen

How to Successfully Navigate Conflict in the Dreamweavers Workplace

"Isn't it just so exhausting?" the overhead lights in the dream stage flicker on to reveal Morpheus standing over the control console, back to his big blue demon form. Mamu, in all her towering glittering glory, stands nearby. Kanasu, Rasui, Yume, and Endri float on Morpheus's other side.

Alora scowls at Endri before turning her attention back to Chernobog. She can see the annoyance on Chernobog's face as he tries his hardest to resist Morpheus's bait. And fails.

"Isn't what exhausting?" he growls as he rolls his eyes.

"Being so dreadfully spooky all the time. The grand entrance, the smoke, the gravitas of it all. It seems like a lot of work. And for what?"

"Hey," Alora says, but the gods either don't hear her or ignore her.

"It's called cultivating a brand," Ikelos, still standing beside Alora, interjects.

"Something you couldn't possibly understand," adds Phantasus from Alora's other side.

"Yeah!" Ikelos confirms.

Behind Alora's back, Morpheus's brothers bump fists.

"Silence!" Chernobog drops his shoulders and whips around. "Where was all your clever incisiveness eons ago when I first told you I suspected corruption in the Dreamscape? You were too busy sulking and languishing, and now look at the mess we're in."

"Hello?" Alora tries again to no avail.

"That hardly seems fair," Mamu responds. "After all, you're the one who poached his brothers. No wonder the poor lad took to brooding for a couple of centuries. Can you really blame him?"

"I don't know about brooding," Morpheus scoffs. "More like quiet, dignified contemplation. Planning my next era, if you will."

"How long is it you've been planning, now, exactly?" Chernobog indignifies.

"Hey!" Alora roars over the gods' bickering, finally quieting them. "What's going on here?"

Mamu steps forward, extending her arms as elegantly as ever. "Our sincerest apologies," she says, eyeballing her fellow immortals. "This must be quite overwhelming and more than a bit confusing, but please give us a moment to explain."

"And you might want to brace yourself," Morpheus adds. "It's a bit of a doozy."

The congregation of immortal gods and human souls circle up in the center of the dream stage at Mamu's suggestion. Some sit in metal folding chairs, some use crates as makeshift seats, and others still stand around.

With everyone settled in, Mamu concedes the floor to Morpheus (Chernobog initially protested against letting Morpheus do the storytelling, but Mamu convinced him that Morpheus, having already built a rapport with the human souls, was the best god for the job).

"We have not been entirely honest with y'all," the big blue demon begins, straddling his folding chair with the seatback in front of him and his arms crossed over its top. "While we gods are rather fond of our incessant infighting, most of what you've experienced has been a bit of a ruse.

"Mamu, Chernobog, and I aren't exactly as disparate as we'd have everyone believe. Truth be told, we've been working together for what would amount to centuries to you mortals."

Rasui gasps, placing a hand on his chest. The rest of the group turns to look at him.

"What?" he says. "If that's not appropriate to gasp at, I don't know what is. Our mentor god and his primary rival—big bad Chernobog over here"—he gestures to the seething, shadowy god—"have been secretly working together this whole time? It's a heck of a twist, is all."

"Is this true?" Kanasu asks with a skeptical tilt of their head.

"He speaks the truth," Chernobog says.

Mamu nods in agreement.

"What about what we saw, back during training?" Alora asks. "Those two ghosts. What you did to them."

Mamu and Morpheus look at her, confused. But Chernobog simply lets out a sigh.

"What is she talking about?" Mamu asks.

Morpheus shakes his head at Chernobog. "Do you want to tell them or should I?"

"Would you believe me if I told you that was just a bit of fun? Hazing, I believe you mortals call it," Chernobog groans.

"You gotta be kidding me," Kanasu exasperates. "All of that was for show?"

"I have a reputation to uphold," Chernobog says, raising his voice. "So, when the new blood comes through, we put on a...bit of a performance to give you a scare."

"And the humans you *transferred*?" Alora makes air quotes through her bedsheet.

"They're fine," Chernobog answers. "They came right back to work after you ran off. In fact, they volunteered to play those parts. And they weren't the only ones. We had to hold a raffle to narrow it down."

"And..." Morpheus motions for Chernobog to continue.

Chernobog rolls his eyes. "And I have neither the power nor the authority to cause any real harm to mortal souls."

"Sheesh," Alora says, placing a hand on her forehead.

"So, all of this," Kanasu says, "is just a big act. Even all your infighting?"

"Why?" Rasui interjects. "Just to fool a bunch of puny mortals?"

"It wasn't all for us," Yume says, looking at Morpheus.

The big blue demon nods. "For a long time," Morpheus sighs, "the three of us operated our pieces of the larger Dreamweavers business as dictated by Maya. At the time, it made sense since she was the most powerful of us and, more importantly, she's the better half of the omnipotent creator of this realm, Vishnu."

"Authoritarian nepotism," Kanasu scoffs.

Chernobog narrows his eyes at Kanasu. "Is that not how it works in the mortal realm?"

Kanasu's eyes widen. "Well, yeah…I guess."

"The point is," Morpheus cuts back in, "Even together, the three of us are not powerful enough to call her authority into question. More importantly, she promised us that this was a temporary measure. That when Vishnu rose from their slumber, they would reclaim control of this realm and take over the company. All we had to do was complete our jobs dutifully until then.

"The only problem with that was that it never came to pass. Maya continued to consolidate power, and Vishnu remained troublingly absent.

"For a time, Maya played the politics well, pitting us against one another and keeping us ignorant of her larger scheme. The creation of the Department of the Mundane was one such play. Her meddling also led to my two idiot brothers defecting to Chernobog's command."

"You're the idiot," Phantasus barks.

"Yeah, idiot," Ikelos echoes, giving Phantasus a high five.

"Quiet, fools!" Chernobog snaps.

"Sorry, sir," the pair says in tandem.

Morpheus rolls his eyes.

"If you don't mind," Mamu addresses the whole group, "I think we'd better move this along."

"Anyway," the big blue demon resumes, "it got to a point where we all came to realize Vishnu wasn't going to wake up and that it seemed like Maya's plan might just be to keep them in their slumber indefinitely. My understanding was that Vishnu and Maya were quite happy together before the creation of the Dreamscape, so what might have driven her to imprison her other half and take sole control of this realm is beyond me. Perhaps it was a crime of opportunity. Or maybe it was always her plan. Whatever the case, there was only one way to fix it."

"To wake Vishnu up," Alora says.

"Bingo," Morpheus replies with a wink. "I brought the idea to Mamu, and she agreed. Then, together, we enlisted Chernobog."

"Not that I needed convincing," the God of Chaos, Misfortune, and Darkness adds, rising from his chair. "I was already in the midst of devising an ingenious plan to wrest control of Dreamweavers from Maya. I had grown tired of her misappropriation of company funds. The Department of the Mundane? *Pshh.* If anything, she should have expanded my Nightmare Department. But she was too busy coddling Morpheus and the foolish humans—"

"Chernobog," Mamu interrupts.

"Right, immaterial," Chernobog says, sitting back down. "But it would have worked superbly, in case anyone was wondering."

Mamu nods at Morpheus.

"Thank you," the big blue demon replies. "Our first hurdle was that we couldn't find Vishnu. We knew Maya likely hid them away somewhere, probably below Dreamweavers HQ and definitely with the help of the Hecatoncheires. Sadly, Cottus and his brothers are contractually obligated to obey Maya, so we couldn't simply ask them to assist us. As such, we were on our own. Trouble is, we just could not find the door."

"Hold the phone," Rasui interjects. "So, you three have been working together for…ages, pretending to be at one another's throats so your boss wouldn't suspect a thing, and the furthest you got in your plans was the very first part of step one?"

"Well, when you put it like that, it sounds pretty bad,"

Morpheus says.

"But yes," Mamu adds. "You are correct. Shamefully, we've made virtually no progress whatsoever."

"I still think my plan would have worked," Chernobog boasts.

"I'm not convinced you ever had a plan," Morpheus responds.

"Of course I do." The God of Chaos, Misfortune, and Darkness leaps from his chair, pointing a shadowy finger toward Morpheus. "And it is ingenious."

"Tell me the first step, then," the big blue demon rises to face Chernobog.

"So you can take credit for yourself when it executes perfectly? I think not!"

"See?" Morpheus outstretches his arms and turns to the rest of the group. "No plan."

"The both of you, quiet!" Mamu steps between the arguing gods and shoves them apart, losing her composure, if only for a moment. After a deep breath, she continues, "All of this is to say that you, Alora"—she outstretches a hand toward the pink polka-dotted bedsheet ghost—"have managed something none of us could do for eons. You found Vishnu."

"Mamu speaks true, human, as much as it pains me to admit," Chernobog says with a scowl.

"You did what we couldn't, kid." This time it's Morpheus. "Don't know how you managed it, but you figured out how to get into the most secure room in all the Dreamscape. And you've given us the means to take down Maya finally."

Rasui starts to clap but ceases abruptly and awkwardly when no one else joins him. "For real? Come on, my dudes, this is some triumphant stuff! Now we can take down the big bad, right? And we've got the rivals-to-friends thing going on with Morpheus and Chernobog. Is nobody else excited by all this?"

"It's great news," Morpheus continues, "really, it is. But we still have a bit of an ordeal ahead of us."

"How can you be sure I found it? That was just some room I found underground. I didn't break in. I walked in."

"You mean to say there were no guards?" Chernobog demands. "No defenses of which to speak?"

"I mean, I met the Minotaur, but it was just like…a big dog."

"Useless creature," Chernobog says.

"Magnificent," Mamu adds.

"Listen," Morpheus says, crouching down before Alora and taking one of her hands in his, "this is very important. Can you recall anything else about how you found that door—anything that sticks out as different or odd? We've been searching for it for centuries, and suddenly you find it out of the blue and just walk right in. There must be something."

Alora furrows her brow for a moment, and then her eyes light up. "Dublin!"

"Kitty cat!" Yume shrieks with excitement.

"Of course, the little pest. I should have known," Morpheus says with a snap of his fingers.

"When I was trying to get away from the Minotaur, Dublin found me and led me to safety. Or that's what I thought he was doing. Maybe he wasn't leading me to safety at all. Maybe he was showing me the way."

"And where is this…kitty cat now?" Chernobog asks.

"Well," Alora's voice drops, "I can't really remember. I was so tired. I just wanted to go to sleep, but he wouldn't let me, and then…these two"—she points to Ikelos and Phantasus—"showed up and grabbed me."

"Imbeciles!" Chernobog bellows, smacking Morpheus's brothers on the sides of their heads. "You forgot to bring the kitty cat!"

"That is unfortunate, but it shouldn't matter too much," Mamu says. "Now that we know where the entrance to the chamber is, we can return to it. Our problem now is that Maya surely knows we found it. She's likely shoring up her defenses, enlisting the citizens of Somnia, and barricading the entrance to Dreamweavers HQ, which would explain why she hasn't come after us here. But we likely don't have much time. She'll come after us once she's certain the chamber is secure. And who knows what she'll do?"

"Mamu's right," Morpheus says. "We need to get back in there and wake up Vishnu, but we're going to need help. We're going to need your help." He looks at the bedsheet ghosts.

"You're preparing to go to war with gods and immortal mythical beasts," Rasui says, "and you want the help of us lowly humans?"

"Gotta say," Kanasu adds, "I'm with Rasui on this one."

"See?" Chernobog says to Morpheus and Mamu. "They think it's a bad idea, too. I told you it wouldn't work."

"Please," Morpheus says, rubbing his fingers against his temples, "tell us what you'd have us do, oh great God of Destruction."

Chernobog crosses his arms. "No. I will not. Besides, it's too late. My plan hinged on guile and cunning, and you've all ruined it by putting Maya on high alert. It won't work now, and it's all your fault."

"That's fine," Morpheus replies. "I have a better idea anyhow. But we're going to have to take a little hike. If there's anything you need to do to prepare before that, now is the time."

Alora turns toward Endri, preparing an angry diatribe. But she's surprised to find that he's already floating toward her.

Somehow, even through his bedsheet, he looks sad.

"Can we talk?" he asks.

☠

As the group of gods and mortals separates, Alora and Endri find a secluded corner of the dream stage. As soon as they're far enough away to be out of earshot, Alora whips around to face her former friend, her betrayer.

"You lied to us," Alora seethes through her teeth, trying to keep her voice to a whisper so the rest of the gang doesn't hear.

"I know, I know," Endri replies, raising his hands defensively. "I'm sorry. Truly and from the bottom of my heart, I'm sorry. I didn't want to do it. I didn't want to be a part of it at all, but Chernobog gave me no choice. It was either obey him and act as his agent, reporting on Morpheus's whereabouts, plans, and whatnot or he was going to…well, I really don't know, but I didn't want to find out."

"I don't care about that. Do you think any of us would blame you for doing what you had to do to survive? Chernobog is a god, and a mean one, at that. If he made you do it, you didn't really have another option. That's not why I'm upset."

Endri lowers his hands. "Then, why?"

"Because you could have told us!" she shouts, realizing too late how much she's raised her voice. She and Endri look around, but nobody else in the room seems to have taken notice.

Endri's head drops.

Alora's voice returns to a whisper. She continues, "If you were just honest with us, we could have helped you. Or maybe we could have used that information to our advantage.

Somehow. I don't know." She throws her hands into the air. "Honestly, anything would have been better. Did you know about Chernobog's little performance, too? That it was all fake?"

Endri nods. "Are you going to tell everyone?" Endri looks up at her with shame in his eyes.

"Well, it doesn't really matter anymore, does it?" she answers. "Does Chernobog still trust you?"

"I don't know." Endri shrugs. "As much as he ever did, I guess. As much as the God of Chaos, Misfortune, and Darkness can trust a human. To be honest, he's kind of always treated me more like a pet than a person. It hasn't been very fun. Until he sent me to watch Morpheus with all of you—that was the first time I really felt like I belonged."

"Yeah, there's something there I'm still wondering about. How did Morpheus not notice that you weren't supposed to be there?"

"I don't really think the gods pay much attention to us humans. Most of them don't even remember what we look like, let alone our names. It's not really high on their list of priorities. Chernobog just teleported me into that room when you all arrived. He said Morpheus wouldn't even notice that I didn't belong. And he was right."

"Or he did know and was just playing along with it," Alora says.

"They do seem to enjoy their little games." Endri perks up. "You know, we might still be able to use this to our advantage."

"What do you mean?"

"Not sure if you noticed, but Chernobog and Morpheus's truce is tenuous at best. Once Maya is out of the way, Chernobog probably still plans to try to take everything over for himself. Even if he had been secretive about it, which he hasn't been, it seems pretty obvious he's just waiting for a chance to pounce."

"The gods are nothing if not predictable," Alora chuckles.

"If he still thinks I'm his little pet, I can still get close to him without raising any alarms."

Alora scratches her head. "If Morpheus's plan is what I think it is, I might have an idea."

Chapter Fifteen

Dreamweaving Works Best When We All Work Together

L eaving the dream stage, Alora notices that the surrounding streets and alleyways of Dreamweavers's part of town are conspicuously empty. There's none of the usual hustle and bustle of human souls wandering from place to place, and all the buildings appear to be locked up tight.

"Where is everyone?" she asks.

"Dorm lockdown, I'm afraid," Mamu responds as gently as she can. "None of the human souls are permitted to leave their rooms for an undisclosed period."

"Your little stunt set all of Somnia on edge," Chernobog interrupts. "It's almost admirable the amount of trouble you've caused in such a short time. You've about unraveled eons of Maya's best efforts."

"Best guess," Morpheus adds, "Maya wants to suss us all out, ensure this wasn't some larger human conspiracy, and deal with each of us on a more…individual basis. Barring that, it can only help her, keeping the rest of you mortal souls out of the way while she ensures Somnia and Dreamweavers HQ are locked down tight. Ultimately, all she cares about right now is keeping Vishnu locked away and preventing us from waking them."

Morpheus leads on, ushering Mamu, Chernobog, and his brothers toward the edge of Somnia—into the same small clearing where he and Alora had once sat, looking up at the impossible sky overhead together. The bedsheet ghosts follow close behind.

Alora can't help but feel a pang of guilt. She never thought that trying to reacquire her own memories would lead to so much trouble for everyone else. It hadn't been her intention to drag everyone—her friends, coworkers, and every mortal soul in the Dreamscape alike—into a knock-down-and-drag-out fight between gods, even if the gods had been planning it all along.

If only she had been satisfied with sticking to her assigned career. If only she hadn't gone poking around. Maybe none of this had to happen. A small, albeit powerful, part of Alora wishes she had just followed orders.

Kanasu rests a hand on her shoulder as if they could read her thoughts. "Hey," they say with a nod and a smile in their eyes. "Look, I don't know if we'll have another chance to talk after all this. So, now seems as good a time as any to say thank you."

Alora furrows her brow. "For what?"

"All of this. Everything. I know this is scary, and, well, it's blown up into something far bigger than any of us anticipated. But I'm glad we're doing it. And I'm sorry I wasn't on your side at the beginning. I was wrong."

"Kanasu's right," Rasui interjects, cutting between the pair and stretching his arms across their shoulders. "Everyone's on board. We're doing the right thing here. I know it. And I'm glad we're doing it together."

"All for one and one for all," Yume agrees, shimmying her bedsheet back and forth.

"With everything that's happened," Endri adds, "I wouldn't want to be going through it with anyone else."

Overwhelmed and unsure how to respond, Alora blurts out the first thing that comes to her mind.

"I love you all."

As if on cue, the five bedsheet ghosts come together in an awkward, clumsy group hug.

"We got this," Alora adds.

She wants to say something more, something deep and inspirational. She wants to assure her friends that she's as steadfast as they are and that she, too, believes in their cause. She wants to say that, despite the insurmountable odds of facing off with the most powerful being in the Dreamscape, she's not just ready and willing, but she's sure they can do it and come out on top.

But she's terrified. As far as she can remember, she's never been more terrified—at least not in her afterlife. She doesn't know if they can get past Maya and wake Vishnu. And she's not sure what will happen even if they achieve their goal.

What if waking Vishnu collapses the entire Dreamscape and blinks everyone in it out of existence? What if Vishnu is just as bad (or worse) as Maya? What if they never get their memories back at all? There were so many unknowns, potential pitfalls, and questions without answers.

"Puny humans," Chernobog calls from up ahead, distracting Alora from her uncertainties. "Cease your strange ritual and join us. Morpheus has informed me that we are to venture into Oneiros. It is dangerous for you mortal souls. I shall enjoy seeing which of you survive." The God of Chaos, Misfortune, and Darkness bellows with laughter. Morpheus's brothers laugh along with him. However, to Alora, their mirth sounds forced and fake.

"Stay close behind and follow our path exactly and you'll be fine," Morpheus reassures them. "I'll take the lead. Mamu and Chernobog, you'll take up the rear with my brothers."

"We do not require her assistance," Chernobog protests, gesturing toward Mamu.

"It is not your assistance I'll be providing," Mamu interjects, scowling at the billowing shadow-demon. "It's theirs," she adds, gesturing to the ghosts. "Wouldn't want any of you three getting bored and shoving one of our friends here off the path."

Ikelos and Phantasus drop their heads in a gesture Alora thinks looks almost like shame. It seems they don't quite enjoy being on their adoptive mother's bad side.

"You're no fun at all," Chernobog replies, folding his arms defiantly. "Do we really need *all* these humans? Surely, we can do without one or two."

"Chernobog!" Morpheus snaps. "Not the time."

"The end of this miserable alliance can't come soon enough," Chernobog grumbles. "You may keep your little pets for now."

"Thank you," Morpheus adds. "Unless anyone else has any objections?"

One by one, the ghosts and gods shake their heads.

"Follow me."

"How much farther?" Chernobog shouts toward Morpheus at the head of the pack.

Alora remembers that their hike to the pomegranate valley took a long time, but it was hard for her to gauge how far they had made it—largely thanks to the ever-shifting landscape. Overall, the route feels familiar, but the surrounding scenery is completely different from the last time they entered Oneiros.

Where she thinks she remembers a crystal canyon morphing into a Technicolor desert, she now watches marbled mountains collapse into glittering flats. And where she remembers a bog bursting into mountains, she now finds icy crevasses filling with warm swamp water, clouding the path with a warm fog.

While the views are breathtaking, this time, she finds joy elsewhere: in seeing her companions enjoy the trek.

It's a welcome distraction for all of them. Alora hears Rasui pointing out landmarks and relating them to the fantasy stories of his human childhood. She sees Yume giggle with glee when the wilderness suddenly jolts and begins to transform. She even catches Endri explaining to Kanasu the different topographical impossibilities that surround them.

Even Morpheus's wayward brothers appear to be enjoying the hike, ribbing and snickering at one another along the way.

After everything that's happened and everything they're about to do, this journey helps to remind Alora that, whatever happens, they're all in it together, gods and mortals alike. And while it doesn't erase her fears of what's to come, it does help to ease their intensity. Whatever may come to pass, Alora finds comfort and revels in this rare moment of gratitude...until Chernobog's impatience gets the better of him.

"I said, how much farther?" Chernobog shouts again, louder this time.

"We'll get there when we get there," Morpheus shouts back,

notes of impatience coloring his tone.

"You still haven't told me where we're going," Chernobog hollers back.

"And I'm not going to. Be patient. We're nearly there."

"I don't see why we can't just teleport there. I can do it, you know. Even with all these," Chernobog sneers, "humans."

"You want to teleport an entire group of us to a place in Oneiros that you've never been?"

"I do. I really do."

"And what happens if you're slightly off and we end up popping up in the landscape just as a mountain drops on top of us or a chasm opens up below us?"

"Every worthwhile venture has a measure of acceptable risk."

"Getting our mortal companions trapped in the landscape for a millennium is not within the realm of *acceptable risk*," Mamu interjects.

"Ugh." Chernobog throws his head back. "This is so boring. I wish to be done with it. Now."

Alora notices that Ikelos and Phantasus have started to distance themselves from Chernobog. Now they stand on the other side of Mamu, whispering to one another.

"We will get there when we get there," Morpheus asserts.

Alora looks forward, seeing the edge of the pomegranate valley up ahead. The ridge is high enough that she can't see the Baku flying over the valley, but she knows they're there, peacefully bobbing up and down in the sky above.

But before they reach the valley, she has one more thing she needs to speak with her mentor about. She picks up her pace and floats up to Morpheus's side.

"Hey, kid," he says to her, his voice as soothing as ever. "Everything okay?"

"Yeah, totally," she instinctively responds. Then, correcting herself, "Actually, no, not really. I'm scared."

Morpheus exhales. "Me, too."

"Oh," Alora replies, clearing her throat to fill the uncomfortable silence.

Morpheus laughs. "Would you have preferred if I lied to you? Should I tell you everything is wine and roses?"

"Well, no, I guess not."

"Good. Because what we're doing here is dangerous for all of us. There's a distinct possibility that we will fail. And it would be foolish to pretend like nothing is at risk when, in fact, everything is at risk."

"Right, yeah…"

"But that also means what we are doing is incredibly brave. And that's because of you, you know."

Alora points a finger toward her own chest.

"Since that first day in my classroom, you've been a menace. You simply couldn't just let things lie. You pushed and prodded and made problems for just about everyone."

"Oh…I'm sorry."

"Don't be foolish," Morpheus chortles. "You're a massive thorn in my side, but one I am eternally thankful for. And not just because you found that infernal bedroom doorway we've been searching for. You're special, Alora. You're the human who moved the gods. That means something, at least to me."

Alora is left speechless.

"I spent so much time playing the part of the broken, lazy lout, I think I was starting to believe that's who I really was. I can't speak for Mamu or, gods forbid, Chernobog, but I can tell you I was ready to give up and accept that perhaps Maya had won and this was our fate. Then you came along and fouled everything up."

"Well, then I suppose you're welcome."

"My pleasure." Morpheus bows slightly. "Was there something you needed?"

"Yes," Alora answers. "The room where Vishnu sleeps. There was something strange about it. These four pillars surrounded the room, each with a different object kind of hovering above them."

"Divine attributes."

"Sorry?"

"Significations of Vishnu's being. Mamu suspects they have something to do with keeping Vishnu asleep. Hard to say for certain but removing them may trigger an awakening."

"That's not it. Vishnu was surrounded by a-a...like a whirlpool of human souls. And there was some machine that was sucking them up one by one."

"I saw that through the portal when my brothers came to get you. I'm sorry to say I don't know what it was. Or why those humans were down there."

"Gyges said they were the Haunted, that human souls can't be unmade. So, what are they doing down there?"

"I wish I could tell you," Morpheus answers, furrowing his brow. "But this is the first I'm hearing of it. I suppose Maya has been hiding more from us than we initially thought, including the limits of her power. I'm impressed she's managed to keep so much under wraps but also a little disappointed in us for not figuring it out ourselves. But it makes sense. If she can't actually control us, clearly fear sometimes does the trick."

"Can we help them?"

"I don't know."

"Will waking Vishnu hurt them?"

"I'm still not certain waking Vishu won't blink this whole realm out of existence."

"Then why are we doing this?"

"Faith, my dear. I have faith in all of this. You. Us. Vishnu."

"But you're an immortal. You're going to be fine."

"Being immortal doesn't mean I can't suffer. Or worse."

"What do you mean?"

"Maybe human souls can't be unmade in the Afterworld. But immortals are another story. See, you live a life in the mortal realm, and then, when you die, you come here. But this place is to us immortals what Earth is to humans. When we die, we don't really know what comes next. What do you think happened to the rest of Cottus's kind, the Titans? How do you think a simple work contract keeps the Hecatoncheires in line?"

"I had no idea…"

"That's why I'm so afraid. That's where faith comes into play. Even if it means my end, this is what's right. I know it, right here." Morpheus taps his chest. "Whatever may come to pass."

Alora has no words.

"Do you have faith in me?"

"Of course I do," she blurts.

"Good. Because I have faith in you, too."

As the words escape his lips, Morpheus and Alora reach the crest of the pomegranate valley. And Alora sees the majestic Baku flying in droves overhead.

"No. Absolutely not. This is why you didn't tell me where we were going. You knew I'd refuse your plan. You tricked me, you foul creatures. May all of you and your families be cursed for an eternity!"

By Alora's estimation, Chernobog has been protesting the descent into the pomegranate valley for around an hour (in Earth time). Apparently, the Baku lore Morpheus had shared with her—that these huge, peaceful creatures eat nightmares—was common knowledge among the gods.

Still, she can't tell if his objections are based on this lore being fact or speculation. In either case, it comforted Alora to know that a god so keen on instilling terror in others is not without his own (potentially unwarranted) fears.

And if the joy in her fellow bedsheet ghosts' eyes is any indication, they're also comforted by the god's discomfort. Especially Endri.

"They're not going to hurt you," Morpheus says again, trying to usher Chernobog forth. "I promise."

"You can't make that promise. The beasts will just gobble you up alongside me!"

"You're being childish," Mamu says. "You're the God of Chaos, Misfortune, and Darkness, are you not? Yet, you let a few docile creatures prevent you from moving forward?"

"You've heard the stories, Mamu! They eat nightmares. To them, I may as well be a three-course meal."

Watching Chernobog's dissent, Alora feels a burst of inspiration. She glides forward toward the towering shadow-god. "I guess Maya was right about you," she says nonchalantly.

"What do you know, human? Stay out of this," Chernobog howls.

"She told me you're subservient. Easy to manipulate. A pawn in her game. She thinks she can control you. If you're afraid of some harmless flying beasts, I can see why she'd think such a thing."

"How dare you speak to me in such a manner! I will end you, little human!"

"You're going to have to catch me first." With that, Alora glides over the crest of the valley and down toward the huge pomegranate tree at its center.

Giggling and bobbing up and down, Yume follows close behind. Then, so does Kanasu, Rasui, and even Endri—the latter giving his boss a defiant shrug as he passes.

Mamu simply shakes her head at Chernobog and follows the humans into the valley.

"How the mighty have fallen," Morpheus says with a guffaw as he marches into the valley behind Mamu and the ghosts.

Ikelos and Phantasus simply look at Chernobog, shaking their heads and giving one another a shrug. They leave their boss standing alone atop the valley's edge and join everyone else heading toward the bottom of the valley.

Scowling and snorting, Chernobog plants his feet and crosses his arms. Glancing up, the God of Chaos, Misfortune, and Darkness sees one of the smaller Baku looking down at him. Ignoring it, he watches the other two gods and the bedsheet ghosts descend into the valley. Then, looking up again, Chernobog notices the Baku looks bigger—no, closer. With a flinch, he uncrosses his arms and follows down toward the pomegranate tree.

Chapter Sixteen

Exploring the Delicate Relationship between Somnia and Oneiros

"Heads up!" Morpheus calls from above, tossing down another pair of pomegranates.

Rasui moves out of the way just as the fruits smack onto the ground right where he had been, both splitting open.

Looking around, Alora sees that Kanasu, Rasui, Yume, and Endri all have their bedsheets pulled up in front of them. They use them like hammocks, cradling dozens of pieces of the sweet, tart fruit.

"This isn't going to stain, is it?" Endri asks, inspecting a wet spot on his sheet.

"Is that even possible?" Rasui asks.

"Juice-stained bedsheets seem like the least of our worries right now," Kanasu adds. "Is this plan even going to work?"

"I trust Morpheus," Alora says. "He's not the same god we met in that classroom."

"He does seem like he's got more pep in his step," Rasui says, dodging another pomegranate.

"Look," Yume says, pointing up.

In the sky above them, the Baku have begun to gather.

When they first arrived at the pomegranate tree, dozens lazily floated around. Now, it looks like hundreds. And more are approaching from nearly every direction.

"I don't think we have any other options at this point," Endri adds. "But I have to say, it's a novel idea."

"Well, I don't like it at all." This time, it's Chernobog. Since they made it to the bottom of the valley, he's stood as close to the tree's trunk as he could muster, keeping his arms crossed tightly against his chest and an eye on the skies above.

"Quit being such a scaredy-cat," Morpheus calls from above as he floats back to the ground. "They're harmless. Come here." He beckons Chernobog forth, holding out a piece of a pomegranate.

"Absolutely not," Chernobog protests.

"You're not really afraid of the Baku, are you?" Ikelos asks.

"Yeah, are you?" Phantasus parrots.

Chernobog shoots the brothers a grimace.

"If one of them hurts you," Morpheus interjects, "I'll hand over complete control of the Department of the Mundane once this is all over. You'll get to be my boss. All three of us brothers under your thumb. How about that?"

Chernobog raises an eyebrow, considering Morpheus's proposal. "No. Too risky."

"The God of Chaos, Misfortune, and Darkness, everyone," Morpheus announces with a chuckle. "Look! Mamu isn't scared." Morpheus gestures to the tall goddess, standing in the valley and gazing at the magnificent creatures above.

"I've always known they were out here," Mamu hollers back, "but I never imagined just how beautiful they were up close. Wonderful creatures, these."

Alora, struggling to hold up her bedsheet basket of

pomegranate pieces, floats over to Morpheus. "I think maybe we've got enough. We should get going."

Morpheus looks down at her, then up at the tree, now practically barren of fruit. "Right. Good point. Everyone, gather 'round."

The ghosts, Morpheus's brothers, and Mamu form up around Morpheus. Even Chernobog takes a step out of the shadows, albeit while keeping a watchful eye on the sky above.

"We've only got one chance at this," Morpheus says. "Does everyone remember their part?"

One by one, they all nod in the affirmative.

"Good. Let's go upset the natural order."

With everyone's arms (and bedsheets) full of pomegranate pieces—save for Chernobog, who refused to participate in this particular part of the plan outright—the trek back to Somnia is a good deal more rigorous, even for floating ghosts. At times, Alora is afraid someone will go toppling into a chasm or bog, but everyone manages to stick to the pathway, only losing a few pieces of pomegranate along the way.

As they come over the final crest between Oneiros and Somnia—a hill so large that it obscures even the sky behind it—they notice something unfortunate, albeit not unexpected.

An army of mythical creatures of all shapes and sizes is waiting for them at the city's edge. Among them, Alora sees fox spirits, djinns, hags, hounds, and nymphs—none of whom look very happy to see them. It seems Maya was able to rally the nonhuman citizens of Somnia to her cause.

While a little disappointing, Alora expected something like

this might happen: that the citizens of Somnia would take Maya's side, and that the golden goddess would exploit their loyalty. After all, Alora's interactions with Somnia's citizenry the one time she had wandered into the city alone had been less than pleasant. Clearly, the seeds of discontent were sown between humans and immortals some time ago. Maya was simply reaping the benefits in her favor.

And it would have been a great strategy under normal circumstances. But what Maya hadn't planned on was that Morpheus was counting on this exact outcome. It was why he had led the bedsheet ghosts, alongside Chernobog and Mamu, out into Oneiros in the first place.

One of the mythical creatures steps out in front of the others—one Alora recognizes. It's the sphinx, the same one that had accosted her while she was searching for Dreamweavers HQ. And while it's hard to tell from so far away, Alora thinks she sees a look of excitement on the creature's face.

"Surrender, and you will be granted safe passage," the sphinx announces, its smile opening wide. "If you do not, Maya has entrusted us with the authority to bring you in by force."

Alora looks up at Morpheus. The big blue demon nods at her. "What is she offering?" Alora cries back.

A scowl replaces the sphinx's smile. "I wasn't speaking to you, filthy human. On Maya's authority, we are offering this opportunity to the gods alone. Surrender, and you will be granted safe passage...and a more lenient punishment. Your humans will not receive any such leniency for their heresy. That's the deal. Take it or leave it."

"Maya always was a shrewd businesswoman," Chernobog grumbles. "Are we sure we don't want to take the deal?"

Morpheus steps forward. "I have a counteroffer," he shouts, tossing a pomegranate back and forth in his hands.

"This is not a negotiation," the sphinx replies, its wide smile returning to its face. "Accept the terms now, or we will capture you by force. And we will relish the opportunity to do so."

"Oh, come now," Morpheus says. "Aren't you even a little curious? Tell you what? I'll propose a counteroffer in the form of a riddle. Don't you just love riddles?"

The sphinx's smile morphs again, this time into a snarl, but it remains silent.

"I knew you couldn't resist," Morpheus continues. "Here goes nothing: I number in the hundreds. I'm far larger than any god. And I love to eat pomegranates. What am I?"

The sphinx furrows its brow. "That's not a riddle," it says. "That's trivia."

"Are you going to answer or not?"

Another moment passes as the sphinx tries to work out the puzzle.

"Obviously, you are Baku," the sphinx finally answers. "You can't out-riddle a sphinx, you fool. But I fail to see how that's a counteroffer."

One by one, Morpheus, Mamu, Ikelos, Phantasus, and the bedsheet ghosts hold pieces of pomegranate up in the air before winding up and throwing them down toward the army of mythical creatures at the bottom of the crest.

One particularly large chunk—almost a whole pomegranate save for a wide crack down its side—rolls right up to the sphinx's feet. With an enormous claw, the creature picks the fruit up off the ground. The fruit's juice squeezes out of the crack and drips down the sphinx's paw.

The sphinx, along with all the other mythical creatures in

Maya's makeshift army, looks back up at Morpheus and his band of misfits—first with confusion and then with horror—as hundreds of Baku come flying over the crest, barreling down toward the edge of the city of Somnia.

In an instant, everything turns to chaos. Many mythical creatures flee back into the city's relative safety. Others drop to the ground in a panic, hoping to get low enough that they might avoid the enormous Baku overhead. Others simply scream and freeze.

But the sphinx, past its initial shock, is too clever for that. Seeing through the ruse, the great creature gets up on its back legs—flapping its enormous eagle wings to steady itself—and pulls its hand—still grasping the pomegranate—backward.

But before it can hurl the fruit back up toward Morpheus, a Baku calf comes diving down, eyeing the fruit cradled in the sphinx's enormous paw.

Midflight, the Baku turns on its side and opens its mouth, moving its elephant trunk to the side and out of the way of its teeth.

At the same moment, the sphinx tries to throw the fruit. But it's too late. The sphinx swings its arm forward just as the gargantuan flying creature bites down. The Baku catches the pomegranate and the sphinx's paw in its jaws. And as it rights itself and sails back up into the sky, it takes the sphinx with it.

Alora can't help but smile as she hears the sphinx scream in horror as it's dragged into the sky and out of sight.

"Everyone, go! Now!" Morpheus calls as he takes flight.

The command shakes Alora from her trance, and she takes off, floating as fast as she can down the ridge toward Somnia. She catches glimpses of Kanasu, Rasui, Yume, and Endri racing alongside her, all of them still cradling pomegranate pieces in their bedsheets.

Alora turns her head back to look up at the crest behind her for a split second. At the top, she sees Mamu laughing with joy, tossing pieces of pomegranate up into the sky above and down toward the edge of Somnia below.

Ikelos and Phantasus flank Mamu, also tossing pomegranates toward the city's edge. For the first time since meeting them, Alora thinks she sees looks of joy on their faces.

Slightly behind them, Chernobog cowers, likely still afraid that the Baku may choose to eat him over the pomegranates at any moment.

The first part of Morpheus's plan has gone off without a hitch and while Alora is riding the high—giggling as she dodges between terrified mythical beasts—she knows they still have a long way to go before they make it to Dreamweavers HQ and enact part two of their absurd, suicidal, bonkers plan.

Except now she's starting to think it might just be bonkers enough to work.

Alora and the other bedsheet ghosts make their way down through Somnia, between the dream stages and deeper into the city—headed for Dreamweavers HQ. Meanwhile, Morpheus, Ikelos, Phantasus, Mamu, and Chernobog run interference—heading off the larger, more aggressive mythical creatures behind them and in the skies above.

But the gods can't stop all the beasts and monsters from going after the bedsheet ghosts. And that's why they're all still cradling pieces of pomegranate in their sheets.

Rounding one corner, Alora skids to a stop. There, a small

group of goblin-like creatures waits. As she turns tail to run in the other direction, she tosses a couple of pieces of fruit behind her. The goblins give chase, screeching with delight at the chance to catch one of the humans, but a Baku dives down into the street, drawn by the smell of the sweet fruit, cutting off the goblins' route.

A few streets farther into Somnia, she comes across a spacious square lined with potion shops, apparel ateliers, and even a small café. But at its center, she sees a bevy of beasts trying to stave off an invading Baku and its calves. And at their feet, Alora notices a small pile of pomegranates. One of her friends must have already come through here. She uses their distraction to her advantage and sneaks by, heading deeper into the city.

Alora also starts to notice that not all the mythical creatures of Somnia are on Maya's side. Some have abstained from the call to arms, choosing instead to watch the pandemonium unfold through their windows, careful not to do anything that might draw the attention of a passing Baku.

And some, even more surprisingly, have taken it upon themselves to help the bedsheet ghosts traverse Somnia.

At one point, Alora feels someone—or something—grab her from behind. She whirls around to find a black hound biting at the edge of her pink polka-dotted bedsheet. The beast snarls, bearing its massive fangs at Alora. And just as she's sure it's going to bring her down, an equally obsidian horse comes galloping up, rearing up on its hindquarters and slamming its hooves into the hound, knocking its jaws open and sending it sprawling out on the ground with a sharp whimper.

"Go!" the horse shouts as Alora skips around a corner and runs deeper into Somnia.

Looking up into the sky, Alora can finally see the top of Maya's white-and-gold tower. Dreamweavers HQ isn't far now.

But there's something else up there, too: a huge winged figure with a woman's head and a lion's body.

It's the sphinx. The beast freed itself of the Baku that had carried it off into the skies above Somnia.

Alora looks around for somewhere to hide, but it's too late. High above, the sphinx spots her.

"You!" it howls before tucking its wings into its side and diving straight for her.

But just before it reaches her, another figure, even larger, comes barreling out from an adjoining street, tackling the sphinx into a nearby building and sending a cloud of dust and debris exploding into the air.

As the second figure rises from the impact, Alora can see its starry, spider-web gown shimmering in the light. It's Mamu, come to her rescue.

And the sphinx, toppled over and lying on its side, is unconscious at her feet.

"Not far now, child." Mamu smiles.

But before they can celebrate, a gang of smaller gargoyles dives down, surrounding Mamu and coming to the sphinx's aid.

"Best be on your way," the goddess says. "I'll hold them off.

Alora doesn't question Mamu's order, checking the skyline for Dreamweavers HQ before taking off once more.

As she approaches the building, she looks down at her cradle of pomegranates, only to discover that they're all gone—either thrown at groups of mythical monsters to attract the Baku to her aid or dropped in all the commotion.

But it doesn't matter. Alora doesn't need them anymore. Because, rounding one final corner, Alora sees the white-and-gold facade of Dreamweavers HQ in all its glory. She made it.

She spies a group of bedsheet ghosts gathered in the building's concourse. It's Kanasu, Yume, and Endri. Alora heads toward them. And just as she approaches them, Rasui comes bumbling out from another of the city's streets.

"Oh, thank goodness," Rasui says as he joins the group, throwing his arms over Yume's and Endri's shoulders. "Everyone made it. That was bananas…" But he trails off, and his eyes go wide when he realizes what they're all looking at.

And then Alora sees it, too.

A huge lotus flower sits between them and the front door to the Dreamweavers HQ.

One by one, its pedals bloom, unveiling a huge gold-and-red mass at its center. And then the mass unfolds, rising high above them and growing even larger.

It's Maya. She now stands several stories taller than normal, and ornate red armor covers her golden skin. In her upper left and lower right hands, she holds massive shields adorned with the same lavish design as her armor. In the other two, she grips enormous, curved tulwar sabers, each with its own stories-tall blade.

She raises an enormous foot into the air and swings it down with an earth-shattering crash, squatting into a battle-ready stance. Then, she brings her shields to bear and bashes the hilts of her swords against them, each strike echoing like a thunderclap.

"I admire your tenacity, humans," she says, her voice shaking the very ground beneath the ghosts' bedsheets, "but I'm afraid your insurrection ends here."

Chapter Seventeen

Dreamweavers' Upper Management Proudly Has a Complete Open-Door Policy

Alora's heart sinks as she gawks at the massive golden goddess standing between her and the entrance to Dreamweavers HQ. She's vastly underestimated her foe. Even if all Maya has is size and strength, they're more than enough to keep a few meager human souls from overtaking her.

Worse, Morpheus and the other gods—the only beings remotely capable of taking on Maya—are nowhere to be found. The makeshift army of mythical beasts seems enough to keep them otherwise occupied. And the Baku—well, they're just animals acting on instinct; it would be foolish to expect them to come to the bedsheet ghosts' aid.

Judging by the smile overtaking Maya's face, the goddess knows she's won. This is the end of the road for the ragtag ghosts and their grand plans of overthrowing an immortal overlord.

Alora wonders what she's been thinking. That she, a mere mortal, might be able to unravel eons of mystery spun together by a literal god. That she might somehow rectify afterworldly injustices simply because she's intrepid enough to give it her best shot.

She feels foolish—no, shameful. Because her meddling hasn't just brought trouble down on her own head; it has brought the wrath of a nigh-all-powerful goddess down on the heads of everyone she's come to care for and then some. There's no telling the infinite, horrible ways they'll all pay for their transgressions.

And for what? To reclaim the memories she had when she was a living human? What good would that really do her, here in the Afterworld? Things weren't even that bad. She had a job—a purpose. She could have made friends and found some version of a family to spend her eternity with. Was getting out from under Maya's thumb truly worth all of this?

All Alora wants to do now is go back to where it all began. If she could just start over, she'd make different choices that wouldn't lead to the eternal damnation of everyone she came in contact with. Everything was her fault, but it didn't have to be like this. She could have made it right. She should have just been subservient like Maya wanted. And nobody would have to suffer.

But it's too late, and she knows that.

"I'm sorry," she says, lowering her head. She wants to look them in the eyes but can't bring herself to do it. "I'm sorry I got you all into this mess. I thought we could win. I really did. I thought we could beat her, but I was wrong."

She feels something on her shoulder—a hand. With a tilt of her head, she sees the familiar geometric pattern of Kanasu's bedsheet.

Alora looks up to see the bedsheet ghosts around her. Not a single one looks defeated—not yet.

"It's okay," Yume says. "We don't have to beat her."

"We just have to get past her," Kanasu says.

"If just one of us can make it through that front door," Rasui says.

"There's still a chance we can win," Endri adds.

"But we'd better be quick about it," Yume says, looking up.

The rest of the bedsheet ghosts tilt their heads one by one to see Maya, who has replaced her smile with a scowl and is raising one of her enormous swords above her head.

"We should probably split up," Rasui says.

"Yes, let's," Endri replies.

As Maya swings downward, the ghosts scatter, each taking off in a different direction. The golden goddess's blade smashes into the ground where they had just been floating, cleaving a huge gash into the ground beneath.

Maya tugs at her sword, but its edge sticks in the ground. She pulls it free with another effort, righting herself and raising her blade back into the air.

She watches the ghosts for a moment, trying to track their patterns, but they all appear to be moving around at random. She swings her sword again, diagonally this time, hoping to catch at least two of them with its long, curved blade. But they scamper out of the way at the last moment.

Too late, Maya realizes the other ghosts have seized the opportunity to get around her backside, making a beeline for the entrance to Dreamweavers HQ.

But just as they're about to reach the door, she brings one of her gargantuan shields down, lodging its bottom edge deep into the ground, blocking their path forward. Once more, the ghosts scatter.

With a heave, Maya frees the shield and brings her weapons

to bear, returning to her defensive stance. "You are only wasting time. You see that, don't you?" she bellows, crashing her swords against her shields again. "There's still time to surrender, cease this pointless uprising, and be shown mercy."

Ignoring Maya's words, the ghosts continue to dodge her attacks, trying to find a way to get up to the tower's front doors.

But Maya thwarts each chance they get. Soon, Alora realizes that Maya's attacks are anything but random. She's not merely reacting to the bedsheet ghosts. She's slowly corralling them together, using her shields to close the space around them and swinging her swords to move them toward exactly where she wants them.

Too late, Alora and her companions realize they're back together at the center of the concourse. And Maya, towering above them, is raising one enormous foot in the air, preparing to bring it down on top of them and ending their so-called insurrection once and for all.

As Maya leans forward, Alora shuts her eyes as tightly as she can, waiting for the inevitable crush.

But when she hears the thunderous impact, she feels nothing.

Slowly, she opens her eyes. Maya's foot is just above her and her friends' heads. Only it's no longer moving. And there's a sixth figure standing between them.

Morpheus has caught Maya's foot above them. He holds it in place with all his might even as the ground beneath him begins to crack and sink.

Though the big blue demon has stopped the golden goddess's momentum, Alora can see the pain on his face as he struggles to brace her colossal appendage.

Morpheus grits his teeth and shoves Maya's foot upward, knocking the towering goddess off-balance. But she catches herself, stabbing the tips of her swords into the ground behind her to keep herself from toppling over.

"What are you waiting for?" Morpheus shouts, readying himself for Maya's next attack. "Now's your chance!"

The ghosts scatter once more, trying to find a pathway around Maya and into Dreamweavers HQ. As the ghosts disperse, Morpheus takes flight, trying to bring Maya's focus up into the air.

Despite Morpheus joining the fray and drawing much of the goddess's attention—buzzing around her head like a housefly—they still can't seem to find a way around her. Each time one of them approaches, Maya swings down one of her swords or shields or stomps an enormous foot in their pathway. And Morpheus's attacks, while forceful enough to sound like thunderclaps, seem little more than a minor annoyance.

But Alora can tell Maya is slowing. Her strikes, while still savage, are growing less frequent and precise. The pink polka-dotted ghost knows that, with time, she and her companions will find a way around the golden goddess. They just need to wait for one misstep to skirt her defenses and make it through the tower door.

And then, the tide turns in their favor as Mamu emerges from one of the concourse's adjoining streets. On her face—normally so serene and kind—she wears a look Alora can only describe as vengeful.

As the elegant goddess marches into the concourse, she spreads her arms wide. A blackness so dark it seems to swallow up the light itself crawls from the tips of the fingers of her left hand up to her forearm, its tendrils stretching past her elbow. And her other hand burns white-hot, gleaming as brightly as a star.

Seeing Mamu approach, Maya swats Morpheus away with one of her shields, sending him careening into the side of a nearby building before swinging that same shield downward, wedging it into the ground, cutting off Mamu's approach.

But the advancing goddess merely places her left hand upon the golden barrier, sending a wave of frost over the weapon's surface, freezing it solid. Then, balling her other hand—still blazing as brilliantly as a sun—into a fist, she punches through it, shattering the shield to pieces. With the bulwark out of her way, she continues to march forward.

Maya reels from the blast only momentarily, raising her now-empty hand and snapping her gargantuan fingers. The thousands of pieces of the shattered shield rise from the ground and, one by one, slam into Mamu, slowly encasing the goddess in a golden sarcophagus.

Mamu extends her hands once again in an attempt to shatter them a second time, but they cover her too quickly, forcing her to outstretch her arms, rendering the goddess unable to reach Maya's makeshift coffin.

As the last few pieces slam into place, Maya extends her free hand and tips Mamu over with a single finger, sending the goddess's body wobbling onto the ground like a dropped coin.

But Mamu isn't finished. Beams of light begin to spring from between the cracks in her golden casket as her entire body burns bright white. Slowly, the gold of Maya's shield melts off her.

Seeing Mamu prepare for another assault, Maya reaches out her free hand, her fingers splayed wide, and tightens it into a fist. The liquid gold, reacting to her power, swirls into a pool beneath Mamu. When Maya releases her hand, the gold bubbles and erupts, sending molten-hot lashes over Mamu's arms and around her neck.

Too late, Mamu realizes the boiling hot metal is draining into the ground beneath her, melting a tunnel through to the rock below. She looks up just in time to see Maya bring down her second shield, crushing Mamu into the shifting landscape of Oneiros deep beneath Somnia.

With Morpheus still recovering and Mamu trapped, Maya turns her attention back to the bedsheet ghosts. "Now, where were we before we were so rudely interrupted?" she growls.

As the words escape her lips, a pool of black shadows bubbles up from under her. Maya tries to lift her feet, but she's too late. The shadows wrap around her ankles and crawl farther up her body.

She swings one of her swords downward, trying to cleave the darkness and free her feet. But the blade merely plunges into the shadows, and it, too, gets caught. She swings the other, but it meets the same fate.

Unarmed and immobile, Maya seethes with rage. "Chernobog!" she growls. "Show yourself!"

And with that, a black figure with great wings and crimson eyes erupts at Maya's feet from the shadows. Chernobog, the God of Chaos, Misfortune, and Darkness, flashes Maya his most impish smile.

"I do so appreciate that you've chosen to do things the hard way, Maya," he asserts. "The takeover simply would not be as much fun were it not so hostile."

Having extracted himself from the rubble of a nearby building, Morpheus flies back down to the concourse and lands alongside Chernobog.

"Nice of you to show up," he says.

Chernobog glares at the big blue demon. "Wasn't it your bright idea to bring those horrible nightmare-eating beasts into this? I could have been here much more quickly if I hadn't needed to battle droves of goblins, gargoyles, and ghouls while also steering clear of the skies above."

"Fair point," Morpheus replies.

"You can't hold me here forever," Maya howls, struggling to free her legs. But as she swats at the shadows swallowing her lower half, they begin to climb up her arms, holding her in an awkward, bent-over position.

"Forever was never the goal," Chernobog replies, turning his attention toward the scattering of bedsheet ghosts. "Humans! Now would be a good time to do your part!"

But Alora and her companions had already read the cue, gathering before the front doors of Dreamweavers HQ.

Alora's relief is almost palpable. Sure, they still had to get down into the restricted records room, find the door to Maya's bedroom, and wake Vishnu, but the hard part was over. With Chernobog holding Maya immobile and Morpheus there to help, they could focus on their task and not worry about an enormous golden goddess trying to destroy them along the way.

With a deep sigh, Alora—joined by Kanasu, Rasui, Yume, and Endri—tugs on the double doors.

But they won't budge. Alora starts to panic.

"Maybe it's a push, not a pull," Rasui says. He glides up to the doors and shoves them, but they remain closed.

"You've gotta be kidding me," Kanasu says, slapping their forehead. "The doors are locked."

"The doors are locked!" Yume shouts, waving at Morpheus and Chernobog.

"Well, break them down," Chernobog shouts back.

Yume turns back to find Rasui and Kanasu taking turns shoving and yanking on the doors. At one point, Rasui puts his shoulder into it, but the portal doesn't so much as budge.

"Chernobog," Maya says, her seething rage cooled to her usual calm smarminess. "You don't have to do this."

The God of Chaos, Misfortune, and Darkness turns his attention back to Maya. "I know I don't have to. I want to."

"Do you really?" she replies. "It seems you want something... something that I can give."

"Don't trust her," Morpheus says. "She's only trying to manipulate you."

"Silence!" Chernobog snaps at Morpheus. "You think me foolish enough not to realize as much?"

"You want power, right?" Maya says.

Chernobog raises an eyebrow at Maya.

"If there's anything this little insurrection has taught me," the golden goddess continues, "it's that I can't keep running this place alone. I need someone I can rely upon. A strong right hand. Someone with shrewd business sensibilities and an iron will."

Morpheus steps toward his demonic counterpart. "Chernobog, don't—"

"I said silence!" Chernobog whips an arm toward Morpheus and grabs the big blue demon by the mouth. When he pulls his hand away, he leaves behind a veil of shadows. Morpheus claws at the shade, but his fingers pass through it like mist.

"You," Chernobog says, turning back to Maya, "keep talking."

Meanwhile, Alora and the bedsheet ghosts have taken to

217

searching the concourse for anything they might be able to wedge into the door to pry it open. In their frenzy, they don't notice what's transpiring between the gods in the center of the concourse.

"I will retain my title and ultimate power, but I can offer you a place as my second-in-command. You'll be my deputy." Maya flashes Chernobog her best smile.

"Not good enough. I want full control," Chernobog counters, shooting a sly smile right back.

"You know I can't do that," she scoffs.

Morpheus waves his hands and shakes his head, trying to draw Chernobog's attention away from Maya to no avail.

"But I might be able to offer something that will satisfy both of our desires," Maya continues. "A partnership. An alliance, if you will. You handle the dirty work you're so fond of, and I'll take care of everything else. We'll be practically equals in nearly every way. How does that sound?"

Morpheus grabs Chernobog by the shoulders and spins him around, staring directly into his eyes. He points at Maya, then at Chernobog, and then draws a line with his forefinger across his throat.

"I hate charades," Chernobog says, waving a hand and removing the shadow-veil from Morpheus's mouth.

"Whatever she offers is a lie," Morpheus practically coughs. "She's only manipulating you into letting her go. Once you do, she'll never keep her part of the deal. She'll probably try to destroy you instead."

"Not if I get her to sign a contract here and now," Chernobog says with a laugh. Then, his voice echoes through the concourse as he yells, "Ikelos! Phantasus! Bring the typewriter."

On cue, Morpheus's brothers emerge from one of the

adjoining alleyways. Ikelos carries a huge typewriter, and Phantasus, following shortly behind, hauls a folding chair and desk. There, in the center of the concourse, they set up Chernobog's writing station.

Chernobog sits down at the desk and—with a flick of his wrist—manifests a largely prewritten contract in the typewriter. "Lucky for us, this shouldn't take too long. I've already mocked up most of an agreement, and I think we'll both find it suitable." He winks at Maya. And the tension in Maya's shoulders begins to melt away.

Morpheus reaches toward the typewriter, trying to snatch the contract off its platen. But Chernobog waves a hand, wrapping Morpheus's body in shadow and yanking him to the ground before he can grab it.

"Stay out of my business," Chernobog barks. "I won't ask again. And I certainly won't play nice any longer."

With fervor and fury, Chernobog smacks at the typewriter's keys, fleshing out the rest of the contract. The clattering is so loud that the bedsheet ghosts—having failed at their repeated attempts to open the doors to Dreamweavers HQ—finally take notice.

"Uhh, folks," Rasui says, pointing toward the gathering of gods at the center of the concourse, "should we maybe be worried about what's going on over there?"

"Oh no," Kanasu says. "Are they—?"

"Looks like it," Yume interrupts. "Worst-case scenario."

"It's okay," Alora says. "We planned for this. Right, Endri?"

Endri nods, pulling a small object out from under his bedsheet. "I'll be right back."

Chapter Eighteen

Curious About Career Advancement? Dreamweavers Promotes from Within!

As Chernobog smashes away at the typewriter keys, Ikelos and Phantasus not-so-sneakily peer over his shoulder with anticipation. But while the God of Chaos, Misfortune, and Darkness hammers out clause after clause, the brothers' faces morph from apprehensive excitement to confused glowers.

"Boss?" Phantasus finally asks.

But Chernobog ignores him, continuing to type away, unbothered.

"What about us?" Ikelos adds. "You're going to secure a spot for us, too, right?"

"We've served you loyally for eons, and you promised us our just rewards," Phantasus says.

"Can he even hear us?" Ikelos asks.

Phantasus shrugs and waves a hand in front of Chernobog's face.

"Stick your grubby mitts in front of my face again," Chernobog hisses, "and you'll pull back only a stump."

Phantasus yanks his hand back and hides it behind his back.

"Sorry, sir. It's just—"

Ikelos adds, "We just thought—"

Chernobog lets out a frustrated sigh, removing his hands from the keyboard and swiveling his chair around to face his bumbling lackeys. The legs of the folding chair grind on the ground below, eliciting a harrowing squeal.

"It's just— We just thought—" he mocks, shrugging his shoulders and waggling his fingers. "Have either of you even once wondered why, in all this time, you've remained in my department? Do you think it's because of your *exceptional* abilities or your *extraordinary* dedication to me?"

Ikelos and Phantasus look at one another, neither sure how to respond.

Chernobog continues, "Or perhaps you've only remained my subordinates for one very simple reason: to maintain a chasm between yourselves and your brother." He gestures toward Morpheus, still enshrouded and silenced a few feet away. "Have they always been so preposterously dense?" he asks the big blue demon. "Oh right."

Chernobog waves his hand and removes the shadow-gag from Morpheus's mouth, giving him a chance to answer. Instead of indulging the shadow-god, Morpheus takes the opportunity to shout a warning.

"Break the godforsaken door down if you have to," he shouts to the bedsheet ghosts still gathered across the concourse at the entrance to Dreamweavers HQ. "Together, they'll be unstoppable. You have to—"

Chernobog swipes a hand through the air and silences Morpheus once more. Then, he rises from his chair, towering over Ikelos and Phantasus.

"Here's the thing," he says with a grin. "Once I've got this contract put together and signed by the big lady here, I'll be a partner at this firm and can finally lord over the entirety of the Dreamscape. As you know, this has been a dream of mine for, well, as long as this realm has existed. I can't say whether you've helped or hindered my progress—likely the latter. What I do know, however, is that I will no longer be requiring your services."

Ikelos and Phantasus both throw up their hands.

"What? No," Phantasus coughs, his crystalline skin turning a sickly shade of pale.

"You can't do this," Ikelos barks, baring his beastly teeth.

With one smooth, lightning-fast motion, Chernobog grabs both of them by their heads and shoves them to the ground, wrapping their bodies in shadow. Then, with a wave of his arm, he sends them skittering across the ground to collide with their brother, Morpheus. The black shades engulfing each of them merge into a single, churning black mass through which nothing is visible.

Alora wants to call out, afraid of what might happen to her mentor and his brothers inside Chernobog's ghastly spell, but she stops. She knows that now is not the time to draw attention to herself or the other bedsheet ghosts, especially because Endri has begun to close the distance between them and the God of Chaos, Misfortune, and Darkness.

"Can we get back to business, please?" Maya says, her limbs still swallowed up by shadows. While her voice betrays an air of impatience, she's no longer struggling to break free.

"Apologies," Chernobog says, returning to his chair. "Where were we? Ah, yes, article sixty-six, section two…looks like we're just about done. Only a few finishing touches and—"

"Pardon the interruption, sir," Endri says.

Chernobog whips around and reaches out, closing his enormous claw around Endri's throat. The bedsheet ghost gags, unable to get any more words out.

"Oh." Chernobog sighs and rolls his eyes. "It's only you. What do you want, human?"

"I thought, maybe, you could use some help," Endri replies, keeping his eyes down and his hands behind his back. "Contracts can be tricky, and I wouldn't want Maya here taking advantage of you."

"And you think you're more well-equipped to tighten up this contract than I am?" Chernobog narrows his eyes at the mortal standing before him. "Keep talking."

"While I don't remember everything about my time in the mortal realm, I do recall the complexities of legal language. I just thought I might offer a second pair of eyes to make sure everything is airtight. It can't hurt to be thorough, right?"

"Surely, you want something in exchange. A guarantee of a position within my new hierarchy, perhaps?"

"No, sir," Endri answers.

"You expect me to believe that you're offering such services *pro bono*?"

"Not exactly," Endri says. "There is something I want." He takes one hand out from behind his back and waggles a finger, luring the God of Chaos, Misfortune, and Darkness toward him.

Chernobog, still seated in his folding chair, leans in, matching Endri's eyeline. "And what might that be?"

"I wanted to get close enough to give you this." Endri pulls his other hand from behind his back and squishes something on top of Chernobog's head. It makes a wet smack, and fluid trickles from atop the god's scalp down his face and onto the sides of his head.

Chernobog erupts with rage, knocking the folding chair out from under himself. He rises to his feet, cocking an arm back and backhanding Endri so hard that the bedsheet ghost goes flying—sailing across the concourse, careening between the other ghosts, and smashing into Dreamweavers HQ's double doors.

Immediately, Alora, Kanasu, Rasui, and Yume rush to Endri's side, checking to make sure he's okay. But Endri points back across the expanse toward Chernobog.

"I think I got him," Endri manages to choke out. "Look."

The bedsheet ghosts rise and turn, gazing across the concourse at Chernobog.

Black clouds billow at the God of Chaos, Misfortune, and Darkness's feet, and his eyes blaze like crimson flames. He reaches a claw up to his face, wipes it across his forehead, and inspects the viscous fluid on his fingers.

Suddenly, his expression shifts from untethered fury to all-encompassing panic. He paws at his head, knocking what Endri had placed upon it to the ground, confirming his fears.

Wobbling on the ground at his feet sits a piece of pomegranate.

But there's something else. A shadow appears below Chernobog and begins to expand. Except this darkness is not his own. It's a shadow of something else—something in the sky above. And it's getting bigger.

Chernobog looks up just in time to see a Baku—one that's younger and more brazen, albeit still enormous—diving toward him, lured in by the sweet scent of the fruit's juice.

With a shriek, Chernobog spreads his giant black wings and takes flight, trying to outrun the hungry beast. But the Baku's dive is too fast.

The elephant-whale catches up to the fleeing god, turning on its side, moving its trunk out of the way, and opening its mouth wide.

Chernobog flaps his wings as hard as he can in a desperate attempt to make up some ground, but the Baku is too quick, too tenacious. The God of Chaos, Misfortune, and Darkness sees the beast's jaws, lined with dozens upon dozens of sharp teeth, surround him.

The creature flaps its tail with one great effort, giving it just enough of a speed boost to overtake the black demon. Chernobog lets out one last blood-curdling scream before the Baku chomps down, swallowing the god whole.

"You did it!" Alora shouts, clapping her hands and turning back to Endri. But he's not there. On the ground where he had been only a moment before, his black-and-white plaid bedsheet lies in a heap—nothing more than loose fabric among the rubble.

"Endri!" she screams, falling to her knees and rooting through the limp cloth. Kanasu and Rasui grab Alora, pulling her back up. "No, no, no, no," she cries, heaving, retching, and clawing at Endri's sheet. "I'm sorry," she mutters. "I'm so sorry."

"He's gone," Kanasu says. "He's gone."

"There's nothing more we can do," Rasui adds.

Alora clutches the sheet close to her chest, still crying and mumbling her apologies.

Yume points back to the center of the concourse. "I don't think this is over," she says.

The shadows enveloping Morpheus and his brothers, as well as the ones immobilizing Maya, dissipate all at once.

Maya rises to her full height and lets out a laugh. "It seems I owe you all a debt of gratitude," she says, looking over at the bedsheet ghosts. "That's one more obstacle eliminated. Unfortunately, that's just not enough to earn your absolution. Shall we get back to business, then?"

But before she makes a move, Phantasus dives between her feet, reaching his arms out wide and entrapping her legs once more—this time, in a thick layer of Technicolor crystal.

Ikelos, hot on his brother's heels, launches himself into her torso, reaching his beastly arms out wide and knocking her off-balance. Together, they tumble back into an adjoining building, smashing through its facade and sending a cloud of dust and debris into the air.

Back on his feet and with his wings outstretched wide, Morpheus calls once more to the bedsheet ghosts. "You have to find a way in! Without Chernobog's help, we can't hold her for long."

"We can't!" Kanasu calls back. "The door is locked! We can't even break it open."

Suddenly, the Dreamweavers HQ double doors creak and crack behind her before bursting wide open. A figure steps through the entryway, rising to an enormous height. Even through her sobs, Alora recognizes its finely tailored suit and hundreds of arms.

Lying in the rubble as she tries to swat Ikelos away and free her feet from Phantasus's crystals, Maya cheers. "Cottus! Finally! Come and help me up, Hecatoncheire. Together, we'll squash this insubordination once and for all."

"Respectfully, ma'am, I'm not here to offer you any kind of assistance or aid," Cottus retorts. "I merely wish to inform you of my immediate resignation from your employ, as this calamity constitutes a breach of contract."

Maya bares her teeth and sets her eyes in a scowl. She flicks Ikelos off her chest with a giant hand, sending him flying through the sky and over the buildings on the other side of the concourse. Then, she backhands Phantasus, sending him skipping and skittering through another building on the concourse's opposite end.

Rising to her feet, shattering and shaking Phantasus's crystals from around her ankles and tightening all four of her hands into fists, she addresses Cottus, "On what grounds?"

"Hostile work environment."

The two giants sprint toward one another, colliding in a cacophony of punches, elbows, slaps, and blocks. While Maya clearly has an edge in strength, Cottus is faster and delivers barrage after barrage of quick hits.

As they battle, their strikes send shock waves through the concourse. Morpheus flies over to the bedsheet ghosts and lands, flapping his wings and sending a plume of dust into the air.

He sees Alora cradling Endri's bedsheet in her arms. He furrows his brow and rests a hand on her shoulder. "I'm sorry, but there's no time," he says. "You have to wake Vishnu. Everything depends on this."

"I know. All of this can't have been for nothing," Alora says, holding Endri's sheet out.

"It won't be," Morpheus responds. "You have to finish what we started."

"But if we leave, what will happen to you?"

"It doesn't matter. If you don't make it, none of this matters."

Alora gives Morpheus an assertive nod. Morpheus flaps his wings and takes back to the skies, joining Cottus in the fight against Maya.

One by one, the bedsheet ghosts turn and float through the doorway into Dreamweavers HQ, Alora still holding Endri's bedsheet tight against her chest.

Chapter Nineteen

Teamwork Makes the Dream Work

Since Alora is the only remaining bedsheet ghost who has been inside Dreamweavers HQ, she leads Kanasu, Rasui, and Yume. They travel through the lobby, passing Cottus's vacant desk—an unsettling reminder of just how upended everything has become—and boarding the elevator down to the lower levels.

When the elevator opens, they find Briareus waiting for them in the records room lobby—standing before his desk instead of sitting behind it. He looks impatient, no doubt worried by the sounds of battle rumbling through the building overhead.

"Alora! Good, you made it," he says. "Shall I escort you through the labyrinth?"

"Cottus told you we were coming?" Alora asks in reply.

Briareus nods confidently, but Alora can see he's anxiously wringing several sets of his hands.

"I think we can take it from here," she says.

"But what of the Minotaur?"

"Go," Alora affirms. "Help your brother."

"Thank you," the Hecatoncheire says before slipping past

the bedsheet ghosts and shrinking into the still-open elevator. The elevator lets out a cheerful chime, and the doors slide closed. But not before another rumble from outside sends a shower of dust down onto the ghosts' heads.

"We should hurry," Kanasu says.

"Where do we go?" Rasui asks.

"This way," Alora answers.

Alora, still carrying Endri's sheet, leads the ghosts through the stacks, under the restricted section's opulent archway, down the spiral staircase, and into the labyrinth.

At the bottom of the stairs, the Minotaur waits for them. It's on all fours, its hindquarters pushed up into the air and its arms stretched out before it. Alora can see the fuzzy green tennis ball in its mouth, covered in even more slobber than before.

But the rest of the ghosts freeze in their tracks, no doubt intimidated by the beast's hulking size and brutish appearance.

"It's okay," Alora assures them. "He just wants to play."

Yume is the first to descend the stairs, excited to meet a new friend. As she approaches, the Minotaur drops his ball and taps it forth with his snout.

The ball rolls toward Yume, leaving a trail of slime on the ground beneath. She tilts over gracefully, picks the ball up, and tosses it down one of the labyrinth's corridors.

The Minotaur follows the ball with its eyes, and on the ball's first bounce, he scrambles off down the hall, knocking books off the shelves in pursuit.

A few moments later, the Minotaur comes scrambling back,

again dropping the ball in front of Yume—only this time, Alora, Kanasu, and Rasui float beside her. Yume picks up the ball and hands it to Rasui.

"Ew, slimy," he says, throwing it as quickly as he can muster and wiping the excess saliva on Kanasu's bedsheet.

"Hey, what the heck," Kanasu protests.

Rasui shrugs. "My bad."

"Come on," Alora says, passing between them. "We still have a way to go."

Together, they traverse the labyrinth, taking turns tossing the ball for the Minotaur as it follows them through each twisting corridor.

Eventually, they turn a corner and find a small black cat patiently sitting in front of a golden door.

"Dublin!" Yume cheers, crouching down to scratch the feline behind its ears. "Good kitty!"

Dublin meows, looking up at Alora.

"It's good to see you, too, buddy," she says.

The cat stands up, walks a quick figure eight, and then leads the ghosts through the golden door housed in its marble archway—which has somehow opened all on its own.

☠

"Once we pass through this door, you're going to start to feel really tired," Alora says, holding the knob that leads into Maya's bedroom. "But you can't give in to that feeling. The four of us are going to split up, and each of us will head to one of the pillars in the room. Then, when we're all ready, we'll remove the objects from atop the pillars."

"And you're sure that will work?" Kanasu asks.

"I just have a feeling," Alora says.

"That's usually how stuff works in video games," Rasui adds. "And if we have to try something else, we try something else."

"Until we get it right," Yume confirms.

"Okay. Here goes nothing," Alora says, twisting the doorknob.

As expected, Cottus's third brother, Gyges, is already waiting for the bedsheet ghosts. But he's not alone. Next to him stands a small, pallid woman in red robes with gold trim. But Alora can't quite make her out, as her head is down and her arms are behind her back.

As they get closer, the woman raises her head. She has a sad, exhausted look in her eyes. Then she removes her arms from behind her back—all four of them.

Alora's heart sinks.

"Maya," she whispers.

The ghosts halt in their tracks.

"Gyges, what in the name of the gods is she doing here?" Alora demands.

Gyges holds up two of his hands, palms out. "Please," he says. "I assure you, you have nothing to worry about. She's still up in Somnia, battling with my brothers. This shade is only a small part of her. And she's too weak to stop you now."

"Then why is she here?" Kanasu reiterates with a sharpness in their voice.

"I'm here to make a final plea," Maya says.

"I didn't ask you," Kanasu barks. "Haven't you done enough already? It's time to end this."

Maya lowers her head and presses two of her hands together. "Please. Just listen."

"Humans," Gyges interrupts. "There's not a being in the

Dreamscape who knows Maya's cruelties more than my brothers and me. You know this to be true. She has kept us indentured for eons, slaving away to help her run this empire of hers without so much as a wink of empathy toward any of us. And that is but a mere fraction of her heartlessness. I am not asking that you acquiesce to her demands. As a final favor, I simply ask you to hear her out."

Kanasu, Yume, and Rasui turn to Alora. But Alora doesn't look back. Instead, she considers Endri's bedsheet still cradled in her arms.

With a sigh, she looks up. "She doesn't deserve it."

Maya closes her eyes and hangs her head a little lower.

"But we'll do it, if only for you and your brothers, Gyges."

"I had my doubts, but it seems Cottus was right about you," the Hecatoncheire says, taking a step back and giving Maya the floor. "Thank you."

Maya steps forward and clears her throat.

"Long ago, there was a mighty god. This god was so powerful that they—alongside their two siblings—created the whole universe as we know it. But the universe was imbalanced, always ebbing and flowing between good and evil, order and chaos. So, this god took it upon themself to become the universe's keeper, helping to nudge it back into balance whenever it shifted too far in one direction or the other.

"For a time, this helped keep the god busy. Some might even say that they were happy. But as time passed, this omniscient being realized that something was missing from the universe. Or rather, there was something they had put into it that they themself could not control or balance: loneliness.

"Perhaps they assumed they would always have the company of their kin, that the three of them would never truly be apart, even in the enormity of their new universe. But their siblings— their counterparts—were always so busy taking care of the universe for which they were responsible.

"This left the god spending a vast amount of their time alone. And there was no amount of splendor or indulgence that could curb their heartache.

"One day, having combed the whole of existence, unsuccessfully searching for something to sate the god's thirst for companionship, they got an idea: just as they created the universe, they could craft a companion for themself—a true counterpart, born of their own flesh.

"In a flash of inspiration, the god removed and repurposed their own left arm—removing it from their body and reforming it into its own being. The god gave this new being a name, and with it came life and sentience—a sense of self.

"*Finally*, the god said, *I no longer have to be alone.*'

"And for a time, things were good. The god showed their new companion, their consort, the whole universe they had helped to create and maintain.

"*Now, you can share it with me,*' the god told her.

"But the consort did not understand. The god was a complete being with an infinite universe at their fingertips. They had everything. And yet, they still chose to create her. Eventually, she got up the courage to ask them.

"*Why did you make me?*' she inquired. *'You have everything. Why do you need me?*'

"*Just as the flower needed a scent,*' the god told her, *'I needed you.*'

"Finally, the consort understood that she existed for one purpose: to serve the god. And just as loneliness had filled the god before they created her, she began to feel something bubbling up inside her—something she knew was real, even if she had no name for it. She called it resentment.

"But she knew the god would not understand. How could they? They had given her life, the universe, everything. How could she not be grateful for all the god had bestowed upon her? How could the god understand that creating her for a life of servitude would never grant her the same completeness the god had sought and now so cherished?

"In the god's defense, the consort never wanted for anything material. Anything she could imagine was hers. In the same instant that an idea crossed her mind, the god would bring that idea to life. But it was never enough, for the one thing she truly wanted—that which she needed to feel her own sense of completeness—was the one thing the god could not give her: freedom.

"Still, the god was good to her. And she tried so hard to be happy. After all, how could the entirety of the universe not be enough? So, she smiled graciously and thanked the god, doing her best to tend to them the way they tended to her.

"*'This can be enough,'* she told herself. *'We can be happy.'*

"But it was not to be, simply because she spoke it. Worse, the god began to notice that not all was right with the consort. Though they did not speak of it, a chasm grew between them. While they met one another with kindness and care, so, too, did they build distance and indifference between them.

"Eventually, the god could bear it no more.

"*'If this is not enough for you,'* they told the consort, *'then I will make something that is. I will make a place just for us.'*

"The consort smiled and accepted the god's will, knowing that they, in all their infinite power and wisdom, had fundamentally misunderstood what it was she was missing.

"The god, using every ounce of their spirit and vitality, built a new universe filled with all the things the consort loved: miraculous landscapes, magnificent skies, strange creatures, and so much more. The god even pulled spirits and lesser deities from around the original universe into this new one, hoping to maintain the same balance they had always sought and fought so hard to maintain.

"But without their siblings to aid them, the new world was too much for the god to bear. They grew tired and weak. They knew they needed to rest. So, they sealed this new universe off, with the consort and all he created for her still inside. And that's where she would remain, entrapped while the god slumbered.

"At first, the consort fell into despair.

"*'How could the god do such a thing?'* she wondered. *'Did they not understand that this place was merely a cage—a physical manifestation of her enslavement to them?'*

"But then she looked out on her universe, the realm created especially for her, and inspiration took hold.

"*'This is my universe to do with what I wish,'* she said. *'Though my god has abandoned me, I will not abandon this place.'*

"And so she set to work, tinkering with her new world. For the first time, she felt a taste of the freedom she so craved. But there was so much chaos. And without the god to balance it, she remained the only being capable of maintaining the scales.

"So, she built systems of control—mechanisms to manage the ever-shifting landscapes of this world and hierarchies to control the beings within it.

"But she was inexperienced and made many, many mistakes. Still, though she was not as mighty as her god, she had enough power to reset and try again. And again. And again.

"She believed that, with enough iterations, she would eventually shape this universe into a place where she could both maintain balance and indulge in her long-sought freedom. There was just one looming threat in her way. She knew that, eventually, the god would awaken once more.

"So she reset the universe. Only this time, she put pieces into place to keep the god in their slumber. So long as they slept, this universe was hers to protect. But she could not do it alone. So she contracted help from three timeless deities the god had trapped in this universe with her. Together, they built a machine to extend the god's slumber infinitely.

"The consort knew she could not reset the universe again for fear of waking the sleeping god. She also knew that not all the spirits and creatures within this universe would understand and appreciate her vision. Even the three timeless deities she had contracted with did not see it as a viable long-term solution. To them, it was merely kindling waiting to ignite.

"But she would not give up what little freedom she had wrenched for herself, even if it only existed in this cage. Her agreement with the trio of timeless deities would keep them in line well enough, but she needed to ensure no other creatures— mortal or immortal—discovered the truth.

"So she gave them all purposes—a social structure and jobs to complete. If all went to plan, they would be none the wiser. Whenever one of them got too close to the truth, she would simply put them to sleep alongside the god until she was strong enough to reset their memory, then reintegrate them into her world's society and try again.

"Better still, she could integrate her system into their work, giving it an air of legitimacy she could not manufacture. The mortals would believe they were making dreams for their counterparts in the world of the living, blissfully unaware that the dreams they constructed served only to help rewrite the memories of their nosy compatriots trapped with them in the Dreamscape. It was exhausting and overcomplicated, but it just might work.

"The other gods and immortals in her universe acquiesced well enough. After all, they were no strangers to falling in line beneath a power greater than their own. But the consort found trouble in an unexpected place: among the mortals.

"These once-human souls never seemed satisfied no matter how much she gave to or took from them. Even with no memory of their past selves, they meddled. Time and time again, they upended her carefully laid plans.

"She admired their tenacity at first. They reminded the consort of herself back when all she wanted was freedom. But she also came to loathe them.

"*'Why is this universe and all I've given to them not enough?'* she wondered. *'They have everything they could ever want. Why are they not satisfied?'*

"It only occurred to her, too late, that she had done to them the very same thing her god had done to her."

"And that brings us to now," Maya concludes.

The bedsheet ghosts can only stare at her, digesting all that the golden goddess had revealed. Finally, Alora breaks the silence.

"I'm sorry that happened to you," she says. "But it doesn't make up for…"—she holds Endri's sheet up before her—"for all of this."

"I know," Maya says. And for the first time, Alora thinks she hears real sorrow in her voice. "I'm not asking for forgiveness. I'm only asking that you not wake Vishnu. I will step down. I'll hand over this entire realm to whomever you see fit to control it. I'll accept whatever punishment you should choose. I just… Don't wake Vishnu."

"Why?" Alora asks, choking on her words. "Why didn't you just ask for help?"

Maya looks into Alora's eyes. There are tears streaming down her golden cheeks. "Why didn't you?" she says. "I thought I could do it all on my own. I had to. I needed to prove it to myself. I never meant… I never wanted to cause this much harm. I'm sorry for everything. But I-I can't go back to a life of servitude."

"You won't have to."

The voice comes from behind Alora through the door to the cavernous bedroom. It's Morpheus, back to his human form. And he's joined by both of his brothers, Mamu, Cottus, and Briareus.

A smile creeps across Gyges's face, erasing his exhaustion.

"Brothers!" he cries, running toward them. "It has been far too long." The Hecatoncheires embrace, their hundreds of hands pulling one another as close as possible.

"Good to see you're all still standing," Morpheus says to the bedsheet ghosts as he passes between them, giving a wink to Alora. "Just hold tight for a moment. Promise, I'll be right back."

"You should have told us," Mamu says as she, Morpheus, and

his brothers approach Maya. "Perhaps we could have helped."

"I didn't think you'd understand," Maya replies.

"Have you met Zeus?" Phantasus asks.

"Or any of the greater deities?" Ikelos adds.

"We understand," Morpheus says. "But that doesn't excuse your transgressions. You must make amends."

"I know," Maya agrees, hanging her head. "There's no other option. You have to wake Vishnu. I can't undo all I've done. Even if I wanted to, I don't... I can't do it on my own. I'm just so tired. I just... I have to get some...some rest."

Maya collapses, her frail body falling into a heap on the rock below.

Chapter Twenty

Notice: Dreamweavers, LLC Is Under New Management

D ublin, who has been patiently meandering about, rolling around on the ground, swatting at dust motes, grooming himself, and just generally doing cat things as all the gods and mortals have been talking, looks up at Alora and meows.

"Hi, buddy," she says as she kneels next to him, scratching behind his ears. "Don't worry, we haven't forgotten about you."

The black cat meows a second time in a way that makes Alora think he understands her.

"We should probably get to it," she says, rising up and tossing Endri's sheet over her shoulder. "Same plan?"

"Seems as good now as it did before," Kanasu answers. "Unless the gods have any better ideas?"

"Your guess is as good as ours," Morpheus says as his brothers shrug behind him.

"Magic isn't exactly a one-spell-fits-all situation," Mamu agrees, crouching down and tending to the still-unconscious Maya.

To Alora, the golden goddess looks so small and helpless,

now lying between the other immortals.

"And if that doesn't work," Cottus says, "my brothers and I have eons of knowledge on sleeping spells that might come in handy."

With that, the bedsheet ghosts split up, each heading for a different pillar surrounding the sleeping Vishnu. As he carefully floats around the pit in the center, Rasui takes a peek—quickly hopping back when he sees the massive, undulating mass covered in bedsheets down at the bottom.

"What is—" he stammers. "Is that a flipping snake?"

Yume skirts closer to the pit and peeks into it for herself. "Ooh," she intonates. "Scaly boy."

"Is that something we should be worried about?" Kanasu asks. "Don't get me wrong, snakes are cool, but…"

"That's just Sheshnag," Cottus calls after them. "Or Ananta. Also, Naagraj, depending on whom you ask. He's the king of all snakes. His soul, like Maya's, is tied directly to Vishnu. He shouldn't give you any trouble."

"You sure about that?" Rasui asks with a leeriness in his voice. "Maya has been nothing *but* trouble."

"I'm quite certain," Cottus answers.

"Okay," Rasui says, but he scampers away from the edge of the pit in a way that makes Alora feel like he's not entirely convinced.

One by one, the bedsheet ghosts float up to their respective pillars. Alora stops before the one with the lotus atop it. Kanasu stands before the club. Rasui eyeballs his pillar with its conch shell upon it. And Yume twirls around the one supporting a discus.

Alora looks up at the huge golden bed suspended in the center of the room. The figure—who she now knows as

Vishnu, creator of the Dreamscape—is sleeping upon it, wrapped up in plush bedding and enveloped by pillows. The slumbering god is also still surrounded by a vortex of orbs— the souls of mortals whose memory Maya was trying to reset.

Alora remembers Morpheus's words—how waking Vishnu could destroy the Dreamscape, potentially destroying even the immortals there and sending the humans scattering across the other realms. For a moment, she hesitates, afraid of the finality of this decision.

Then, she feels something down around her legs. Dublin is walking in his figure eights and rubbing his face on her bedsheet. And it reminds her of something else Morpheus told her—about his own faith and his certainty that, no matter the risk, waking Vishnu is the choice he would make without hesitation.

"Everybody ready?" she asks, looking at each of her three companions.

"This one's for all the marbles," Rasui says.

"Ready, captain!" Yume squeaks.

Kanasu gives Alora a nod.

"On three," Alora says.

"Whoopsies," Rasui says.

The three other bedsheet ghosts turn to look at Rasui, who is already holding the conch shell from his pillar.

"Sorry, sorry, sorry," he says, trying to put it back up atop the pillar, but the shell just won't stay balanced.

A huge clang rings throughout the room, and the enormous bed starts to descend, clicking and clanking as the gargantuan chains holding it up begin to unravel.

Then, all of a sudden, the bed comes to a halt—just a few feet lower than it was before.

"Okay, I think we're good," Rasui says in a way that makes Alora think he's trying to convince himself more than everyone else.

Suddenly, the clang rings out again, and the bed once again starts descending.

"My turn," Yume shouts, holding the discus high above her head.

"I guess we're just doing this," Kanasu responds, pulling the club from atop the pillar before them.

Kanasu looks at Alora, and Alora shrugs, grabbing the lotus from her pillar.

The bed continues to descend until it hangs at ground level above the pit in the center of the room. And then it stops, and the room goes silent.

"Shouldn't there be some kind of big magical explosion or something?" Rasui asks. "An all-powerful god waking up after however many centuries seems like it should have more...I dunno...flair?"

Morpheus splits off from the rest of the immortals and joins Alora, scratching his head and looking across the chasm at the sleeping Vishnu.

"You know," he says, "I really thought that would work."

"What do we do now?" Alora asks.

"What's that in your hand? A lotus? You could try throwing it at them. That usually wakes me up."

"You sure that's a good idea?"

"On second thought, getting bonked on the head usually makes me pretty grumpy, so maybe scratch that idea."

"Wait, where's Dublin?" Alora asks, looking around at their feet where the cat should have been.

She turns around to see the black feline crouching toward

the wall behind her. With a push, the cat launches himself forward, sprinting toward the center of the room.

"No, buddy!" Alora cries, trying to grab the cat as he sprints past her, but she's just not quick enough.

At the edge of the pit, the cat leaps, sailing across the chasm and landing on the edge of the bed. Having safely landed, the cat casually—*too casually*, Alora thinks—sits down and grooms his ears for a moment before hopping atop the sleeping Vishnu in the center of the bed.

Dublin sits again, kneading its paws into the sleeping god.

Vishnu stirs, rolling around under the blankets and pillows. "Five more minutes," they say. Their voice sounds gravelly and harsh, which Alora chalks up to centuries of slumber, but it also echoes through the room with silken smoothness.

The god's voice is unlike anything Alora has ever heard—somehow both comforting and commanding, serene and spooky.

But Dublin continues pestering Vishnu, swatting at the grumbling god with his tiny paws.

"Ugh, fine," Vishnu says with a tremendous yawn. The god's breath is so powerful that Alora can feel her bedsheet swaying in its breeze. And it smells of flowers in the springtime.

Alora watches with awe as Vishnu rises from the bed, the god's skin a vibrant shade of cerulean. But the sheets and pillows do not fall from the god's body. Instead, they shapeshift and coalesce into the most beautiful prismatic garments Alora has ever seen—shimmering, color-shifting, and delicate.

A garland of flowers blooms around Vishnu's neck and, below it, an ornate collar of gold. A similarly adorned belt forms around the god's waist.

Vishnu's mane falls from their head, across their shoulders, and down their back in thick black curls—descending more like a velvet curtain than locks of hair—and a bejeweled crown of gold and peacock feathers forms atop the god's head.

But Alora notices something strange. In contrast to Maya, Vishnu has only one arm, which they stretch out toward the black cat, who is walking tight figure eights around their feet.

"Garuda," Vishnu says, smiling. "You've come back to me. It is wonderful to see you." The god crouches down and scratches the cat behind his ears.

"Looks like your kitty wasn't a stray, after all," Yume shouts across the chasm at Alora.

"Guess not," Alora chimes in. She realizes that the lotus she had held in her hands only moments before is suddenly gone—it has vanished into thin air.

But there's something else that draws her attention. Vishnu picks up the black cat on the bed and holds him close, pressing the feline into their chest. And like paints blended together, they merge into a single being.

The cat's essence undulates and transforms, sprouting from Vishnu's shoulder like vines and forming a second arm.

"Thank you, my friend," Vishnu says, clenching their new fingers into a fist before stretching and splaying them wide.

Suddenly, the room begins to rumble and shake, sprinklings of dust falling from the cavernous roof above. For a moment, Alora thinks the battle overhead has resumed—forgetting that all the remaining immortals are here in the cavern with her.

Then, she notices the bedsheets at the bottom of the pit undulating and shifting. The snake—the one Cottus told them was named Sheshnag—has awoken from its slumber. It lifts its head up and out of the pit, resting its nose against the bed and stretching its spine toward the pit's edge.

"Good morning to you, too, Lord Naagraj," Vishnu says, bowing their head. The god steps forth, walking across the snake's head, down its back, and coming to a stop at the edge of the pit.

The snake then begins to slither up and out of the pit. The ghosts skitter back, trying to distance themselves from the titanic serpent. But the snake seems even more familiar with its surroundings than they, deftly meandering around the pillars as it shifts its body and shakes the myriad bedsheets from its back.

Alora can see its gorgeous scales, free of the fabric covering them, shimmering in the same prismatic Technicolor of Vishnu's garments.

The serpent slides around the pit until it approaches Vishnu once more. Then, shrinking and deflating almost like a balloon, it wriggles itself into Vishnu's body, just below the god's right arm, twisting and reforming itself into a third appendage.

"Welcome home, old friend," the god says with a smile. But Vishnu's smile fades when their eyes settle on the scene before them. "Oh, Lakshmi, what have you done?" they ask with deep sorrow in their voice.

Vishnu looks around the room, noticing the great machine built into the ceiling and the swirling vortex of human souls overhead. Then, the god looks at Alora.

"Garuda tells me I have you to thank for waking me," Vishnu says.

"Garuda?" Alora stammers.

"He also tells me that you know him as Dublin. This is a strange name for an eagle, no?"

"Dublin...was a cat," Alora responds.

"Yes, of course. To you. Garuda comes in many forms. To me, he is a great eagle and one of my dearest friends. When my slumber began, he separated from me. He was to wake me when the time was right. But it seems Lakshmi, my consort, had other plans. She kept us apart. And he sought help from the mortals—the only beings in this realm who stood against Lakshmi's plans. So, he chose a form you might recognize—one that Lakshmi would not. It was a clever disguise. Perhaps too clever since you and your friends were the first to heed his call. Though I can hardly fault those he approached before. To a mortal soul, a cat is usually just a cat." Vishnu furrows their brow. "I'm sorry, this must all be so confusing."

"It's okay," Alora replies. "I think I get it. Mostly."

"In any case, I owe you my thanks," Vishnu continues. "It seems some things have been taken from you. I'd like to return them. Let's start with this."

Vishnu raises a hand and stretches it out, palm up. Endri's bedsheet lifts from Alora's shoulder and hovers before her. From above, one of the many ghostly orbs in the swirling vortex of souls separates and flies down, dipping under the black-and-white plaid bedsheet and then back up into it.

The bedsheet sheet swells and fills, and Endri wakes, gasping and coughing. He settles in the air before Alora, looks around the room, and asks her, "Where am I?"

But Alora doesn't answer. Instead, she pulls him forward, hugging him as tightly as she can.

"Whoa, hey," Endri says. "I'm okay. It's okay."

"I thought you were gone," Alora says. "What happened? What was it like?"

"I don't know," Endri says. "It was like...like I took the best nap of my life. Or afterlife, I guess. Wait. Did we win?"

Alora nods her head emphatically. "Yes. We won."

"Well, hey, that's wonderful news," Endri says. Then, looking around, he asks, "Who are all these other people?"

Alora hadn't even noticed that the room had filled with hundreds of bedsheet ghosts. And the swirling vortex of souls overhead is gone. Whatever was keeping them up there, Vishnu had apparently reversed, waking each and every bedsheet ghost trapped in the cavernous bedroom.

"Welcome back, everyone," Vishnu announces with warmth and gentleness. "I hope you are all well rested. Now, if you'll all hold very still, I would like to give you one more thing."

With that, Vishnu claps their hands together, and like a wave crashing on the shore, all of Alora's memories return to her.

The first thing Alora remembers is her mother. She was kind, caring, and loving. She didn't have much, but she gave all she could to her daughters—both of them. And that's when the second memory floods Alora's mind: she had a sister.

They were poor, living in a small apartment in the city alone, but they were not lonely. They had their mother, and their mother had them. But most of all, they had one another. Despite their struggles, they were a happy family.

Then, one day, Alora and her sister were left alone in their apartment. Their mother told them she would be right back. But then it got late, and she still hadn't returned.

Alora and her sister were too young to understand and too small to care for themselves, so they sought the help of a neighbor. Another woman lived on the same floor of their apartment building and sometimes watched them when their mother had to work late. But too much time had passed, and the friendly woman did not know what to do, so she made a phone call.

Soon, the building's hallways were crowded with unfamiliar folks, some in uniforms and others in suits. They took Alora and her sister and promised that they would be safe. But their mother made them feel safe, and she still hadn't returned.

One day turned into two, two days turned into three, three into four, and then a man took them to a room together and told them a story. Their mother was not coming back. She was gone. Forever.

Worse, Alora and her sister would have to live with other families. They asked if they could stay together, for that was all they had. The man assured them they would do their best. But the man and his coworkers split them up only days later.

Alora never saw her sister again.

Years went by. Alora moved from a foster home to a group home and eventually aged out. But she was smart and resourceful and had gotten good grades in school. So, she applied to college and was accepted.

It wasn't easy. Alora could barely afford to live. She had few friends and no family, other than a black cat—a stray, just like her, that she found in an alleyway near her apartment. She named him Dublin.

Though she could say overall that she was happy to pursue her dreams, Alora had to make many sacrifices. But she did it. She achieved an undergraduate degree in social work and then a graduate degree, and she was in the midst of applying to a doctorate program, determined to rise as high as she could to help children—other strays like herself, her sister, and Dublin.

Expecting letters of acceptance—and praying she wouldn't get any rejections—she kept a close eye on her incoming mail. But she was not expecting to get a handwritten letter from an unfamiliar name at an unfamiliar address. And she did not know that this letter would change the course of her life forever.

In the note, written in beautiful penmanship, the author claimed to be looking for someone with Alora's background. Specifically, they sought an orphaned girl who had been split up from her only remaining family—her sister. Alora could not believe what had happened. Her sister had finally found her after all these years.

They did not wait. They could not. The pair made plans to meet immediately, even though it would require a cross-country trip and would strain both of them financially.

In no time, Alora packed her car and hit the road. And then a truck hit her car. And Alora woke up in the afterlife.

But that was not the end of their story. Alora was determined to find her sister in the afterlife, no matter how long she had to wait or how far she had to search.

It turned out that her sister perished only a few years after Alora, falling to an incurable illness. Once in the afterlife, she also set out on a quest to track down her sibling.

After what felt like years—but could have been eons—of wandering from realm to realm, Alora and her sister found one another again, defying the odds. It was not the reunion they had planned, but it was a welcome one all the same.

Together, they were happy, traversing the Afterworld and sharing all they had missed during their separate lives in the mortal realm. It was more than either of them could have ever hoped for.

And then, just like before, they were ripped apart—thrown into a strange new realm and separated. Worse, someone erased their memories, and they once again became strangers, alone in an unfamiliar world.

☠

Alora remembers the woman from the dream, back before the dominoes fell, and Alora brought her friends and coworkers into a war with a vengeful god. The two of them recognized one another—it didn't matter that one was human and the other was a soul-stuffed bedsheet. And it wasn't some coincidence or trick. It was real. It meant something. It made Alora want to pursue waking Vishnu and unraveling Dreamweavers in its entirety.

And now she remembers why. The woman with her big bouncy curly hair was—no, *is*—her sister.

Alora scans the cavern, knowing now exactly who she's looking for. And then she sees her. Or rather, her sister sees her, raising her hands high in the air and waving them around like a maniac.

She's wearing the same pink polka-dotted bedsheet as Alora—the same sheets they both had on their beds back in that tiny apartment in the middle of the city.

The two ghosts rush toward one another, dodging other bedsheet-clad ghosts who are having similar realizations and reunions. When they meet, they collide, falling on the ground in a laughing, crying heap of pink polka-dotted cloth.

"If you're going to do something," Nia says, pulling Alora as close as she can.

"Do it right," Alora replies—finishing the mantra their

mother had taught them both as children. "All this time, I knew the words, even if I couldn't remember why."

"You knew in here," Nia says, poking Alora in the chest. "That's what matters."

"It's so good to have you back," Alora replies. "Again. You've missed so much. I'll tell you. I'll tell you everything. But I have something else I have to do first."

"Of course," Nia says with a laugh. "You were always so busy. Come back to me when you're done. I'll be here, waiting."

Alora rises and meanders back through the crowd, dodging the other ghosts, remembering, catching up, and embracing. Yet, surrounded by so much happiness, she can't help but feel worried for what comes next.

Now that Vishnu is awake, the god who created the Dreamscape will see all that Maya has done. And they may not be happy. There's still a chance, however small, that Vishnu will want to erase everything and start over. She cannot fathom all the power the god has, but wiping the slate clean and returning this place to their original vision—

"Alora!" Morpheus interrupts her train of thought. He waves at her, still surrounded by all the other immortals. Only this time, Vishnu has joined them. And in his arms, he cradles the body of Maya, holding her close and smiling the most sorrowful smile Alora has ever seen.

"So much pain," Vishnu says as Alora joins the congregation of immortals. "How could I not have seen it? In my hubris, I thought I had delivered paradise. Instead, I had built a prison. She did not deserve this. Nor did any of you. I must make amends. I must set things right, though I cannot imagine how."

"I might have some ideas about that, actually," Alora says, raising a hand. "If you'll hear them."

"For the girl who moved the gods," Vishnu says with a smile, "anything."

Dream Log #4

Courtesy of the Department of the Mundane

Earth Date: Holocene Period, Age of Humankind, Year 729 Ab Urbe Condita, 25 BCE (Earth calendar)
Corporeal Location of Subject: Sulmo, Italy (Earth)

Subject: Human, male-identifying, orator, aged approximately twenty-two (Earth years)

Start log.

A young man with a short curly haircut tucked beneath an olive wreath sits in a white chair before a white table in an all-white room. As he scrutinizes his surroundings, he straightens out his blue-trimmed pallium—a cloak worn by people of Ancient Rome. He notices there is only one door on the wall opposite and that the space is otherwise unadorned and unremarkable. A fluorescent light flickers overhead.

The young man looks around, curious but not confused or panicked—almost as if there's something familiar to the chamber, as if he knows what will happen next.

The door opens, and a ghost in a pink polka-dotted bedsheet

floats in. The ghost is holding a manila folder stuffed with loose papers. She closes the door behind her, glides over to the table, and sits down in the chair opposite the young man.

They sit in silence for a moment as the ghost gets situated, opening its folder and flipping through some of the pages. Finally, they look at one another.

"I thought this was supposed to be against the rules," the young man says.

"Special dispensation," the ghost responds. "Took a while to get approval. We had to lobby for it, actually. But after a fair amount of convincing—and several rounds of character testimony—we got approval."

"Still trying to follow all the rules, I see." The young man smiles. "What's the catch?"

"You're not going to remember any of it."

"Figures," the man says, leaning back in his chair and kicking his sandaled feet up on the table. He squints at the ghost. "How many times have we done this before?"

"I'm not at liberty to say," the ghost responds with a tilt of her head.

"What difference does it make? I'm not going to remember anyway."

"You got me there," the ghost says. "But rules are rules."

"How about if I guess? You don't have to say anything. Just nod if I'm close. Deal?"

The ghost stares at the young man. "You know, this whole thing was your idea," she finally says. Lowering her voice in a mocking tone and moving her arms like a robot, she continues, "If I want to understand these mortal souls better, I should live the life of one. They've done so much for me; this will help me better prepare to return the favor."

"Okay, alright," the man says with a chuckle, holding his hands up, palms out. "That's fair. So, what are we doing here? Seems pretty droll. Couldn't have spiced this place up just a little? Maybe hang some pictures or get a plant or something."

"You know, we're on a timer," the ghost replies.

The man lowers his feet and leans forward, trying to peek at the papers fanned out on the table before the ghost.

The ghost closes the folder, tucking the papers back inside. "Isn't it enough that we miss you?"

"No. I don't think it is," the man answers. "A lifetime on Earth is a flash in the pan in the Afterworld. How long have I been gone, anyhow?"

"Not long," the ghost says. "Truth is, we have a few things to go over before you return. And since I'm the head of Mortal-Immortal Relations, that falls on my shoulders."

"You got a promotion?" The young man's smile widens. "Congratulations. Much deserved. You did miss me, though, right?"

"Maybe a little."

"I'll take it."

"So, what's everyone else up to? Do we have time for that?"

"We can probably spare a few moments." The ghost opens the manila folder back up, thumbing through the pages. "Where do we start…"

The young man kicks back in his chair again, plopping his feet up on the desk.

"Vishnu made a big show of their reawakening. I guess they liked a lot of what Maya had done with the Dreamscape, but they also thought it needed a lot of tweaking to get it back closer to their original vision. Somnia and Oneiros are a lot more integrated than ever before. All citizens now have access to regular schedules of the shifting of Oneiros, and the wild lands are no longer off-limits.

"Segregation between mortals and immortals is ended. Mortal souls are now allowed to—and even encouraged—to move into other districts in the city. A few immortals didn't think this was appropriate—stragglers from Maya's makeshift army—but they've since been enrolled in mortal sensitivity training. For the most part, it's going very well.

"To be fair, a lot of the credit is owed to Rasui. He's become Vishnu's Mortal Cultural liaison. All that pop culture knowledge comes in pretty handy, after all. They're setting up an arts and entertainment district in the city—a place where mortals and immortals alike can come together to learn about one another's history through art installations, live performances, food festivals, and so much more.

"Funny enough, Yume is actually going to be putting on one of the first performances there—a ballet about the creation of the Dreamscape. But when she's not directing and starring in that, she's been working as Dreamweavers' stage choreographer."

"Right," the man says. "The pilot program. How is that going, by the way?"

"Well, we're still in the early stages. But everything is going great. Obviously, most of what the departments were doing was bogus. But Vishnu found inspiration in the overall concept. Once the Dreamscape reopened and travel between the other realms was possible, they thought letting the mortal spirits visit their still-living friends and families back on Earth was a fantastic idea.

"It's complicated and doesn't come without risk, of course. But overall, everything has been running extremely smoothly—thanks in no small part to the fact that Mamu is helming the project. Letting people visit the ones they love—if only in dreams—has gone a long way toward smoothing over all the bad faith Maya—sorry, Lakshmi—built up."

"She's still on Earth, too, I take it?" the man asks.

"She is." The ghost nods, flipping through some of the pages in her folder. "She seems pretty serious about making amends. She's living as a Sanyasini nun in a small city in India called Vellore. I don't think she's aware of the irony, however."

"What irony?" The man cocks his head.

"In a few centuries, the very grounds she's living on will be home to a temple in her honor."

The young man lets out a belly laugh.

"Once this lifetime of hers is over," the ghost continues, "She'll meet with Vishnu and a council comprised of immortals and mortals alike. At that time, they'll decide whether she should return to the Afterworld or if her sentence living as a mortal should extend for another lifetime."

"You know, another mortal might have lobbied for her annihilation. And she may have deserved it."

"Maybe," the ghost replies. "But it wouldn't have undone what Maya did. And it wouldn't have made any of us feel any better. This way, she has as much freedom as any other mortal—all without the trappings of immortal knowledge. She can pursue a life lived however she so chooses. There's freedom in that."

"Do you think she would agree?" the man asks. "Or is this just another prison?"

"Considering that she's in her third lifetime as a mortal already—her choice, by the way—I'd say things are going well."

"What about everyone else? Cottus and his brothers?"

"Vishnu liquidated the Hecatoncheires' contracts. They were free to go wherever they wanted, but they all decided to stay here. Together, they're all running the day-to-day operations of Dreamweavers and are in charge of Dreamscape's entire infrastructure. Of course, now they have a full complement of staff working along with them.

"And that brings me to Endri. He actually went right back to work. Under the Hecatoncheires, he took over as head of the records room. And he's found a new best friend in the Minotaur. They both seem really happy down there surrounded by their books. Endri's actually been teaching the Minotaur how to read and even set up a word board so they can communicate with one another—although the Minotaur still seems mostly concerned with playing."

"What of my brothers? Still getting themselves in trouble?"

The ghost laughs. "You're not going to believe this, but Ikelos and Phantasus retired from Dreamweavers entirely. Something about the grind"—she makes air quotes—"*making them lose touch with what really matters.* Now they own a café in downtown Somnia. The food's not for me. I don't really know who it's for, actually. But it seems like enough for them. They still bicker, but I don't think either of them would have it any other way."

"I'm sure it helps that Chernobog isn't around to boss them around anymore," the man says.

"About that," the ghost replies with a shrug.

"You're kidding. He's alive?"

"And kicking. I guess Baku digestive systems can't exactly process gods they've swallowed whole. He spent a few months worming through the beast only to come out the other side better for it. Something about the Baku's gastrointestinal tract acted like a kind of filter, stripping all the resentment and bad intentions he's built up over the eons. He and the Baku have apparently reconciled, and he's been learning groundskeeping practices—helping to integrate the flora and fauna from Oneiros into the city of Somnia. His first project was to turn Dreamweavers' concourse into a green space. And I have to give it to him: it's truly beautiful."

"What about Kanasu?"

"That's why I'm here to talk to you today. Kanasu is actually going to be taking over for me as the acting head of Mortal-Immortal Relations. They were reticent to the idea until I told them why."

The man puts his feet down and sits forward.

"I'm leaving the Dreamscape," the ghost says. "Indefinitely."

"I see," the man says. For the first time since their conversation started, his cheeriness has faded. "Why?"

"Mamu has some connections in the other realms of the Afterworld. She thinks she might know some folks who can help my sister and me track our mother down. So, we're going to do that."

"So, this is goodbye," the man says.

"This is goodbye," the ghost replies, "For now."

"And I won't even remember it until after I die," the man says, choking back tears.

"You will," the ghost says, rising from her chair and picking up her manila folder. "If only in dreams."

"Before you go," the man says, rising to meet the ghost. He leans across the table and pulls the ghost toward him, wrapping his arms around her. "I'm going to miss you, Alora."

The ghost drops her folder and embraces the man in return. They just stand there for a long while, holding one another, until the man is suddenly gone.

The ghost in her pink polka-dotted sheet stays there for a moment longer, standing beneath the flickering fluorescent light before picking her manila folder up off the table.

With a deep breath, she turns around and walks out of the door, closing it gently behind her.

End log.

Character Name Glossary

Humans/Mortals

Alora: Bantu (Botswana) for "My dream." Wears white sheet with pink polka dots. (she/her)

Dublin: Middle Irish (Ireland) for "Blackpool." Beloved domestic feline, black. (he/him)

Endri: Albanian (Albania) for "Dreamer." Wears white and black plaid bedsheet. (he/him)

Kanasu: Hindi (India) for "Dream." Wears off-white bedsheet with an intricate multicolored geometric design. (they/them)

Nia: Swahili (Tanzania, Mozambique, and other East African countries) for "Purpose" and "Aim" or "Goal." (she/her)

Rasui: Egyptian (Egypt) for "Dream." Wears light gray bedsheet with science fiction imagery—rockets, astronauts, and shooting stars. (he/him)

Yume: Japanese (Japan) for "Dream" or "Vision." Wears light pink sheed with little drawings of fruit. (she/her)

Nonhumans/Immortals

Morpheus: Greco-Roman, God of Dreams. (he/him)

Chernobog: Slavic, God of Chaos, Misfortune, Darkness, et al. (he/him)

Briareus/Aegaeon: Greek, Hecatoncheire (hundred-hander), Titan; brother of Cottus and Gyges. (he/him)

Cottus: Greek, Hecatoncheire (hundred-hander), Titan; brother of Briareus and Gyges. (he/him)

Gyges/Gyes: Greek, Hecatoncheire (hundred-hander), Titan; brother of Briareus and Cottus. (he/him)

Ikelos: Greco-Roman, God of Dreams (Animals); brother of Morpheus. (he/him)

Mamu/Nyx/Ratri: Mesopotamian, God of Dreams; Greek, Primordial Deity of Night; Vedic (Hindu), God and Personification of Night; adoptive mother of Morpheus, Ikelos, and Phantasus. (she/her)

Maya/Lakshmi: Hindu, God of Wealth, Fortune, Prosperity, Beauty, Fertility, Sovereignty, and Abundance; consort of Vishnu. (she/her)

Phantasus: Greco-Roman, God of Dreams (Inanimate Objects); brother of Morpheus. (he/him)

Vishnu: Hindu, Principal Deity and God of Preservation. (they/them)

About the Author

Sean M. Tirman is the author, creator, and custodian of the *Marrower* and *Dreamweavers* universes and has been published in both *Infinite Worlds Magazine* and *Infinite Horrors Magazine*. He lives in Rochester, New York, with his wife and two remarkably entitled, small, old dogs. *Dreamweavers, LLC* is his second novel.

A Note from the Author: If you've made it this far, I hope that means you've finished reading *Dreamweavers, LLC*. For that, I'd like to thank you from the bottom of my heart. It genuinely means the world to me that you'd take the time to read my work. Now that you're done, I'd love for you to take the time and share your thoughts by leaving a review. As a largely one-person operation, I cannot overstate how important and impactful reader community evaluations are to me and my books.

You can connect with me on:

🌐 https://seanmtirman.com

Also by Sean M. Tirman

Hounds of Gaia

Foxhound doesn't care about the gaps in her memory. Being a Contractor, a kind of spacefaring mercenary, keeps her occupied enough. Rather than dwelling, she rockets around the farthest reaches of the solar system, earning a steady paycheck hunting down ne'er-do-wells and enjoying a semblance of freedom most folks in the outer colonies can't dream of.

So when she receives an urgent prisoner transfer request from a cult starship, she accepts the gig. She figures that transporting a bone marrow-eating serial killer from the cult's colony back to Earth is just another well-paying job that'll keep her mind off things. Upon discovering that the suspect in custody is an orphan girl—one that could pass for her much younger doppelgänger—she decides it's time to get some answers.

Before she can piece together who the girl is and how their lives intertwine, a group of violent prisoners aboard Foxhound's starship breaks free. As the once-peaceful cultists take up arms in response, the Contractor teams up with her mechanized AI assistant and two of the cult's wayward members to stop the barbaric escapees and elude the grasp of the cult's radicalized leader. And when that's done, she can focus on figuring out the secret behind the mysterious, potentially dangerous girl—but will she even want to know the truth?